BEWILDERMENT

A NOVEL

MICHAEL ONOFREY

TAILWINDS PRESS

Copyright © 2017 by Michael Onofrey
All rights reserved. Except as permitted under the U.S. Copyright
Act of 1976, no part of this publication may be reproduced,
distributed, or transmitted in any form or by any means, or stored in
a database or retrieval system, without the written permission of the
publisher.

Tailwinds Press
P.O. Box 2283, Radio City Station
New York, NY 10101-2283
www.tailwindspress.com

Published in the United States of America
ISBN: 978-0-9975742-0-3
1st ed. 2017

For Suzuyo

BEWILDERMENT

PART 1

CHAPTER 1

The living room is full of people, some standing, others seated. Children are on the floor. There is overflow, all adults, all standing—kitchen/dining area, two doorways to the kitchen/dining area, doorway of a hall that leads to bedrooms, and then another doorway that leads to the front door.

He seats his mother on a straight-back chair that's next to a sofa. The chair's back and seat are padded, but since the chair is new, or at least not broken in, the brocade-like fabric encasing the padding is stiff, as is the padding itself. So there's no give, particularly in the case of his mother, for she is very thin. Thus, she sits as if perched, and she smiles in the same manner, stiffly. Someone had courteously gotten up to allow Paula, Wade's mother, the chair.

Paula is wearing a cream-colored blouse and a pastel orange skirt. White Keds are on her feet. Her jacket, a tan-colored corduroy garment that she wore on the way over in the car, is on a bed in a bedroom, jacket on top of other coats and jackets. It's not exactly cold outside, but it's not exactly warm, either. It's a sweater/jacket night in Southern California. It's Christmas Eve.

A low counter separates the kitchen/dining area from the living room, and this works out nicely in terms of inclusiveness, for all anyone in either room has to do to see anyone else is turn their head, right or left depending.

People have plates of food, real plates, genuine crockery, not paper plates, and the same can be said for cups and glasses, utensils as well, no plastic. Napkins, though, as Wade soon discovers, are paper, a thick beige paper that is textured with raised lines that represent flowers, daisies perhaps.

On a table in the dining area and on the kitchen counter there are casseroles and platters and bowls and large rectangular pans—carved turkey, Italian sausage, enchiladas, eggplant Parmesan, raviolis, sliced ham, mashed potatoes, brown gravy, candied yams, several kinds of salad, several kinds of bread, cookies, pumpkin pie, cheesecake, and so on. Wade, in addition to bringing his mother, brought two cheesecakes, one plain, the other raspberry, each in its own cardboard box, thin white cardboard, very chic. Those boxes haven't been opened. They got slid into the refrigerator. Presumably their time will come when counter space opens up.

Wade sets to work fixing a plate of food for his mother, modest helpings. Christmas music is in background, a Muzak effect, volume low. Also in background is conversation, or more accurately a number of conversations, which lend themselves to blending in Wade's ears because he isn't participating in any of those conversations. The conversation-sound is spiked with ups and downs, volume and pitch rising and falling, especially with exchanges involving children.

There is a decorated tree in one corner of the living room, but Wade can't detect its scent. The food before Wade kind of has a scent, a warm scent. In addition to that, now and then there's a whiff of cologne or aftershave or perfume. Food is Wade's focus, then a napkin, and then a heavy silver fork.

He makes his way over to his mother and hands her the plate of food, which she takes with two hands. Wade places the fork on the plate next to small pieces of turkey. Everything on the plate was selected with the idea of fork-able, thus eliminating the need for a knife.

Wade puts the napkin on Paula's lap. Paula didn't bring a bag or a purse, so there isn't that to deal with, for a bag or a purse would have meant finding a place for it once Paula's plate of food arrived to occupy her hands and lap. Wade had noticed his mother's no-bag/purse status when they were leaving home, and he had deemed this good even though it probably wasn't consciously conceived on Paula's part. More likely than not, it had slipped her mind, but Wade silently approved because that automatically negated the possibility of misplacing the bag or purse.

Paula looks at the food that's on the plate. She smiles anew, but it's still a stiff smile. Wade asks if she needs anything else. Paula looks at him. She is wearing glasses. Her eyes have a blue tint. Wade repeats himself, but this time with more force behind the words and with more space between the words. Paula's view returns to her plate of food. After a moment, she says, "This is fine."

Wade returns to the kitchen and pours himself a cup of coffee. No alcohol of any sort is present, but that's okay because Wade is driving. Wade also notes that no one is smoking, or if anyone is they are doing it outside in the backyard.

After adding milk and sugar to his coffee and stirring it, Wade is then faced with the quandary of where to stand. He solves this by taking a couple of steps to his left where he establishes himself next the refrigerator.

Sipping his coffee, Wade thinks about not knowing, or not recognizing, anyone. He imagines his mother might be confronting the same issue, but she has a plate of food to occupy herself, yet offsetting this might be confusion that varies in intensity depending on how she is feeling. Hopefully the food won't confuse her. Looking between a couple of people who are standing in the doorway of the kitchen that gives out onto the living room, Wade can see his mother, who seems to be doing okay, fork moving between her mouth and the plate.

It was Art Perez and his wife, April, who invited Wade and his mother over for Christmas Eve, and they of course greeted Wade and Paula when they arrived, but after that Wade and his mother were left on their own.

Right now, Art is busy in the vicinity of the Christmas tree where he is handing out wrapped gifts to children.

A pair of scissors makes its way into the hands of a boy, who cuts the ribbon off a fairly large box. The scissors are dropped and the wrapping paper shredded and then the boy is into the box with his eager hands. A serious water cannon emerges, and evidently this is just what the boy wanted, for he springs to his feet with a gleeful smile on his plump face, and he starts making noises while pointing the bloated squirt gun around the room. Fortunately the device did not come with water.

As for Art's wife, April, she is in and out of the kitchen on errands ranging from napkin procurement to checking on the level of coffee in a glass coffeepot that's nestled in a sleek, black coffeemaker.

When pouring himself a cup of coffee, Wade noticed that there was no coffee aroma, or at least none that he could detect. Probably the coffee's smell got lost in the kitchen's moist warm air, which is warm and moist because of people and food. Curtains, covering windows, prevent

Wade from seeing any glass, but he imagines condensation even though it isn't that cold outside.

Wade shifts his weight and sips his coffee. There must be at least thirty-five people within eyesight, four generations represented, but of the eldest there are only Art's father and Wade's mother, and one other lady, whom Wade doesn't recognize in the least.

Wade's afraid to speak to anyone for fear that he might have known them from a long time ago but can't recognize them now. He figures a blunder like that might be embarrassing.

A fleeting thought has Wade thinking about who is going to wash all the dishes, and with this he realizes that the dishes and cups and saucers all match, and so does the silverware, which means that everything was either rented or stored in boxes and kept somewhere in the house to be brought out for occasions such as this. Art did mention "yearly Christmas Eve get-together" when he called to invite Wade and Paula over. Art also mentioned "family gathering" and "lots of good food."

But now, as Wade sips his coffee in tiny increments with the intent of making it last, something else takes over, something other than the practicalities of clean-up and cutlery and china and coffee, something that carries a stepped-back feeling, a feeling that is mixed with perception, and it is this feeling/perception that has Wade viewing the scene as if he were an onlooker, which in essence he is. It's just that now it feels like he's really "watching," as in watching a movie, for there is this movielike perception and feeling that has taken hold.

In back of this movielike watching, but coming to the forefront, there is a conversation to Wade's left that he has begun to listen to with increasing interest. This makes Wade an eavesdropper in addition to an onlooker, but he's not looking at whom he's eavesdropping on, but he has a vague idea, or image, of who is to his left. It's two middle-aged men, and they are talking about religion. Wade saw both men a few minutes before in the living room, the men attending to a couple of young children, who were handling presents while also dealing with plates of food. Upon finishing with the children the men returned to the kitchen to take up their former place to Wade's left, but what these men had been talking about before going to the living room Wade has no idea. He wasn't eavesdropping then. Now, though, he is paying attention, and he understands that the two men are talking about Christianity, and they are talking about it in such a manner as to suggest heavy involvement. Church and Jesus are part of their vocabulary, yet they are not all jazzed up in a radical way. Their voices are not loud, yet not hushed, and the tone of their conversation is normal. It is a normal conversation, but . . . there is this little something that draws Wade's attention.

The two men are talking about someone whom they know, a mutual friend, who hasn't picked up on the spirit of the Lord, and it strikes Wade that the men view their friend as unenlightened. It's not exactly a put-down, but there is a distinct sense that their friend is out of step and unfortunate, and so there is a sense of criticism, but it's not heavy or malicious. It's more of an in-group-slash-out-group discernment.

Wade wants to turn and look at these men because he wants to see their expressions and gestures as they talk, but he doesn't want to enter into conversation with them, for he doesn't want to talk to them about religion. But, he wants to hear what they have to say about it, and he wants to hear what they have to say about their friend who isn't part of their group. If Wade could look at these two men so as to see gesture and expression, he feels this would help him understand what these men are trying to express.

Also, while not daring to look at them for fear of having to participate in their discussion, Wade's afraid he might know these men from a long time ago, which means he *should* know them. But, after having stood for so long without saying anything to them, Wade doesn't want to commit to recognizing them because they might interpret that as rude, as in: "Why did you ignore us for so long?" Remaining strangers, or supposed strangers, is a safe stance, or kind of a safe stance. Wade is acutely aware that he doesn't have a clear stance.

One of the men would be about the right age to be Art and April's son, and the other might be Art's very younger brother. So while the embarrassment and awkwardness of maybe having known them, but not having said anything, serves as a deterrent, there is, in addition to wanting to see gesture and expression, a strong temptation to look at them for purposes of identification, for Wade would like to know if the one is really Art's son and the other Art's younger brother, but that would entail some heavy-duty probing of their faces, which is out of the question.

Another thing that strikes Wade is that these two men, along with others at the party, haven't greeted Wade and haven't tried to engage Wade in conversation, and this is probably for the same reason, or reasons, that Wade hasn't approached anyone, which means that the same dynamics are at work—embarrassment and etiquette, Los Angeles etiquette. It would, after all, be kind of rude for someone to come up to Wade and say: "Who are you?" Or, "Do I know you?" Or worse yet, "Why are you here?" Of course it probably wouldn't be put so bluntly, but in the end that would be the question, or questions.

The two men to Wade's left have moved on to another subject. They are now talking about schools. They mention names, and Wade understands that they are talking about private schools, but then they mention other names, and these seem to be public schools.

Wade's thoughts drift, and even though still an onlooker there is now another dimension, a back-and-forth quality, a dual quality, for in addition to the scene before his eyes there are fleeting thoughts, little clips that are like snapshots, appearing, disappearing, radical turns of thought. He sips his coffee, and then he sees his mother put her fork down on her plate, which brings him back from wherever he was. She's eaten about half the food. Wade leaves his post next to the refrigerator and makes his way over to Paula, where he says, "You about finished with that, Ma?" She seems relieved to see him. She says, "Yes."

Wade takes the plate from his mother's lap, napkin under the plate remaining on Paula's thighs. Wade regards the napkin. In Wade's one hand there is the plate with the fork, and in his other hand there is his coffee cup, and it's at this point, while thinking about how to pick up the napkin, that he discovers a serious tactical error, for his mother says, "Could you get me a cup of coffee?"

This is a major setback because Wade was about to suggest leaving, and maybe it was the cup in Wade's hand that set his mother to thinking about coffee. Wade should have set his cup down on the kitchen counter before leaving the kitchen or in one of the two sinks where people had begun to stack dirty dishes. What could he have been thinking about to have left the kitchen with that cup in his hand?

CHAPTER 2

The well was where two roads met, the one road paved but severely damaged, the worse for wear and lack of maintenance, the other road red dirt. There was no traffic, and there was no one around except for him at that Y-junction between the two roads. Circling the lip of the well mortared stones rose a foot off the ground. Overhead orange clouds ran like skid marks in a mauve sky.

He pulled down and then pushed down at one end of a long wooden pole, the pole a lever that he then swiveled on its fulcrum to bring a bucket of water to the ground near the well, bucket at the end of a length of rope.

Maroon gym shorts hung from his hips, rubber flip-flops on his feet. His limbs were long and his muscles were the same way, long. Raised veins trellised his arms. His ribs showed.

He went down on his haunches and began scooping water from the bucket with a tin can. When his body was wet, he lathered with a bar of soap. His hair was light brown and sun-streaked, and it was thrown back. He looked like a mendicant.

He raced to soap his skin and he raced to rinse off, and when he toweled off he moved with the same haste, for he had begun to shiver. He knew this would happen, so he was in a hurry from beginning to end. He needed to bathe. Bathing was important because cleanliness and health were linked, or so he believed, and to sink further into what was upon him was unthinkable.

When he finished toweling off he stepped away from the slick red mud that he had created in his washing. He stepped out of the goo and onto dry dirt and wrapped a *lungi* around his waist and pulled his wet shorts down and off his legs. He had chosen this time of day in an attempt to slip between the day's heat and its dusky darkness, and now, as he sat on a flat stone cleaning mud from his rubber flip-flops, feet held up, he began to shiver in earnest.

Pitter-patter, pitter-patter, pitter-patter on palm fronds. It was almost soothing as he woke to listen to it.

Earlier, he had thrown his sleeping bag open because he was burning up. Before that, though, before sleep, he had been shivering from having come in from the well, sleeping bag offering warmth, which finally stopped the chills. But then the room began to spin, palm-frond walls and ceiling, daylight fading, surroundings barely illuminated, no electricity. He had candles and a flashlight, but why bother? He was on his way out. It was a repeat of the previous four nights—stomach cramped, intestines knotted, vision berserk, bones aching, head pounding, body wrapped in uncontrollable chills that rattled his jaws. There was nothing to do but to get inside his sleeping bag and wait for warmth. And so that's what he had done. When the chills stopped, sleep took him away.

Sometime after that he woke up in pitch-black darkness. He was burning up. He threw the sleeping bag open and took his *lungi* off and put on a pair of jockey shorts that he positioned below his money belt that was limp around his waist like a spent garter. The reason for the jockey shorts was to protect his genitals from mosquitoes.

Reaching down from his cot, he picked up his water bottle from the floor. He drank some water, but in short order that water started swishing around in his stomach and he hoped he wouldn't vomit. He went prone on top of his sleeping bag and looked up at the darkness. He slipped off again, but how cruel that he had no awareness of sleep's relief except for brief moments of entering and leaving.

Pitter-patter, pitter-patter, a soft sound that offered respite from the night's warm humidity. He heard no mosquitoes at his ears and noted that mosquitoes hadn't been a problem in this room, a room raised six feet off the ground by way of wooden poles, an elevated structure of four palm-frond rooms in a row with frond-doors that opened and closed on hinges of course twine, framing and flooring rough-cut wood, two-by-four approximations that were irregular along their lengths. There was a ladder from the ground to a three-foot-wide walkway, walkway situated in front of the frond-doors. His door, though, was the only one in operation because the other three rooms were vacant.

He was alone except for the husband-and-wife team who ran the place. The couple had a small child, the three of them residing in a mud-brick house that had a connecting patio with a frond awning, four wooden benches and two wooden tables under the awning. The patio was termed a restaurant courtesy of a hand-painted sign that hung from the eaves—RESTAURANT—all in upper case letters. The mud-brick house and its open-air restaurant were about fifteen yards away from the elevated, palm-frond rooms that the couple rented out for a reasonable price—ten rupees a night, about one dollar.

Pitter-patter, pitter-patter. Water was dripping on his legs and at first it struck him as inconsequential, but then he realized it wasn't.

He swung his legs off his cot and reached down for his flashlight that was on the floor. He turned the flashlight on and directed its beam up at the ceiling, which was the same as the roof, ceiling and roof of the same fronds, an A-shaped ceiling/roof. He had to get out from under the leak. He ran the beam of light around the room, a surprisingly large room, and he found that water was streaming down from any number of places. Pitter-patter was turning into a deluge. He saw it in the flashlight's beam and he heard it on the palm-frond roof, gentle sound gone.

He dropped the flashlight on his cot and pulled the cot to the side, but it wasn't a smooth operation because the floor's hand-cut boards were uneven. In the flashlight's beam he saw water jumping from irregular floorboards all across the room, but, at the same time, that gapped flooring allowed for swift drainage. There were no puddles.

Picking up the flashlight, he searched the room for an area where no water was coming down.

Thunder and lightning began. An explosive clap shook the room and everything flashed silver like a photograph in reverse, a blonde negative. In his eyes there were spots that lingered.

Locating an area spared from streams of water, he dropped the flashlight on his sleeping bag and grabbed the cot's wooden framing with two hands and dragged the cot across the room, wooden legs bouncing off the floor. Bang, bang, bang. When he got to where it was dry, he let go of the cot and picked up the flashlight and pointed its beam upward. The ceiling/roof over this area was holding.

He then thought about his possessions, which were in a cloth bag and in a couple of canvas saddlebags. The beam of his flashlight found those bags near a stream of water. He walked barefoot across the room and picked up his bag and saddlebags and went back to his cot and stowed his things under the cot. Using a hand towel, which he used for a pillow, he dried himself the best he could.

He then stood and wondered what to do, but he didn't think about this for too long because he heard the rain slowing, and then he heard it stop, and not long afterwards the streams of water stopped. Isolated dripping remained. The night was suddenly quiet again except for thunder in the distance. He remembered that it was windy when it was raining, but now the wind was gone.

Chills began and he felt them move into his body from his skin. He took his wet jockey shorts off and got into his sleeping bag, which had wet patches that he now tried to avoid by bending his body. He was shivering and his teeth were chattering.

In his sleeping bag, he began to feel warmth, as if warmth were something delivered, and with this he felt a sense of luck, for if warmth failed to arrive he'd be in grave trouble.

His flashlight was still turned on, and it was lying on the floor next to his cot. He wanted to keep it on because it offered a degree of comfort and discouraged dizziness, but he couldn't keep it on because the batteries would run out. The flashlight, beyond all else, had to remain operable.

He reached down and turned the flashlight off and with this he felt his arm getting cold and he felt that coldness go up into his shoulder and this surprised him. He yanked his arm back inside his sleeping bag and put it against his chest.

The room was dark and he tried to find something to look at, but his eyes found nothing to grab onto and things began to spin even though he couldn't see anything. It was a "feeling" of spinning, and it was like he was falling and spinning in blackness.

He was on his side and he was curled up like a baby. His head was pounding and his eyes felt like they were going to pop out of their sockets and his stomach was twisted and his bones hurt. He wasn't cold, but that was the only thing good about what he was, for everything else was wrong.

He passed out.

The sky is blue and there's not a cloud in sight and he's in the open-air patio that's termed a restaurant and he's trying chai and *bhaji* and a roll. The roll is a piece of bread the size of a baseball and the *bhaji* is bean *bhaji* that's spicy and hot, but not too hot. He tried these the previous mornings, tea, *bhaji* and bread, and now he's trying them again. From where he sits, he can see waves lapping at white sand, and he remembers that he heard waves sometime around first light when grayness entered his room like a mist.

The man who runs the place stands in the doorway of the kitchen watching him while smoking a *beedi*. The man's son is nearby. The boy is wearing a little white T-shirt, but nothing else, pee-pee and buttocks exposed, along with a couple of chubby legs. The child is barefoot and he teeters while walking. A piece of torn bread is in the child's one hand. A yellow dog, which is the family pet, sits on its haunches and watches the child. The child uses his free hand to grab onto benches for support. The child is of an age where he's learning to walk.

Thus far the chai is okay. He's taken a couple of sips and it's in his stomach and his stomach and the chai are not fighting. He tries the *bhaji* and then the roll. He picks up his glass of chai and sips again. He is about to spoon more *bhaji* into his mouth, but then he feels it.

He gets up from the table. He needs to get out of the patio. He needs to make it to the bushes that are in back of the raised structure that houses his room. It's where he defecates and urinates, but now he's got to get there so he can vomit. The man is watching, and he feels the man's eyes following him as he makes his way across the clearing to the bushes, but once he's in the bushes he finds that he can't vomit. His guts are tossing, but he can't throw up.

Bent over, he emerges from the foliage and goes to the ladder that leads to the walkway. He climbs the ladder and walks on the walkway and opens the frond-door of his room.

He sits down on his cot. The room starts to spin. His head is pounding, his bones ache, his stomach is a mess. He lies down and he tries to fight the pain, but the pain is out of control. He loses track of time, but there occurs a moment when he understands that sleep is right there within his perception.

She is sitting on the edge of his cot next to his right leg and she is looking at his face and she is smiling and he has no idea what she is doing in his room.

It must be afternoon because there is strong sunlight coming from under the eaves. It takes a few moments, cognition assembling pieces. He was walking back from the well, shaking with chills, and she was at the side of the dirt road. She said something to him, which he didn't understand, and he said, "Sorry?" And she said, "Oh. You speak English. You are not German." And he said, "No. I am not German." She said something more, and he said something in response. He was in a hurry, light fading, bats slicing the air. His skin was livid with chills.

There is a flower, perhaps an orchid, wedged behind her ear where her hair leaves off, short-cropped hair that is blonde and thick. He feels a flash of panic and looks down to see if he is wearing any clothes. Yes, he's in his *lungi*, no shirt, though. Only his madras *lungi*, but that's enough, because that's what he was concerned about. He smiles tentatively. He feels calm. The room isn't spinning. He has no fever. His stomach is okay.

"You must eat ginger," she says.

Her face is sun-red and so are her bare arms. She's wrapped in light green cloth that is almost translucent. Her eyes are blue.

"Ginger?"

"Yes, of course. It will make you well."

She speaks with an accent. He recalls that she had laughed when he asked if she was German. This was at the side of the road, and she had responded, "Of course. Is it not obvious?"

"Ginger?" he questions again.

"Yes, of course."

He smiles at this.

"I will bring you ginger," she says, and then repeats, "It will make you well."

Her eyes go down over his body, a frank examination. If she told him her name the day before, he has forgotten it. He raises his right hand and places it on his chest. He is calm, but exhausted.

"How do you know I'm sick?"

"The thin man at the restaurant told me."

"The restaurant? You mean, this restaurant here?" He gestures.

"Yes."

"He told you I was sick?"

"Yes. He said, 'Sick man.'"

He chuckles while thinking about the man's English, which is limited.

"How did you find me?" he asks, and on top of this, "Why did you come here?"

"You pointed, yesterday."

He looks at her. She continues to smile. Her teeth are slightly gapped.

"I will go to the village and search for ginger."

He waits, but she says nothing more.

"Okay," he says, but this response is only to satisfy the need for a response because for him ginger registers as nothing, if not bizarre. Actually, the entire scene since opening his eyes strikes him as surreal.

She sighs and says, "There are many Germans here."

Again he waits, and again she says nothing more, and it's as if her statement were hovering. He's vaguely aware of other lodgings along the beach, but he doesn't know anything about them or who might be staying in them.

"I'm sorry," he says. "I've forgotten your name."

"I am Herta."

This doesn't sound familiar. Maybe she didn't tell him her name the day before, but then again maybe she did. He's not sure.

"I'm Wade."

"Yes," she says. "Wade." She pronounces this carefully, but whether or not she heard it the day before he can't tell.

Wade smiles. Herta smiles. She is not fat. She's medium. Through her arms and shoulders there is strength. The green cloth outlines the contours of her breasts, no bra.

"I came here to get away from Germans," she says, "but there are Germans here as well."

He listens to this, and then he says, "Where did you come from?"

"The beaches north of Panjim."

"I was at one of those beaches," Wade says. "Chapora."

"Chapora," Herta says. "It is nice. But of course there are Germans there too."

"Yes, among others."

"And you arrive here by bus?" she asks.

"No. I arrived by bicycle."

"Bicycle?" questions Herta.

"Yes."

"Did you buy the bicycle in Panjim?"

"No, I bought the bicycle in Amritsar."

"Amritsar?" she says. "In the Punjab?"

"Yes."

"You have come by bicycle from the Punjab?"

"Yes."

Herta falls silent. Her smile is gone. She stands up and looks down at him.

"Where is your bicycle?"

"It's chained to a pole under this building."

"Outside?"

"Of course."

She reaches down and picks up a colorful cloth shoulder bag from the floor. The bag's little mirrors and design designate Rajasthan. She loops the wide strap of the bag over her shoulder.

"I will look for ginger in the village," she says and turns to go to the frond-door where she puts her hand through a hole and raises the door and shoves it outward, which initiates a blast of sunlight.

Wade's eyes are squinting as he looks at Herta's silhouette going out into the sunshine like a ghost. The door closes with a brushing sound, sunlight extinguished.

Wade hears footsteps, and then he hears a different sound and understands that Herta is going down the ladder. The ladder-sounds end and Wade listens, but there are no sounds. He thinks that maybe she is standing at the foot of the ladder looking at his heavy black bicycle. Perhaps the yellow dog is on its way over from the patio to sniff at Herta's leg. Wade continues to listen, but he hears nothing more.

It is hot and there are wispy clouds in the sky and Wade has bought two coconut shells of yogurt, half shells that form cups, bought them at a kiosk-like place on a dirt road five minutes away from his room, and he has walked back to his room and has gotten a spoon and has removed the square piece of paper from on top of one of the shells, paper to protect the yogurt from flies. He now sits on the walkway outside his room where he spoons runny yogurt into his mouth. The yellow dog has come over to settle on the ground six feet below where Wade is sitting. The dog is looking up at Wade.

Three-quarters of the way through the first shell of yogurt Wade's stomach begins to knot and with this panic sets in, for it's a familiar pattern.

The coconut shell falls to the ground below the walkway. The spoon as well goes down there. The other cup of yogurt, the full one, is kicked when Wade struggles to his feet. There's a thud that the full shell makes when it hits the ground.

Wade's bent over, hands coming to his stomach. As he turns toward his room, he sees the dog down below. The dog's orange-red tongue is moving in and out of a coconut shell, slips of white slush lacing the dog's muzzle, silver spoon nearby in the reddish dirt.

He pulls the door to his room open and goes in and pulls the door shut and goes onto his cot. The room begins to spin and he tries to stop it by focusing on a wooden table that's away from his cot, but the table starts spinning as well. He closes his eyes, but this makes things worse. He opens his eyes, and at first there's no spinning, but within moments the palm-frond walls and ceiling begin to turn. He's on his back on his cot, and then he's on his side, but it makes no difference. He can't stop the room from spinning. His stomach feels like it's digesting shrapnel.

He moves his legs from side to side. He grabs a hold of the cot's frame, but nothing helps. He wants sleep to arrive, but at the same time he fears its arrival because things are so out of control that he thinks he might not wake up. The thought of dying crosses his mind.

The image of the dog slurping white yogurt with its orange-red tongue flashes in his brain and quickly turns into a repetitive movielike reel that oscillates between slow motion and frenzy, a true phantasmagoria that he carries into sleep.

Herta is holding a gnarled root in her hand. Wade blinks his eyes and senses that it's late afternoon. He doesn't know if she woke him or if he woke on his own. He didn't hear anything. He just opened his eyes and there she was, looking down at him with a root in her hand. She is wearing the same green cloth, which extends from her chest to her knees. There are folds and tucks, and the cloth is arranged so that from the waist down it's loose. He imagines her walking with definite strides.

"You should eat this," she says and smiles.

"Is that ginger?"

"Yes."

The root has gray skin that appears flaky.

"How do you eat it?"

"Cut it into pieces with a knife and eat the pieces." She continues to smile. "Do you have a knife?"

"Well," he begins. "I do, but … maybe if you could put the ginger on the table over there, and I'll get to it later."

His fever is gone. His vision is normal. He looks down at himself and sees that his flip-flops are on his feet. He's wearing his *lungi*. He puts his feet over the side of the cot and gets rid of the flip-flops. He feels skinny, he feels empty. He's certain that he has lost weight.

Herta sets the ginger down on the table and then takes a flower from behind her ear, a larger flower than what was behind her ear the day before. She puts the flower on the table next to the ginger. The flower has petals that are pastel orange. A toothbrush and a tube of Colgate toothpaste and a candle and a box of matches are also on the table. But now, with the flower, the table has been transformed. It now looks like a still life waiting to be painted. Herta walks over and sits down on the cot next to Wade's hip. Wade is prone.

"You must eat ginger. It will make you well."

Wade says, "Yes," but this is simply a courtesy. Herta looks at his body, head to foot. Wade feels drained, but comfortable.

Herta begins talking about Christmas in Nuremberg, which is where she is from. She tells Wade about the night market in Nuremberg's central square, which takes place on Christmas Eve. She talks about how it is cold, and how there's a ceremony in the square along with the market, everyone turning out for the ceremony—families, young people, old people. Wade listens. Herta's English is very good, and there are ways that she puts things that are amusing and interesting, and there is her accent, which is intriguing. Her voice, at Wade's ear, is soothing. He's glad she is talking. She tells him that ten days ago she was in "Goa, Anjuna, for Christmas."

Herta continues to talk. She tells Wade about her room down the beach, and about Goa, and about her parents' house, and about trains and buses in India. She glides from one subject to the next, Christmas, Easter, summertime in Nuremberg. Wade inserts a "yes" here and there. He wants her to continue. English doesn't seem to be a burden for her.

"And here it is," she says. "A fresh year—1975. Do you have a resolution, Wade?"

"Yes. To get well."

She smiles. Her eyes squint when she smiles.

"And you?" says Wade. "What is your resolution?"

"To see India."

And now it is Wade's turn to smile, but his is a crooked smile, which Herta looks at with interest.

"Why do you smile like that?" she asks.

"I fell off a swing when I was four years old. A nerve got pinched. The left side of my face, between my eye and my mouth, is paralyzed. It doesn't move. It doesn't bother me. It's just that my smile is aslant."

"I like it," Herta says. "It is unusual."

Herta reaches for Wade's water bottle that's on the floor.

"Wait a minute," Wade says. "It's best not to drink from that. I don't know what I've got, but whatever it is, you don't want it."

Herta looks at him, water bottle in hand.

"Even sitting here," Wade says, "might not be all that safe."

Herta sets the plastic bottle back down on the floor. Birds are calling. Sunset must be nearing. Herta stands up.

"I will return tomorrow," she says. "Is there something I can bring you?"

Wade still doesn't understand the context of her kindness. She is standing and waiting. The strap of her colorful bag is over her shoulder.

"Pepsi-Cola," Wade says. "If you can find a couple of bottles of Pepsi, that'd be great."

"Pepsi-Cola?"

"Yes."

"I will try."

It's when he's urinating in the bushes in back of his room the next morning that he understands what he has. His urine is purple. A half hour later he squats and defecates, and this confirms what he suspects. His stool, what little there is, is chalk-white. Ten minutes later, with a hand-held mirror, he looks at his face and sees yellow in the whites of his eyes.

When Herta shows up in the early afternoon, Wade is sitting on the walkway in front of his room. Herta walks to beneath him and looks up. "Hello," she says. Near her sandaled feet there are the two empty coconut shells. The spoon, however, is gone.

"I have hepatitis."

Herta continues to smile as she says, "Did you eat ginger?"

Herta is wearing a skirt and a short-sleeved blouse, both with floral designs, but the designs don't match. Wade wonders if she understands what hepatitis is. She walks to the ladder and starts up. When she comes to where Wade is sitting, she stops.

Wade has been to the patio-restaurant and has brought his own glass and has asked for chai. He has drunk two glasses of chai, and so far it's okay. He feels weak, but the tea didn't cause him any stomach problems nor any fever or headache or spinning vision. He feels content sitting on the walkway while looking out at the scene before him— red dirt, mud-brick house, emerald palm trees, white sand, blue sea, yellow dog sleeping.

Herta reaches into her bag and brings out two bottles of Pepsi-Cola. Wade looks at the bottles and says, "Terrific."

"Do you have an opener?" Herta asks.

"Yes. I'll get it."

"No. Tell me where it is. I will get it," Herta says.

"It's in my bag under the cot. Green and red and blue bag."

Herta goes into the room and then returns with the opener and sits down on the walkway. Wade takes the opener from her and uncaps the bottles and hands one bottle to Herta. They raise their bottles and drink. The cola is not cold, but it tastes good. Wade imagines that he needs glucose.

"What do I owe you for the Pepsis?"

"Owe me?"

"How much did you pay for the bottles of Pepsi?"

"It is not a problem," Herta says.

Wade sits for a moment, and then raises his bottle and drinks.

"Do you know what hepatitis is?" Wade asks.

"Of course. This is India, is it not? Everyone knows hep."

Wade has noticed that Herta favors "of course." She uses it often.

"It's a contagious disease," Wade says. "You can catch it from me."

Wade waits for a response, but Herta only looks out. The dog has stood up and is arching its yellow-furred back.

The dog circles twice before settling back on the ground. The dog looks like a thin Labrador.

"We will have to wait," Herta says.

"Wait? Wait for what?"

"Wait for your health to return before we kiss."

Herta moves into the room next to Wade's. She supplies him with Pepsi-Cola and she tells him stories about her life and she talks about her thoughts and ideas, but Wade's not sure where the stories end and the thoughts and ideas begin. She tells him, for example, "Walking on the beach at night, next to the silver sea in the moonlight, without clothing, is wonderful. It is freedom, and how could it be otherwise?" Wade doesn't doubt this, but whether it's experience or imaginings that speak, he can't ascertain.

They go to the well and wash while standing in red dirt that becomes mud. The days and nights pass. Wade is on the mend, but he is weak. His urine has lightened. He is eating more and Pepsi-Cola continues to taste great. He only wishes that the Pepsi was cold.

It rains one night, and the next morning Herta sits on his cot and reports that her room is completely dry, no leaks.

They take exploratory walks, and one afternoon, while walking on the beach midst marvelous weather that is typical for southern India during the winter, they spy a gaggle of nude bodies in the distance. Herta declares them German, and with this they turn and head back to from where they came.

"What is it that you have against Germans?" Wade asks.

"I left Germany to see something else, but in Jodhpur, Delhi, Agra, Goa, I found Germans."

Wade nods.

"I came here, very south Goa, but even here there are Germans, until I saw you."

Small waves collapse and throw spume up onto the beach. Wade is carrying his flip-flops in one hand, Herta her sandals in one hand.

"And there was my boyfriend. He was German."

"Your boyfriend?"

"We split up in Goa, Christmas Day, in Anjuna."

"I didn't know that."

"It is not important."

He now possesses an appetite. He makes requests, and Herta returns from the village with those requests, but sometimes not. It is, after all, a small village.

He spreads strawberry jam onto the baseball-size rolls that are served in the patio/restaurant of the mud-brick house. He drinks chai and brings his own glass to the patio for the woman to fill.

It was in the shop that sells Pepsi-Cola that Herta discovered the jars of strawberry jam. She has described the village to Wade. He thinks he might want to give the village a try for a haircut.

Herta informs him that the bus stop is just beyond the well. Herta says the bus comes hourly, twenty minutes past the hour, and it's always on time. Wade finds this hard to believe because nothing in India is on time.

They decide to go to the village, and indeed the bus is on time. In addition, the vehicle isn't crowded. Wade says, "Double miracle." Herta says, "I told you so." Her English continues to amaze him.

The bus is a recycled school bus. Its front door never closes. They reach the village in fifteen minutes, road paved, but riddled with chuckholes. There's hardly any traffic on the road, only a motor scooter now and then.

A single street defines the village. Herta and Wade stroll. In an open-air barbershop with a hard-packed dirt floor, Wade gets a haircut and a shave, straight razor in the hand of a lean man who wears thick glasses. Wade's hair is taken down to a nub. When he emerges from the barbershop, Herta laughs and tells him, "You look like a convict."

They load up on essentials—bread, Pepsi-Cola, hard candy, soda crackers, strawberry jam, bananas, limes, toothpaste, matches, candles, incense, and six tins of sardines imported from Portugal. Herta wants to buy ginger at a spice shop, but Wade reminds her that he's still got the root that she gave him a couple of weeks ago.

The bus leaves on the hour from the center of the village. They board. The driver gets in and starts the engine. There's no glass in the windows of the bus except for the front windshield. Horizontal bars have been welded across the window openings, four steel bars to a window. Wade wonders what happens when it rains.

Prior to Herta's entrance each morning, there is her chanting voice, low in volume and faint for language and enunciation, and along with this there is a strong whiff of incense that drifts into Wade's room. It is the same every morning, chanting and incense from Herta's room that's adjacent to Wade's room, palm fronds separating the two rooms. It is this that wakes him each morning.

And now, as Herta sits on the edge of his cot, she looks down at his body as she does every morning, but now her reconnaissance stops where his *lungi* is tented.

Wade looks at Herta's sun-red face. An aroma of coconut oil clings to her vicinity. Above the *lungi,* Wade is bare-chested. Outside birds are announcing the day.

"You are well," Herta declares.

Wade can't think of a reply, so he says nothing. Herta brings her hands up as if to show them to Wade, but then her hands go down to untie the knot of Wade's *lungi* where it is bound below his bellybutton. She does this slowly and carefully, and when she opens the folds of the *lungi* it is with the same care. She holds the cloth open for an extended moment, looking, before allowing the cloth to drop on either side of his body.

Wade is aware of his breathing, and at the same time there is the moment, which is suspended, for what has transpired seems to have been ceremonial. He is now waiting for what comes next, and it occurs to him that it will be no less surprising than what has just transpired. He has no idea what's coming next.

Herta stands up. Her smile is gone, and for this Wade's smile falters. Herta brings her hands up to in back of her neck and unties the knot of her green garment and lets the cloth fall to the floor. She is naked.

It all seems so logical, but it is only logical after the fact, which is when it seems natural for its directness and simplicity.

Herta continues to stand as if to invite examination. Her feet are in sandals, but other than sandals there is only flesh and dabs of hair at strategic locations.

She slips her feet out of her sandals and steps over to the table and takes that day's flower from behind her ear and sets the flower on the table next to the previous day's flower. A half-burnt candle nearby is secured in a puddle of hard wax, candle unlit. As Herta walks back to the cot, Wade can almost feel the weight of her breasts.

A text of sorts begins where none existed before. Wade unties his money belt from around his waist and drops the money belt on the floor.

Herta puts her left knee on the cot next to Wade's hip. Her hands come to either side of Wade's shoulders where they press down on the cot as she brings her body over his. She reaches under herself and directs Wade's erection while easing back and lowering her weight. There is a gasp, but nothing more. Her hands are now free as she sits on top of him, her torso vertical. She begins a faint smile while rocking back and forth, no embarrassment. Wade is looking up at her. She moves with intent.

Wade is surprised that he can be thinking about description and intent, for given the immediacy of the situation he should be more involved. He attributes this to the way things have transpired, and now, as he watches Herta start to quiver, he wonders about voyeurism, but how is voyeurism possible given his involvement? He senses that he is not only watching Herta, but watching himself as well.

Herta's hands come to the tops of her thighs and her fingers dig in. She shudders.

When Herta falls onto Wade's chest, he puts his arms around her. She is breathing heavily, but this soon calms. She remains prone on top of him, and Wade can almost hear her thinking.

She pushes herself up and rocks a couple of times to see if he is still there. He is. She smiles. Her cheeks are more puffed up than usual and this gives her a brattish look. She starts talking in English, voice accented and guttural. "Is it not nice, Wade? Do you like?" She rocks back and forth in a languid manner as she looks at him. She is smiling, but it is different from before, for now, in addition to candid, there is mischief. She knows what he wants even though he doesn't know it until it arrives. Under her tutelage Wade's body gathers itself and tumbles as if clairvoyance were at work.

Taking a seat on one of the wooden benches in the patio/restaurant, they watch the proprietor approach, a smoldering *beedi* between his fingers. The man accepts their order and calls the order to his wife, who is standing in the doorway of the kitchen eight feet away: "Two chai, two bun." The wife turns to go into the kitchen, thus leaving her half-naked son to stand alone in the doorway. The boy's large eyes latch onto the dog, and with this the child totters across the red-dirt floor of the patio to where the dog waits.

Wade and Herta have brought a jar of strawberry jam. Wade, though, has forgotten his glass, but no one seems to mind. When the tea and rolls arrive, Wade produces a pocketknife to spread the jam.

The man returns to stand in the doorway of the kitchen. His wife joins him, and together they watch Wade and Herta eat and drink. Occasionally the wife's eyes go to the child, who is with the dog, child and dog at the edge of the patio where the shade from the awning leaves off.

Wade and Herta don't talk. They eat, they sip chai, they look at the Arabian Sea. All is calm. The glow of their love making lingers.

"Baba," says Wade. "More chai, more bread." The man responds, "Two chai, two bun?" Wade says, "Yes. Two chai, two bun." The man turns to his wife, who is standing next to him, and the man says, "Two chai, two bun." The wife goes into the kitchen.

After breakfast Wade and Herta return to Wade's room. Wade's stomach is fine and so is everything else. Wade and Herta undress as if it were assumed.

"You have energy," Herta reports.

"Yes, I do."

"I do, too."

The day's proceedings alternate between Wade's room and the patio. In the late afternoon Herta and Wade go to the well to bathe.

He sleeps and he dreams, and when he wakes in the morning he remembers that he didn't dream when he was sick and delirious.

The morning is the morning-after. Wade is sore, but he's sore in the right places.

When Herta enters his room after incense and chanting, she says with a smile that she is sore, and with this she proceeds to show Wade exactly where it hurts.

The man and the man's wife are in the doorway of the kitchen, looking on. On the table in front of Wade and Herta there is chai and bread and strawberry jam. The child is nowhere to be seen. Perhaps the child is asleep. The yellow dog, though, is in evidence, but not in the patio. The dog is peeing on bushes at the perimeter of the cleared ground that surrounds the mud-brick house and the patio and the palm-frond rooms.

Wade and Herta have determined that they need to go to the village. They are running low on supplies, particularly strawberry jam.

Wade now begins, "I'm just curious—" But Herta cuts him off by saying, "I take the birth control pill. I do not want to kill a baby in my belly."

Wade looks at her. Her expression is neutral. Wade looks out unto the clearing and sees the dog trotting back toward the patio, gait spry.

"I take the malaria pill for the mosquito. I take the birth control pill for the baby."

Herta picks up her glass of chai and sips.

Wade says, "That's important and I'm glad you told me. But, what I was going to ask about is: When was it that you decided that we were going to have sex? You know, it seems to me—"

"I knew when I saw you at the well."

"At the well?"

"Yes. That first time at sunset. You were washing, and then we met on the road. I knew then."

"You knew then?"

"Yes. I knew you were phallic."

"Phallic?"

"Yes."

Wade picks up his glass of tea.

"Where did you learn English?" Wade asks.

"I told you. There was school, and there were movies. I like watching movies."

"In English?"

"Of course."

Wade's glass of chai is elevated as he holds it.

"I don't think I've ever heard the word 'phallic' used in a movie."

Herta shrugs a shoulder. "It is the correct word, is it not?"

Wade continues to hold his glass of tea as if it were stalled en route to his mouth.

"That's what I saw," Herta says. "Phallic. And that's what I felt."

The dog is standing in the shade of the patio where it looks out toward the sea.

"The body knows before the mind knows," Herta says. "The mind dictates strategy, the body dictates need. It is when we ignore the body that there is trouble."

Wade listens to this as it replays in his head. This isn't uncommon when he's conversing with Herta, for when she is speaking there is her accent that garners Wade's attention. So there is often a delay in cognition, for he has to go back over her words with the intent of extracting meaning.

Wade looks at his tea glass and sets it down. The glass is almost empty. Wade looks toward the doorway of the kitchen and says, "Baba. Two chai, two bread."

The man turns to his wife and says, "Two chai, two bun." The wife leaves the doorway to go into the kitchen.

"So," Wade begins, "it was at the well, three weeks ago, when you first saw me, that all this was determined?"

"No," Herta says. "None of this was determined, but something was decided. You came by, and I spoke to you. The next morning I came here and asked Baba if there was a man here who spoke English. Baba, of course, doesn't really understand English, but he pointed and said, 'Sick man.'"

Wade nods. "Weren't you kind of . . . you know . . . nervous or scared?"

"Of course. Nervous. Nervous is a better word. But I was also excited. I was looking for something, and that is always exciting."

"And when you found me sick?"

"Yes. I found you sick, but I found you *alone*."

Wade moistens his lips with his tongue. His lips are chapped.

"I waited. You allowed it," Herta says.

Wade waits, but Herta adds nothing more.

"You helped me through my sickness," Wade says. "It was . . . It was you sitting on my bed and talking. And you kept coming back. I was . . ." He raises a hand in gesture, but words don't follow. Wade lowers the hand.

"Of course. You were sick, and I waited."

"Yes," Wade says, and wants to continue, but it's like he's out of words. Herta is looking at him. So he says, "And now what?"

"And now," says Herta, "we do what we are doing. This will continue until something else arrives, and that something else will be next. Can it be any other way?"

The man comes to their table with an aluminum tray and transfers two glasses of chai from the tray to the table and then does the same with two small plates, a roll on each plate. He picks up the empty glasses and sets them on the tray and does the same for the two small plates from the previous serving. The man goes to the doorway of the kitchen and hands the tray to his wife.

Wade looks at Herta and says, "Well, what do you think is next?"

"One day you will leave this place."

"Yes, I will."

"Take me with you."

Wade is stopped. He looks at Herta's sun-red face and sees a half-smile.

"I'm on a bicycle."

"I will purchase a bicycle."

"Purchase a bicycle?" Wade questions. "I'm headed south, Cape Comorin, southern tip of India."

"Yes. You told me. It is where the three seas of India gather. It is a holy place."

Wade picks up one of the glasses of chai and sets the glass in front of Herta and picks up the other glass and sets it in front of himself.

"Did I say it was a holy place?" Wade asks.

"No, I don't believe you did. But everyone knows it is a holy place."

Wade picks up his glass of chai along the lip of the glass. The glass is hot. He sips tentatively, aroma of cinnamon funneling into his sinuses.

"You are thinking that it is difficult," Herta says. "You have told me, and I have listened—weather, hills, mosquitoes, food, roads, punctured tires, sickness, exhaustion—I understand."

Wade sets his glass down.

"But look at you," Herta says. "It shows."

"What shows?"

"India."

"India?"

"Yes. And it is what I came here for."

Wade can only look at her.

"When did you think of all this?" Wade asks.

"When I sat on your bed, when we talked. You told me you were on a bicycle. I went outside and saw the bicycle."

Wade nods.

"I understood your *body* at the well, and I understood the rest when I saw the bicycle."

Wade watches as Herta picks up her glass of chai and sips.

"And now," Herta says, "I understand even more—and so do you."

Wade listens to this, its delivery and then its replay in his head.

"If you say 'yes,' or if you say 'no,' next will begin," Herta says.

"I imagine it will."

"Don't think," Herta tells him. "For it is not your mind that moves you. It is your body. Your mind would never undertake a journey such as yours. Your body and its energy have put you on the bicycle, and it is this that moves you from north to south—is it not?"

Wade moistens his lips with his tongue.

"And it is your body that has determined what has taken place here." Herta raises a hand. Wade looks at the hand, but then his eyes shift to Herta's mouth as she speaks.

"What does your body say? Not your mind, but your body."

CHAPTER 3

He was in the kitchen doing dishes when he heard the countdown. Coming into the living room, he saw Times Square on TV. His mother was in her armchair, an over-stuffed piece of furniture, feet resting on an ottoman. She was smoking a cigarette and the TV was loud. The camera panned the crowd, everyone in coats and mufflers and hats, and then there it was, a huge glittering ball at the end of its famed descent. The camera looked for jubilation and found it. Wade saw a couple of women wearing big plastic glasses that said—2005—novelty items that would become keepsakes.

Wade, dishtowel in hand, turned to his mother who seemed to notice, for she looked at him and said, "Happy New Year." And even though it would remain 2004 for another three hours in Los Angeles, Wade said "Happy New Year" back to her.

With the holidays over, Wade went looking for work. By way of classified ads in the newspaper, a Valley paper, he tried two warehouses. At the first one, an obese man behind a gray-metal desk told Wade that they'd call him if they wanted to interview him. Wade's application was in front of the man, front side of the form glanced at, backside ignored. Wade figured that it must have been Wade's looks, or more precisely his age, that caused the man to ignore the application.

At the other place, a casually dressed woman, Loren Snell, mid-thirties, examined Wade's application with interest, particularly the backside, which was the work-history side. Looking up from the form, Loren said, "This is remarkable." Wade smiled in a small way, for on the one hand "remarkable" was a positive comment, but on the other hand maybe it was too positive. Wade waited for follow-up. Loren, whose title was warehouse manager, said, "You were really in those places?" Wade was about to reply, but then he saw Loren doing some calculating with regards to dates, finger moving over the "from/to" sections. Loren's lips were moving as she silently added things up.

"Gee whiz," Loren said. "From beginning to end it comes to about thirty-two years. Is that right?"

"Yes."

Loren seemed to be an energetic person, the way she gestured with her hands, the way she turned her head, the way she looked at Wade with a pair of lively brown eyes. Her hair was short and thick, chestnut in color. The warehouse she was in charge of dealt with PVC piping.

"I'm tempted to say you're over qualified, but that's not exactly it. It's more like . . . I'm not sure exactly what it's like. But . . . I think you'd find this work boring. Besides, you're what . . . " She flipped the application over to the front side. "Fifty-six years old." But then Loren seemed to catch herself by dismissing this with a wave of a hand, as she said, "But that isn't of any real consequence." She smiled, and as Wade looked at her smile, "age discrimination" flashed in Wade's mind, for the term had become part of media-lexicon, along with a lot of other phrases and terms relating to discrimination. Loren had to be careful about such things.

Getting down to business, expression on Loren's face indicating, Loren said, "Part of the job description is 'heavy lifting.' The job requires someone who can lift fifty-pound boxes frequently."

"I can do that."

Loren looked at Wade with renewed interest, but whether this was good or bad, or something else, wasn't clear.

"We are going to make a decision in about a week. If you don't hear from us by next Friday, you can assume the position has been filled."

Wade nodded and thanked Loren for her time.

At the state employment office even more diplomacy was at work, but the results were the same.

Wade drove to a nearby Home Depot, and in the paint department he picked out two pairs of white pants, Dickies. At a cash register he paid for the Dickies along with two pairs of work gloves.

At home Wade took off his khakis and put on a pair of Dickies, which satisfied his idea of an outfit: sport shoes, white pants, gray sweatshirt with the sleeves cut off at mid-forearm, and a billed-cap without any sort of logo.

From the garage he got an aluminum stepladder, a claw hammer and a pair of pliers. Setting the ladder up at one corner of the house, he climbed the ladder and began removing the cracked and warped fascia from the ends of the rafters where the roof left off.

The roof had been re-shingled five years previous, as Wade happily discovered by way of a receipt and a ten-year warranty that he came across while going through a torrential pile of papers and mail, which was one of the first chores he attended to after returning home just before Thanksgiving—mail. So, the roof was in good shape.

But, there were other discoveries amongst that mail that weren't so cheerful, such as a five-hundred-dollar water bill that Wade unearthed early on because he attempted to start with the most recent mail. Looking up from that water bill, his view went out the dining room window to the backyard where some doves and sparrows were bathing in a puddle of water under an elm that was shedding leaves. Wade got up from the dining room table and went to the kitchen and got a large, rectangular Tupperware container, three inches deep, and went out to the backyard, sparrows and doves taking flight. He walked over to a faucet that had a garden hose attached to it and turned the faucet off. This stopped the water at the other end of the hose from feeding the puddle that the birds had been bathing in. Setting the Tupperware container down near the puddle, Wade put the end of the hose in the container and went back to the faucet and turned it on. When the container had two inches of water in it, Wade turned the spigot off. Paula really liked birds. She fed them seed every day and kept them well supplied with drinking and bathing water via a 24/7/365 flow from the garden hose.

Other problems buried in the mail weren't so readily solved, such as lapsed insurance premiums, house and automobile outstanding. To some extent, though, the automobile was understandable because Paula had stopped driving. Of course the true nature of this status wasn't clear to her because she thought she was going to start driving again as soon as she got better, and better meant: "When I'm feeling better." So the uninsured car, even though okay while sitting in the garage, wasn't purposeful. In a sense, it was symptomatic of the general state of affairs regarding her and her home. Dishes, for example, that Wade found in the kitchen sink upon his arrival home were dirty and moldy and fetid, and the same could be said for laundry in the washing machine. Forgotten and unattended described the situation: expired food in the cupboards and refrigerator, yellowed sheets on Paula's bed, sour-smelling towels in the bathroom.

It had taken Wade two weeks to sort through the mail and to figure out where things stood, which in terms of the automobile was further complicated because Wade didn't have a valid California driver's license, which in effect was like being crippled vis-à-vis Southern California and its insistent automobile lifestyle. So, he had to wing it by driving unlawfully without a license and without insurance to the DMV, where he took a paper test and then a driving test in his mother's eight-year-old Pontiac that was nearly new in terms of mileage on the odometer. Fortunately the licensing fee for the car had been paid, 2004 sticker in place on the rear license plate. With a driver's license in hand, Wade went to the registration department with the car's pink slip, which he had had his mother sign along with a bill of sale, and switched the car's ownership over to his name. Returning home, he called the Auto Club and asked about obtaining insurance. Yes, he could get insurance, but it would be "assigned risk" because Wade hadn't been an insured driver the previous year. "Assigned risk" meant expensive.

The next-door neighbor had been helping out with grocery shopping, and Wade's long-time friend from childhood and early youth, Art Perez, had been driving Paula to the doctor's office as well as picking up fifty-pound sacks of wild bird seed at a pet shop slash feed store. It was when Wade called home in November that the next-door neighbor answered the phone and told Wade he had better get home because things were out of hand. Two days later Wade was on an airplane. It was a long flight, transit points part of it—Penang to Los Angeles.

When he walked in the front door, it wasn't that Paula didn't recognize him, or so he thought. It was more that she didn't care, as if maybe he hadn't been away, like maybe he had just stepped out and was returning from the supermarket. A warm Southern California day, Wade getting out of a taxi and crossing the lawn to step up onto the porch and open the screen door, and then to step into the living room, his mother in her chair, a reupholstered armchair, feet up on a footstool. She was watching a game show on TV.

"Howdy, Ma. I'm home."

She glanced up at him as he stood with a small burgundy-colored suitcase in hand. Paula's face was white and thin, and it was lined with wrinkles. There was no expression.

Wade smiled. Paula's view went to where a cigarette was balanced on the lip of an ashtray. She picked the cigarette up with her yellow-tipped thumb and index finger and brought the cigarette to her lips and inhaled, and in this way Wade began to understand the consequences of time.

The exterior of the house needed painting, and painting required new fascia, as well as stucco patching. The new wood would get a primer/sealer. Other wood, such as doors and window trim, would be sanded and patched and sanded again before getting a primer/sealer. After that, the paint would go on, paint for the wood, paint for the stucco. Wade had done this kind of work as a teenager, and then at times while abroad he had done similar work, Greece and Israel, the early part of his travels when he was still in his twenties. So, the work wasn't unfamiliar. But it had been a while and products had changed, and Wade had aged.

It was after the prep work was done and when he was rolling paint onto the stucco with a long-napped roller that a woman came up and said, "Hello. Are you Paula's son?" Wade was working on the front side of the house. The woman was wearing large, round glasses and her hair was brushed back with a slight wave, length to the nape of her neck. Wade said, "Yes, I am." The woman said, "I'm Ruth. I know your mother. She was in the hospital where I work. I'm a nurse." Wade took this into immediate consideration, and perhaps Ruth saw it, for she said, "You didn't know? About a year and a half ago. Fortunately, it was relatively minor. She had hurt her back. She was discharged in a week, most of which was spent in therapy." Wade nodded. Ruth shifted her weight and gestured. "I see you're working on the house." "Yes," Wade said. Ruth was wearing a bone-colored sweater and a pair of blue jeans. "Well, I have this big crack in my kitchen ceiling from that earthquake a few years ago. I put spackling paste on it and then tried sanding it, but that was hard on my arms and the dust fell on my face, and… And so I still got that crack in the ceiling and it's got hard, white paste on it, which makes it look worse. Anyway, I'd like to have that crack taken out and the kitchen painted. Do you think you could come over and take a look and maybe give me a price?"

"Sure."

CHAPTER 4

They set out along the coastal road heading south, and in those introductory days the weather was pleasant, but in the afternoon it got hot, but not nearly as hot as it was going to get once they gave up the narrow coastal plain for the Deccan Plateau, which would coincide with February turning into March, hot and dry, temperatures commonly above 40 degrees Celsius, 104 Fahrenheit. The only relief on that huge plateau would be an occasional hill station, until the monsoon rains arrived around the beginning of June. Hepatitis, and Wade's recovery from that illness, had set his timetable back a month, a critical month in terms of heat-related weather.

Two days before embarkation from that southern Goan beach with the palm-frond rooms and the yellow dog and the half-naked child and the stout woman and her skinny husband, Wade and Herta took the bus to Panjim, Goa's version of a metropolitan city, which in actuality was a leftover Portuguese port town of a colonial variety, a somewhat sleepy town with cobblestone streets and wine merchants. At a bicycle shop, Herta purchased a used bike, manufacturer Hero, color black. The one Herta chose came with a little bell on the handlebars along with a reed basket that hung over the front fender, while at the rear of the bike there was a sturdy steel rack over the rear fender. Thus, Herta and Wade's bicycles were alike.

Next came a tailor's shop. Wade had brought the canvas saddlebags that a tailor in Amritsar had made under Wade's instruction, saddlebags fashioned so that they hung from the rear rack of his bike. He figured he could show the bags to a tailor in Panjim and have the bags duplicated, which was what transpired. Tailors in India were very adept at custom tailoring. They could put together just about anything, and on short notice. Herta and Wade went and had lunch, and when they returned from lunch the saddlebags were ready, bickering about price having been done before any fabric was cut, so it was simply a matter of checking to see if the job had been done right, which it had.

At the bus station in Panjim they put Herta's just-bought bicycle on the roof-rack of a bus that was headed south. An hour later, with multiple stops at no-nothing places, Wade yanked a cord that rang a bell, which signaled the driver to stop at an intersecting dirt road, which was where Herta and Wade got Herta's bike down from the roof-rack via a steel ladder at the rear of the bus.

And so, that night there were two bicycles chained to poles beneath their palm-frond rooms. The next morning they set off, husband, wife, child and yellow dog seeing them off, everyone waving except the dog.

The pace was off. Wade noticed it almost immediately even though his concerns were about his physical condition with regards to stamina, for he hadn't been on his bicycle for a month and he figured that he'd be out of shape. So he was thinking about that, but what was obvious was that Herta's mode of pedaling and Wade's were very different. There wasn't too much traffic, and for stretches at a time the paved road was dappled with shade, tall coconut palms on either side, grove upon grove, and within that canopy there was a soft green hue. Pedaling was rather easy, for in addition to the shade there was no incline.

When Wade and Herta were side by side on the road, it wasn't too bad, their respective speeds matching somewhat, but this was only because Wade had downgraded his pace in order to stay parallel with Herta. But when a vehicle would approach from the rear they had to give this up, which meant that either Wade or Herta would fall in behind. At first, Wade sped up to go ahead of Herta, but when he did this he'd soon outpace her and then would have to wait for her to catch up.

So Wade tried falling in behind Herta when vehicles were approaching from the rear, which of course meant on their side of the road, and that was another thing—paying attention to the sounds of cars or trucks or buses coming up from in back of them, which wasn't all that difficult because drivers almost always blasted away on their horns well in advance in order to tell pedestrians and cyclists to move over so that the drivers wouldn't have to give up any speed. But when Wade tried this, the Wade-in-back-of-Herta alternative, Herta would slow down, and the longer Wade was behind her the slower the pace got until it was like dawdling, as if maybe Herta was doubtful about direction. And then, of all things, on the third time that this was tried, Herta slowed down to the point of pull off onto the dirt shoulder of the road to stop and straddle her bicycle, as if to wait up for Wade, who was right in back of her and who was wondering what was going on. If it had been a truck or a bus blasting away on its horn, a very distinct sound, then going off onto the shoulder might have been necessary because of draft-impact that those vehicles carried, which could knock a cyclist over. But it was cars going by, and more to the point it was Herta stalled midst indecision or confusion.

The tandem side-by-side cycling could only work when there were no vehicles, and even then it was a mode that required surveillance because there was always the possibility of traffic developing from the rear, so Wade and/or Herta had to be thinking about that. The tandem condition would be hard to maintain if they wanted to cycle any kind of real distance, for long-distance cycling requires an ease of concentration that allows for non-thinking. If they rode one in back of the other, they could mostly disregard traffic approaching from the rear, and so be done with that. Naturally, it is in this mode, non-thinking mode, that the mind can wonder, daydreaming and free thoughts prevalent, a form of relaxation while moderate exertion continues. Conversely and oddly, though, it is also in this mode that the mind can take notice of ongoing surroundings that are passing in reference to the bicycle's movement.

Wade thought it was necessary to work things out, particularly after they were stopped on the side of the road with Herta asking, "What are you doing?", irritation in her voice, and with Wade then replying, "I wasn't doing anything. I was behind you. Why'd you pull over?" "I pulled over to wait for you." And so Wade, faced with this, explained the necessity of one of them in back of the other when there was traffic, and then he went on to explain about how it was necessary to set a pace, a one-in-back-of-the-other pace, so that they could get somewhere without having to think so much. But then Herta said, "I know that." And perhaps she did because Wade might have said something about this before. So Wade said, "You got to pick up the pace. You got to go faster. This isn't like bicycling in the park with your family. We got to get from point A to point B, otherwise we won't get anywhere." In response to this, Herta said, "Are we in a hurry?" Meanwhile, a crowd of local kids had gathered to look at them, and along with the children a few adults were on their way to join the kids in their gawking, not an uncommon occurrence, people from seemingly out of nowhere gathering to look at foreigners.

"No, we aren't in a hurry, but we got to get on with this. Come on. Let's go."

The issue of pace continued as a source of friction that got worse in the afternoon when they were navigating the edge of some mild hills. Fortunately, those hills receded where the state of Goa ended and where the state of Karnataka began.

They spent the night near Kumta Beach in a room-to-let that was part of a sprawling house where the husband and wife spoke a little English and where the husband had approached Wade and Herta as they were walking their bikes down a dirt road that led to the beach from off the main road. "A room?" the man had said, and gestured toward his concrete house that was set back from that diminutive red-dirt track. It was late afternoon and Herta and Wade wanted to try the beach, a swim perhaps. But more than that, where there's a pleasant beach there is almost always accommodation of one sort or another. And so, as the man had guessed, they were looking for a room, thus it was easy to arrange and easy to strike a deal in terms of money.

An extended family lived in the house, and as it turned out Wade and Herta's room was an add-on with its own entrance that faced a clearing where a concrete outhouse stood, and beyond that clearing tall coconut palms rose up into a blue sky, sea breeze swaying the palms.

"No," Wade said, in response to dinner that the man offered, with the inherent understanding that the meal would have to be paid for. "We brought food," Wade explained, and indeed they had: bread, strawberry jam, processed cheese, peanuts, bananas, and Pepsi-Cola. But more than the price of a meal was the consideration of health, for the food Wade and Herta carried was safe, which was to say, free of water-contamination, for water was often the cause of sickness in India, so the more they could stay away from water the less risk.

There were two cots in the room along with a wooden table and a couple of rush-seated chairs. A candle in a tin-framed square with little panes of glass, a lantern of sorts, was on the table, too.

They brought their bicycles into the room and changed into swimsuits and left for the beach, Wade locking the room's plank door with a padlock that he carried in his saddle bags, padlock fitting through a hasp on the door, not an uncommon arrangement, which was one reason why Wade carried a padlock.

The beach was a sandy stretch, no people. They jammed their money belts into a plastic container that had a tight-fitting, screw-on lid. They waded out into the water and jumped around in the small waves that were rolling in, Wade holding the circular container with the money belts above the waves with one hand, a container that doubled as a receptacle for peanuts. They thought of taking off their swimsuits and going naked, but since they didn't know the local rules or how the situation might change, deserted beach suddenly filling with people out to see the sunset, they kept their swimsuits on. The water was fairly clean and it revived their spirits, as did the sunset, a huge orange ball sliding into the Arabian Sea.

And that's how it would go, their spirits rising and falling in the course of a day and/or night, sometimes together, both of them high or low at the same time, or sometimes not together, when they'd be on different frequencies, each involved with his or her own attitude and disposition, a private construct that was indulged silently or noisily. The only constant was change, internally and externally, for India was a reflection of self, a play between inner and outer, a paradigm of extremes.

Their bicycling, of course, represented a change from the lifestyle they had adopted during Wade's illness and recuperation, and their room near Kumta Beach represented a change as well, for now they were sharing a room as opposed to having separate rooms.

When they woke that first morning together in the same room, Herta said, "I want to chant, but I feel funny about it." Wade said, "I'll go outside." And that's what he did.

Outside, Wade lowered himself onto his haunches and started chewing on peanuts, shells falling onto the ground. A few children gathered and Wade gave them peanuts, everyone shelling goobers and chewing. Wade wondered about school for the kids, for they were elementary-school age, but they weren't dressed for school, and it seemed that they had nothing to do but to stare at Wade. There were four of them, two boys and two girls. The four kids could say, "Hello" and "Thank you," in English, and they could smile, and their teeth were white, albeit slightly squiggled. Naturally a dog appeared, ribs showing, but obviously the family pet.

After about fifteen minutes Herta opened the door and stood in the doorway and smiled and said, "You can come in now."

Wade went in and shut the door, thus shutting the kids out, which made him wonder what they would do now. There were two windows in the room, but neither one had glass or a screen. There were wooden shutters, though. Herta had closed the shutters for privacy in order to chant. The night before, after the candle was extinguished, Wade had opened the shutters to allow for ventilation, but of course that also allowed for mosquitoes. So before opening the shutters Herta and Wade had put their cots together and then positioned their bicycles on either side to jerry-rig a frame to hang Wade's mosquito net from, a large double net, for there were no hooks on the ceiling or walls for mosquito netting, nor were there canopies over the cots.

So, entering the room with its closed shutters, Wade found his eyes adjusting to the candle-lit enclosure with its concrete walls and ceiling, with Herta saying, "Come on," while rubbing at Wade's *lungi* to get him hard. The room smelled of incense and Wade's mind was bouncing between the bag of peanuts in his hand and the candle/lantern on the table and Herta leading him over to the table and then untying her wrap-around cloth and letting it fall to the floor and untying Wade's *lungi* and letting that drop to the floor, which left Wade with only a pair of sandals and a brown T-shirt, and then Herta's hand working busily, erection on the make, with Wade putting the bag of peanuts on the table and then fondling Herta's weighty breasts, with Herta then hopping up on the table to sit on its edge and to raise her legs up to where she put her feet on Wade's shoulders, and Wade sliding into her so easily because she was all moist, which made Wade wonder what she had been thinking about while chanting.

They are similar in dress as if following a dress code: sandals, khaki shorts, floral-print cotton shirts. Sometimes there is a billed cap and sometimes a pair of sunglasses.

For suntan lotion, they share a bottle of coconut oil that has a nice fragrance.

Wade keeps a journal in which he notes kilometers and miles, and on their first day of cycling he registered forty miles, sixty-four kilometers, that he calculated by using a map and measurement. When he relayed this information to Herta, she said, "By George, we have done well!" It was obvious that she was proud, obvious in her smile that plumped her cheeks, which were aglow with the day's sunshine and exercise.

But Wade knew that forty miles was not remarkable. Actually, it wasn't even average. But Wade wasn't really into averages or remarkable mileage or impressive mathematical data. For Wade, each day of cycling was its own creation. Terrain and weather and accommodation and points of interest and road conditions and tiredness and sickness were the determinants of how far he would get in a single day, or night, of pedaling.

So in response to Herta's excitement about sixty-four kilometers, Wade smiled as if to accept her conclusions, but this was a fib of sorts, for what he would have liked to have said was that this wasn't a report-card activity. Mileage and/or kilometers were part of description that Wade put down in his journal along with other descriptions, such as weather and hills and food and people at work or at leisure. He also noted his feeling and thoughts about what he had seen and experienced that day, and experience might encompass such things as loneliness or boredom or fascination, and in this he sometimes found that the outside world and the inside world were not so easily divided. But he didn't say anything about this to Herta because she had entered into his journal entries, for she had entered into his world, a world composed of description that oscillated between outer and inner. Wade wanted his journal to remain free, as in freedom of expression, so he didn't want to talk about his journals because then Herta might be curious and might want to read it. But he did tell her: "We bicycled about forty miles today, roughly sixty-four kilometers."

Simple numbers, as Wade tried to see them, were theoretically impartial, but Herta took off on them, and Wade had let that be. There was nothing really wrong with this, nothing wrong with Herta's sense of accomplishment and subsequent excitement. After all, the same processes were at work within Wade—personalization of the outside world and the experiences it delivered via interaction.

A choice had presented itself, and choice meant decision, and so they were committed to that decision, which they made before spending the night near Kumta Beach, and if they had decided the other way, for there was a fork in the road, they wouldn't have spent the night near Kumta Beach. They would have pedaled uphill and ventured inland, which was the direction almost all the traffic went, but Wade had thought it easier to continue along the coastal route, which wouldn't have presented a choice if it weren't for a river with no apparent bridge over it, or so Wade's map indicated, a topographical road map that included railway lines and the relative size of towns by way of boldness and size of typeface. It was a good map, and it was constantly in use. Wade had purchased the map in a bookstore just off Syntagma Square, in Athens—Indian Subcontinent.

As Wade explained it to Herta when they were at the side of the road in the shade of a palm tree, fork in the road up ahead: "We could continue all the way to Cape Comorin without leaving this narrow coastal strip." He showed her by fingering the map. "But then we'd be seeing mostly what we're seeing now, which is like what both of us saw in Goa—coastline and a lot of greenery. Also, we'd have to go through Mangalore." "Yes," Herta said. "On the other hand," Wade resumed, "if we went up through the Western Ghats, this long range of mountains," and here again he fingered the map, "that'd put us on the Deccan Plateau, which is the largest plateau in India, and in a sense it is that landmass that makes India like a triangle." He gestured at the map, which was spread out on the ground. Luckily there was no wind, but it was hot and somewhat humid, and both Wade and Herta were perspiring, and what an odd place to make such a decision and to explain all the things that needed explaining in order to frame that decision. But on the other hand, Herta now had an inkling of what was at stake, for she had been pedaling a good part of the day, fatigue and muscle pain coming to bear. So maybe Wade's saving this until they got to the fork in the road and how that translated on the map wasn't so haphazard. Yet Wade wasn't sure if he had consciously worked this out in his head beforehand. Perhaps it was a matter of laziness, as in putting things off until the very end, when they can no longer be put off.

"So either we stick to the coast, or we go up onto that plateau." "Yes, I see that," Herta said. "If we go up onto the plateau, we can fashion our journey through Mysore and Madurai, thus avoiding both Mangalore and Bangalore, which are rather industrial. Three years ago, on my first trip to India, I was in Mysore and Madurai, and I found both cities to be interesting, and for the most part they weren't industrial."

Herta looks up from the map to where her eyes lock onto Wade's eyes. "I didn't know you were in India before."

"Yeah, I was, but I wasn't on a bicycle. I was traveling the regular way, trains and buses."

"Why didn't you tell me you were in India before?"

"It didn't come up."

"I'm not sure if that's a reason."

"It's the same reason that I didn't tell you about the high school I went to or the first job I ever had or the first Bob Dylan song I listened to—it's not pertinent until it's pertinent. After all, we can't say everything about our lives. We don't have time for it. And besides, I'm not so talkative."

"I noticed that."

And so there they were, down on their haunches with a map spread out on the ground, their bicycles nearby, sweat on their faces and arms and legs, while overhead crows cawed as if maybe Wade and Herta were signaling food-activity, always a drawing card, while on the opposite side of the road a dozen children had gathered to stand and gawk. A few cars had slowed, one of them honking its horn as if to stir irritation.

Wade stood up and went to the wicker basket of his bicycle and got a half-full bottle of Pepsi that was corked with one of a couple of corks that Wade carried for the purpose of corking half-full bottles, which were inevitably never cooler than lukewarm. After taking a swig, he went over to Herta and stooped down and handed her the bottle. Herta drank some cola.

"Okay," Wade said. "If we go that way," and with this he pointed to the road that forked left, which was just beyond where the kids were standing, "that'll take us this way," and now he directed Herta's attention back to the map where he traced a course inland with his finger. "But if we go straight," and here he continued with his finger on the map, "we come to this dead-end at the river." Herta nodded. "But the road picks up on the other side of the river, so I'm guessing that there's a ferry of some sort that crosses the river to connect these two dead-ends. I mean, it's just logical. A business opportunity for someone, don't you think?" Herta raised her view and looked at him. "We're going to go up into the Western Ghats anyway on the other side of that river," Wade said, "but we'll be going directly up instead of this long way around and up. Both ways will get us to exactly the same place on the plateau, but if we chance the ferry deal, and it works out, we'll be saving ourselves a lot of kilometers through the hills."

Herta looked down at the map and then looked up at Wade. "What if there's no ferry?"

"That's why we're here talking about this, because if there's no ferry, then we have to backtrack about fifty kilometers, which amounts to one hundred kilometers roundtrip, and then go up into the hills anyway."

So after the chanting and the peanuts with the children and the episode on the wooden table, they put shorts and shirts on and mounted their bicycles and pedaled back to the paved road, which was the shortcut road with the potential of maybe becoming a long-cut road. The day before Wade tried getting information from the man who rented them the room, but the man either couldn't understand Wade or didn't know about a ferry, so the ferry was still a matter of speculation.

On their left, a dull stream moves sluggishly under overhanging bushes. Now and then there is a kingfisher perched on a branch, a small brilliantly colored bird, metallic green accompanying orange and turquoise. The bird is deft at dive-bombing for small fish. Wade keeps looking over with the hope of seeing some action. He says to Herta, "Look," and points. Herta and Wade are side by side on the road, which is quiet for lack of traffic. Herta looks and says, "What?" And Wade says, "Kingfisher." And Herta repeats this, but with a question mark, "Kingfisher?" "That colorful bird." Wade stops pedaling and comes to a stop, so Herta stops, too. Wade points and says, "Right over there on that branch." Herta looks, but doesn't say anything. And then, like magic, the bird comes off the branch and goes into the water with its wings folded back, sharp beak leading the way, and it's all so quick, and so is the bird's emerging with a little fish in its beak, a minnow perhaps. Returning to its branch, the bird takes a moment as if to savor its prize, head and tail of the fish sticking out from either side of the bird's beak. And then the fish is swallowed.

"Oh," says Herta, tenor of her utterance telling, which satisfies Wade, because he knows that she saw it.

There is a small town at the end of the road just before the river, and at the river there is a ferry dockside. They board that overcrowded small boat with their bicycles just as others have boarded with their bicycles. The boat sets off across brownish water carrying forty people and twenty bicycles and Wade hopes that the boat doesn't capsize or lose power, engine asthmatic and puttering, exhaust black puffs of smoke. The entire scene with the colorful clothing of the women and the skinny men in *lungis* and the children with wide eyes and dark faces and the straw-woven baskets with bananas and coconuts is so typical that it almost seems scripted for National Geographic.

But it's not scripted. And even though Wade's seen it over and over again, he still has to tell himself that it's real. It is this feeling, this perception, this impression that reminds him all so emphatically that he is an onlooker, and even though the bicycle erases some aspects of "onlooker," this perception persists. Of course the myth of "going native" he gave up years ago, but what continues to mystify him is the idea of "adventure," for he continues to wonder if adventure is merely the narration of experience, in which case "adventure" would always be cast in past tense, for midst experience there is simply that occurrence, which might or might not ignite feelings of excitement or fear or exhilaration or beauty, but never "adventure."

Wade is certain that Herta has projections as well, speculation about "adventure" and "going native" and "seeing the country" and "getting off the beaten path." But Wade and Herta haven't really talked about these things, at least not yet. And maybe they never will.

They disembark and they head inland along a paved road, and for a little while that road parallels the river, the river they just crossed, the Sharavati, and it could be said that the shortcut paid off. After all, they guessed right, they made the right decision, they took the correct road, which led them to a ferry that saved them a lot of pedaling through up-and-down country. But they didn't say anything about that when spotting the ferry or after disembarkation. They simply got on the boat and they simply got off the boat and started pedaling, and for this Wade feels that maybe Herta has fallen into the temper of this mode of transportation, the equanimity of pedaling.

It wasn't long before they were pushing their bicycles up a steep hill on a winding road, hot and humid, pedaling impossible. During this ascent they saw Jog Falls, but there wasn't much water falling, a few thin streams. It was too early for the spectacle that these falls were famous for, a spectacle that would begin when the monsoon rains arrived.

Before reaching Sagar they were again pedaling, and that's how they entered the town, on their bicycles. They were now in the Western Ghats at the edge of the Deccan

Plateau, but between them there were no expressions of accomplishment, perhaps because they were exhausted, or maybe it was that their immediate needs dictated food. Or, maybe it was that thing about equanimity again.

A chai wallah, like a chemist midst alchemy, is on the dirt shoulder of a road that runs with traffic, and nearby on that same dusty shoulder Wade and Herta sit on a couple of low stools with rush seats and sip spicy tea in thick glasses, while in front of them on another low stool there are pieces of cut-newspaper spread out, and on those sheets of grease-stained newsprint there are potato *wadas*, *bacoras*, and *samosas*. Shade from a two-story building in back of the chai master offers a degree of comfort, which is maybe why there are other customers on low stools who are sipping tea and taking a late afternoon break from either an indoor job or an outdoor job, clothing and depth of weathering on their complexions indicating one activity or the other, but amongst this corps of chai connoisseurs there are no women—except Herta. But of course she is a tourist or traveler or foreigner, which exempts her from a lot of social custom that governs native women. Surprisingly no one is staring at either Herta or Wade, and that's how it sometimes goes—anonymity. But it is a fickle event, and what determines it is kind of a mystery, for identical circumstance often breeds staring, gawking, giggling, and crowd-gathering.

Herta seems content, but it's not just Herta who sits with the satisfaction of tea and finger-foods after having struggled with her body by way of the bicycle. It is Wade as well, for he can feel his muscles, and it is not a bad feeling even though it is a tired feeling. He wonders if he is out of shape from his bout with hepatitis. Yet, hepatitis or no hepatitis, he understands this feeling, for he has had it often, and in this regard Herta was correct in diagnosing what moves him, for it is indeed physical activity that charges him, his muscles working and the feeling of that work, and then the aftermath of such exertion, which leaves him feeling calm.

He looks over at Herta and he wonders if he is reading what he feels into what he sees in her posture and expression, as well as into the way she sips her tea and picks up those greasy morsels from off the newsprint and puts them in her mouth and chews.

"Are you tired?" he asks.

"Yes."

There seems to be irritation in her voice, and it seems to imply that Wade is responsible for this, responsible for her fatigue, as if he's forced something on her—exertion, tiredness, exhaustion, heat, humidity.

He says, "I'm tired, too," as if to alleviate this implied tension that he senses between them.

Herta sets her glass of tea down on the newspaper with the bacoras and stands up and walks away. Wade turns to watch her as she goes to the window of a tobacconist that's in the building in back of the chai wallah. She makes a purchase and returns and sits down next to Wade. A pack of beedies and a small box of wooden matches are in her hand. She opens the beedi pack and takes out a beedi and lights up. She offers the pack to Wade, but he declines. She puts the pack of beedies and the matches in her pocket and picks up her glass of tea.

Wade's not against beedies, but he can sense that Herta thinks he is, and he can also sense that no matter what he says about beedies or about being tired or about the weather nothing will change between them. So he says nothing.

They finish their tea and they finish their food, and Wade takes their glasses and hands them to the chai wallah. Herta stands up and Wade picks up the pieces of newspaper and crumples them in his hands. They walk to where their bicycles are and Wade tosses the wadded-up paper on the ground at the edge of the road where other trash has accumulated. Herta lights another beedi and they get on their bicycles and pedal away, with Herta manipulating the beedi between her lips and her fingers.

Picking up a railroad line, they continue on a course paralleling to the tracks. Nearby there is the shore of Linganmakki Reservoir, a huge body of water, and it is in this locale that they come across some buildings with a sign: *Traveler's Bungalow*. The bungalows, like small cottages, look well maintained, and they are spread out over a maintained area that gives the complex a spacious feel as opposed to a crowded space. The bungalows have little porches, and on the windows there are screens. It looks too good to be true, and Wade can't imagine that there isn't a hitch, like maybe these bungalows are reserved for civil servants.

They stop pedaling and dismount, and Wade leaves Herta with the bicycles while he goes into a building where he finds a man and a woman at respective desks behind a counter. The man rises from his desk with a smile and comes to the counter and says, "May I help you?" He is slim and dark-skinned, and he looks healthy. "Do you have a room, a bungalow, a vacancy?" "For how many persons, may I ask?" "There are two of us." "Certainly, sir. The charge is ten rupees per overnight." "Ten rupees for two? Five rupees apiece?" "That is correct." Wade fills out a card, shows his passport, and pays for one night. He is given a key, and the man gestures to indicate the direction of the bungalow. Wade goes outside, and together with

Herta they walk their bicycles to the bungalow and go inside. The room is simple, clean, and spacious. There is an Asian-style toilet behind one door and a bathroom (shower) behind another door. Both the toilet and bathroom are clean, and there are even towels.

Herta is sitting on one of the beds and she is testing the springs by bouncing up and down. Wade says, "I can't believe it. I'm going to go back and pay for two more nights." Herta nods enthusiastically.

CHAPTER 5

Ruth's partner is Barbara, and Barbara is a tax accountant who works in a four-employee office on Lankershim Boulevard, clientele small businesses and individuals, one of whom, as it turns out, is Wade's mother, Paula. So it's not only Ruth who knows Paula; it's Barbara as well. Wade has looked at his mother's recent tax forms, standard 1040, and has understood that an accounting firm has been doing his mother's taxes, but that is as far as he has gone with it.

Barbara's office is well north of the NoHo Arts District on Lankershim Boulevard, which for Wade is a new district because it wasn't there thirty-two years ago, but of course Lankershim Boulevard was there thirty-two years ago, so Wade knows where Barbara's office is after she tells him the nearest cross street, this coming to Wade's ears as the three of them, Wade, Ruth and Barbara, are having coffee in Ruth and Barbara's living room after Wade finished disappearing the big spackling-paste smeared crack on the kitchen ceiling, newly purchased palm-sander employed, and then prepping the entire kitchen (cracks and spackling paste and sanding) before putting on a primer/sealer and a coat of paint. Ruth and Barbara are very pleased with how the kitchen turned out. In addition to coffee and chitchat, Wade is given a check.

Both Ruth and Barbara are middle-aged, and they both like doing yard work, which they sometimes term "gardening." Their complexions and forearms are tanned, and all four of those forearms have muscle tone. Neither woman is dainty in body or voice. They laugh freely and seem to be happy. They keep a neat house, and their backyard has flowers and fruit trees.

It's not surprising that new things and new terms and new patterns of speech have arisen in Southern California during Wade's absence. "Partner," for example, in its current usage, is new to Wade.

In this after-painting-the-kitchen conversation Ruth and Barbara talk about a recent trip to Disneyland that they took with a bunch of their friends. Ruth talks more than Barbara, but Barbara contributes. Wade sits and listens while sipping coffee, which is a little weak for his taste. The conversation slides into a reference about going to church on Sunday, "Sunday mass," which leads to more information about Ruth and Barbara, who, as Wade learns, are practicing Catholics who take their faith seriously. Wade doesn't ask, but he does wonder how the idea and situation of "partners," particularly two same-gender partners, jives with Church doctrine, but Church doctrine doesn't come up during the conversation, but what seems apparent to Wade is that neither Ruth nor Barbara are bothered about this. Ruth and Barbara talk freely about going to confession and receiving Communion.

After thanking Ruth and Barbara for the coffee and the work, and after the two women thank Wade for "transforming" their kitchen, Wade walks home feeling pretty good about having a check in his pocket.

A Saturday afternoon, there's a phone call. The man's name is Roger, and he's been over to Ruth and Barbara's, and he's looked at their kitchen, and he wants to know if Wade can come over to his house and give him a price on a living room and a kitchen that need painting. There are some cracks in both rooms that need repairing, cracks from earthquakes, as is common in California. Wade says sure, and takes down Roger's phone number and address, along with directions on how to get to Roger's house, which, as it turns out, is a couple of blocks off of Lankershim Boulevard, just south of the NoHo Arts District.

Wade's already been to a copy shop to have some business cards made, and he's already replaced his mother's simple telephone with an answering-machine telephone, and he's already gotten himself a cellphone and written that long number down in black marker on a letter-size piece of white paper and taped that paper to the dining room table next to the brand new telephone, so that if his mother needs to get a hold of him all she has to do is punch in the numerals on the new telephone's push-button buttons. He's gone over this carefully with Paula, and she's indicated that she understands.

Wade has also been to Home Depot again, and he has purchased more drop cloths and picked up additional color charts.

Regarding transportation, Wade has fitted a couple of old surfboard racks, which were in the garage gathering lots of dust, onto the roof of the Pontiac for carrying ladders, and he's removed the backseat, which then created a continuous space from the back of the front seat all the way through into the trunk. Since it's a four-door vehicle, easy access to that space is afforded from either side of the car as well as from the trunk.

If things work out the way he hopes, Wade'll need to go over and consult Barbara at her accounting office on Lankershim Boulevard about income tax and about paying into Social Security, for after having understood and dealt with his mother's situation Wade deems Social Security benefits a necessity (monthly bank transfers and Medicare), because to be without them in old age would be disastrous, unless someone was tremendously wealthy. So, in order to put into Social Security and be legal about it all, meaning paying income tax in its various forms, federal and state for example, Wade needs to understand the know-how of all this, for he will be self-employed, which will generate its own breed of paperwork.

Also, Wade needs to contact an insurance company to see about purchasing breakage insurance, for without it where would he be if he dropped a can of paint on someone's piano?

Wade and his mother, Paula, and Art Perez and his wife, April, are in a vermillion tuck-and-roll Naugahyde booth in the "bar section" of an Italian restaurant in Burbank. The "bar section" is a room that has a bar and some booths and tables, and the reason they are in the bar section instead of the main dining room is because Paula had vetoed the non-smoking dining room in favor of the smoking-okay barroom. Of course this is the restaurant's way of accommodating smokers. Paula is a heavy smoker, and she is proud of it to the extent that she brags to her doctor about continuing to smoke two packs of cigarettes a day, this in response to Dr. Green's telling her that tobacco contributes to ill health. Paula uses an asthma inhaler frequently, and Wade has watched her use the device while smoking a cigarette, which in a sense is hardly surprising, considering the frequency of Paula's smoking during waking hours, a cigarette burning almost continuously. Wade has waited for signs of adverse reaction from the immediacy of tobacco smoke and medicated spray, everything going down the windpipe and into the lungs nearly in tandem, but, so far, he hasn't detected any drastic reactions.

When Wade and Paula and Art and April entered the restaurant and were met by the *maître d'*, who promptly asked about smoking or non-smoking, Paula had spoken up, and because of that they had to wait fifteen minutes before a table was vacant in the smoking section, which was the barroom. The fifteen-minute wait seemed to suggest that the bar/smoking section was popular, and this turned out to be the case because the barroom was full of people and full of smoke and full of voices that translated as noise, as in noisy. Wade found that he had to raise his voice to be heard, but since he didn't talk much, he didn't have to do this very often.

It's obvious that the food menu in the bar section is the same as the menu in the restaurant section. Actually, everything is the same except the issue of tobacco, because in the restaurant/main dining room liquor is A-Okay. Wade saw this during those fifteen minutes they were waiting for a table to open up in the bar section, for he had to go to the bathroom, and in order to get there he walked through the main room of the restaurant, which was spacious, quiet, and clean-aired, people sipping at drinks and eating food, and of that food there was an appetizing aroma, an aroma that was distinctly missing in the bar section for reasons that had everything to do with tobacco smoke. Wade is a non-smoker and so are Art and April.

When Wade was beginning to tell his mother to forget about the bar/smoking section as the *maître d'* was saying that there'd be a wait, April had interceded by saying that the bar section would be fine and that they'd wait. April did this while putting a hand on Wade's forearm and while flashing Wade an expression that said, "This is okay. We understand," and what was understood was Paula's condition, which Wade was still grappling with and contesting even though he had been dealing with it for the past two and a half months. In a way, Wade couldn't get used to it, for it was hard for him to believe, even though he was trying to believe it. And yet it should have been easy to believe, considering the obvious evidence of dementia and its progression. Perhaps this belief-slash-disbelief quandary had to do with Wade being Paula's son, whereas Art and April were friends, which might have made it easier for them to see and understand, and accept.

After the *maître d'* departed, which left the four of them waiting in the small waiting area near the front door, and after Wade returned from the restroom, April, engaging Wade privately while Art and Paula talked, told Wade: "She can't help it. It's part of the illness." Wade nodded and said, "I know, but there's this meanness about it, which is just plain mean, like she wants to be mean." With this, April looked at Wade as if to say, "Can't you see it?" meaning: "Can't you see that she is ill?" But in addition to this, there was April listening to what Wade said and then nodding, as if to acknowledge that Wade might have been seeing things at home with his mother that were in fact "mean" in a purposeful way, aside from the illness. So April, who had a strong disposition and was outspoken, was soft in this instance, and this instance not only involved April talking to Wade about his mother, but also listening to what Wade had to say.

Wade was instantly grateful for April's input and for her listening to him, which translated into tenderness, the first tenderness he had experienced since returning home. Wade attempted to express his gratitude by saying, "I really want to thank you and Art for helping out while I was away. I had no idea it had gotten this far." And even though this was true, it was short of what he really wanted to say, for what he wanted to say had to do with tenderness.

Of course Wade had told Art a couple of times that he was really thankful for Art's stopping by to help Paula out while Wade was away, and, as it was, this dinner at a restaurant of Art and April's choice had been termed "a little bit of thank you/payback," as expressed by Wade when he phoned Art and April to invite them to dinner. But, since the Pontiac no longer had a backseat, would Art mind driving?

Wade looked over at Art, who was smiling while listening to Paula talk. Art was a big fellow with a wonderful disposition that was expressed in his smile, a great big beautiful smile. Everyone liked and appreciated Art, but none more so than Paula. Art was the son Paula wished she had had.

Wade took Paula to the doctor, Dr. Green, every Tuesday afternoon, which was her regular appointment time. This particular schedule had been set up to accommodate Art's working hours, for Art worked for the City of Los Angeles, a job that had him starting early in the morning and ending in the afternoon. Along with this, Dr. Green's office hours figured in, so between Dr. Green's hours and Art's hours Tuesday was the day, four in the afternoon the time. Wade, seeing no reason to change this, left it that way.

It was the first Tuesday after Wade arrived home in November that he was introduced to the doctor's-office routine, Art swinging by after work to take Wade and Paula to the doctor's office in order to show Wade where the doctor's office was and what was involved—receptionist, waiting room, maybe consultation with Dr. Green, medications, check signing, next appointment scheduling. In addition, there was the idea of easing Paula into the switchover, and perhaps Dr. Green and his receptionist as well.

Art had been taking Paula to the doctor's for the past three months, which was when Paula stopped driving due to getting lost and confused on her way to or from familiar destinations, such as the supermarket or pharmacy or doctor's office.

Since Wade had only talked to Art on the phone since returning, this would be Wade and Art's first face-to-face meeting in thirty-two years, so while Paula was seeing the doctor Art and Wade could sit in the waiting room and catch up on things, which was what took place, or sort of took place, because what took place was Art talking about his job and family and hobbies and house while Wade listened, which was okay with Wade because he wanted to find out what was going on with Art.

As it was, Art began by telling Wade that he and April were concerned about their two daughters because neither one was married and neither one had a good job. About their son, though, they were happy with how he had turned out—job, marriage, family, house, church. More than anything, though, Art was happy with his job because working for the city meant excellent benefits and a decent paycheck. Art said that he was looking forward to retirement because that would mean he could play golf three or four times a week, if he stuck to public courses. And that was a noticeable part of what Wade was hearing—footnotes, add-ons, riders—such as "public courses," for running concurrent with this picture of suburban well-being was a continual reference to saving money—changing the oil on his and April's and his daughters' cars, shopping for groceries at warehouse-type supermarkets, taking advantage of specials at fast-food venues, and buying clothes at outlet stores.

Art was doing well, but he seemed to be living in the shadow of penny pinching, which might have been a leftover habit from thirty-two years ago when Art and April were renting a house and struggling with expenses, but of course Art wasn't working for the city then. But on the other hand, Wade had this idea that maybe middle-class, or even upper middle-class, living required careful economizing in the face of, or because of, cable television, multiple automobiles, utility bills (water in particular), numerous insurance policies, cellphone(s), flat-screen TV (initial outlay), computer, Internet connection, annual Christmas shopping, movies, restaurants, and so forth. Wade had a suspicion that this wasn't necessarily extravagance. Rather, it was middle-class or upper-middle-class living, and even for those with good jobs things were tight.

Of course Wade wasn't really sure about why Art's financial well-being was seemingly under threat, if indeed it was under threat. Clarity, Wade felt, would come with time, for he had just returned and was nowhere near up to speed. Yet there was this other thought, which was already incubating even though premature, and it was that maybe he would never understand what was going on in suburbia.

When Paula emerged from one of the examination rooms, and was standing at the side window of the receptionist, Art stood up and went over to assist. Wade followed, and then there was Dr. Green who emerged, everyone converging at the side window of the receptionist, which was the window that faced the hallway that led to the examination rooms.

Art said, "Dr. Green, this is Wade, Paula's son."

Dr. Green, a slim man in his forties with a neat beard, nodded, which kind of deleted Wade's natural response, which was to shake Dr. Green's hand. Suddenly a handshake didn't seem the correct etiquette, so there was no handshake and no purposeful eye contact. Eye contact was reserved for Art, as were instructions about a slight change in medication, which amounted to a change of dosage, for the pills would remain the same, but one of them had to be cut in half, but only the morning pill. The evening pill would remain the same, a whole tablet. Dr. Green briefly explained to Art the reason for the change by way of some terms that Wade didn't understand, and that Art probably didn't understand either, for neither Art nor Wade were chemists, but what Wade did understand was that medication and its dosage were predicated on the results of blood tests. In listening to this, particularly as a third party, Wade wondered if Dr. Green was reciting these terms in order to keep them fresh in his memory, an exercise for himself as opposed to an explanation that would connote communication, for there was no attempt at lay language.

And then, that seemed to be it, Art nodding, Paula looking at her arm, Dr. Green about to turn away. But then Wade said, "Well, what about the asthma medication, the inhaler?"

Instantly everyone was looking at Wade, which was disconcerting and puzzling, for it was like he had done something wrong. Dr. Green stepped right up to Wade real close, which to Wade seemed an invasion of personal space, kind of aggressive and challenging. It all happened so quickly, and Wade could only think that for whatever reasons Dr. Green didn't like him, and that Dr. Green wanted to establish dominance, as if to let Wade know who was boss. Midst this baffling circumstance, Dr. Green told Wade that there was an ongoing prescription for the asthma inhalers, implication being that there'd be no change and that it was beyond question that there would be. Wade wanted to nod to indicate understanding but held up because he was afraid of head-bumping Dr. Green.

So instead of nodding he smiled dimly, and evidently this was response enough, for Dr. Green turned and walked away.

At this point Art re-introduced Wade to the receptionist, Shirley, an obese woman in her late forties. Of course Art had already introduced Wade as Paula's son to Shirley when they first entered the office and went to the receptionist's window that faced the waiting room, but now it seemed that a re-introduction was necessary because now it was time to write a check. Evidently Art wanted to make sure that Shirley spoke to Wade, for Wade would be writing the checks from then on. So Shirley looked at Wade and said, "Fifty dollars." Simple enough, except that while Wade was writing the check Paula stepped forward to sign the check as had been the procedure with Art, who had been writing the checks and who had been having Paula sign them, all of which Wade understood when Paula said, "Give me the pen. I'll sign it." But with Wade it was different because he could not only write everything out but sign the check as well, for Wade had already been to the bank with his mother to create a joint checking account, which had been absolutely necessary considering what he had discovered at home, mail neglected and a mess, immediate check-writing slash check-signing a must.

"It's okay, Ma. I can sign it."

And with this, not only did Paula look at Wade, but so did Shirley.

In addition to this change of procedure there was Wade pocketing the checkbook instead of the checkbook returning to Paula's purse. Of course it was Wade who had drawn the checkbook out of his pocket to write the check, which created a bit of confusion for Paula because she started looking for the checkbook in her purse when check-writing time came, which was after Dr. Green's instructions and departure. Fortunately, Paula noticed Wade with the checkbook at the counter of Shirley's window, and so desisted with searching her purse.

On the way home from the doctor's office, Wade asked Art about filling the prescriptions, upon which Art told Wade where the pharmacy was and that all Wade had to do was phone before going over and they'd have it ready and waiting. The phone number was on any one of the plastic bottles of pills that were in the kitchen cupboard. Wade, though, already knew about the phone number and the address of the pharmacy because he had looked at those little bottles of pills carefully, for Paula had said any number of times, "Oh, I forgot to take my pills," or "Let's see, what do I take now? or "Did I take my pills already?"

"When the pills get low, or when the asthma inhalers get down to one," Art said, "that's when you phone."

And that's how things went—Dr. Green, Shirley, blood tests, fifty dollars, medication.

Of course there was Medicare, which Shirley, with the help of two assistants, whizzed along via a paperwork corridor that defined the true challenge of her job, and in this way Shirley was invaluable.

Also, as in expected and ongoing, the drawing of blood for the blood tests left Paula's arms forever bruised because she was on blood-thinning medication, or so Wade thought. Beyond speculation, though, there were Paula's crape-paper skin and arms like sticks.

With the onset of diarrhea, which burst upon the scene in July, stool samples were called for. A nursing assistant at Dr. Green's office handed Wade a stool-sample kit, sample to be taken at home and then delivered to the hospital (hospital lab) that was next to the medical building that housed Dr. Green's office. Dr. Green was on staff at the hospital.

As time passed the general proceedings at Dr. Green's office evolved—monthly office visits turning into weekly visits because of deteriorating health, more blood tests, ongoing medication adjustments, and stool samples as needed.

Yet the obvious remained unsaid, for dementia was never mentioned.

CHAPTER 6

They are munching on chickies and sipping Pepsi-Cola in their bungalow, Traveler's Bungalow. Chickies come in two varieties: peanut and coconut. They have a supply of each, but it's apparent that they favor coconut. Chickies are like peanut squares, but with the coconut variety bits of coconut are substituted for peanuts.

They've had a good night's sleep thanks to screened windows that kept the mosquitos outside while allowing a breeze to enter their room, and they've been to town, Anandapuram, on their bicycles, and they've lounged around in their room and on the porch of their room, and they've copulated three times, the second and third times unhurriedly, particularly the third time.

Their spirits have been revived and their sexual activities expanded. A good night's sleep probably accounting for this, and at the same time there is their room, which is clean and comfortable, and compared to their previous accommodations, the palm-frond room where Wade was sick and then the side room of the house near Kumta Beach, this bungalow is the Ritz. There is decent furniture, and there is electricity that powers a couple of table lamps as well as a ceiling fan that has three speeds. There are even sheets and pillows and a light blanket on the two beds, and they are indeed beds, not cots.

The day has progressed pleasantly, and yet it began somewhat strangely, for in the morning there was no chanting and no incense. Wade, upon waking, heard Herta in the bathroom that has a sink and a mirror and a shower. When she came out of the bathroom she was in her bicycling clothes, which surprised Wade because they had the room for three nights, which meant that there'd be two non-traveling days before they started journeying again.

"Let's go to town and buy a lot of food," Herta said.

"Okay," Wade answered and got out of bed. "We don't have to go back to Sagar. There's a small town nearby, up ahead."

"Good," Herta replied, face bright with a smile.

"What about chanting?"

"No chanting today," Herta said, and left it at that.

It was a nice morning for bicycling, not too hot, surroundings green, traffic sparse, birds in full chorus. Groves of areca palms, source of betel nut, stretched into the distance. They stopped a couple of times to listen to the birds.

And so it became clear that their bicycles had two functions: one, long-distance pedaling, and two, leisurely sightseeing pedaling. Yet long-distance pedaling had its sightseeing aspect as well, but it was different than leisurely sightseeing pedaling, for having a place to stay meant they could bicycle around leisurely as opposed to pushing toward a destination where there supposedly would be accommodation, which was how long-distance cycling was chopped up into manageable pieces, one accommodation-place to the next.

Wade drew Herta's attention to this, the subject of leisurely cycling, by telling her that when he was in various places, such as Chapora in Goa, he did this leisurely type of exploratory bicycling, which was kind of a bonus to traveling by bicycle because other people couldn't do this unless there was someplace to rent a bicycle, which was rare. Herta seemed attentive to Wade's observation but she didn't comment. Instead, she lit a beedi.

In town they had chai and flat bread, and after locking their bicycles up with a chain they walked about and discovered that along with betel nut fresh cinnamon was abundant. They bought a small bag of cinnamon, cinnamon like short broken pieces of thin bark. It smelled great. Herta said, "We can add this to our tea."

And so, after a lot of fun things from morning till late afternoon, here they are in their room, Wade on a chair next to a table, Herta nearby on a bed, Wade in a pair of gym shorts, Herta with a cotton shift on, inward-closing shutters of the windows open, no one outside, which lends itself to the idea that Wade and Herta are the only ones renting a bungalow, and perhaps they are. Birds, stirring from their midday slumber, are beginning to call.

Herta has begun talking about Khajuraho, and Wade has begun to understand the source of Herta's inventive postures that Wade was instructed to participate in during the day's sexual activities. As was natural, or accommodating, these purposely assumed positions increased in number and variety proportionally with each organism, vis-à-vis Wade, intervals of time between ejaculations necessary, a recharging of Wade's sexual batteries, which Herta understood very well. Between bouts they ate chickies, drank Pepsi-Cola, and talked, but in those talks there was no mention of Khajuraho. Those in-between-sexual-activity talks were relaxed and varied, subject jumping from one thing to the next, a whiff of stream of consciousness: When did you discover chickies? Have you tried betel nut? Do you like my tits? Do you think we can stay here forever? Do you dream in English or German? Are there monkeys here? Have you ever been in an orgy? How many people are necessary for an orgy? Have you seen any traffic accidents while bicycling? What does an erection feel like?

But now it's more focused, more subject oriented.

"Did you go to Khajuraho, Wade?"

"Yes."

"What did you think?"

"Well, as with so many things, particularly famous things, so much of what we think has to do with our circumstance when we see these famous places. Circumstance might be the weather, or how we feel, or who we are with, or how old we are, and so forth and so on."

"Of course."

"I arrived in Khajuraho after traveling due east from Jodhpur in Rajasthan, about four hundred and fifty miles, seven hundred plus kilometers. This had me coming out of the Thar Desert up into the Aravalli Range, and so that meant uphill, which wasn't real, real bad, because the Aravalli are old mountains. You know, they're not the Himalayas. After that I was traveling on the Malwa Plateau, Central Highlands, which is north of the Deccan Plateau. It was hot, but not like the Thar. So again, it wasn't real bad, but it wasn't real good, either. Anyway, when I got to Khajuraho I had been pedaling every day for over a week and I was tired. But what really did it was that I got hit with diarrhea."

"Oh, no."

"So that's how I arrived at those erotic temples, or erotic stone carvings on the temples, which constitutes only about ten percent of the stone images on those temples. The overwhelming majority of those stone sculptures are about everyday life. But of course it's that ten percent that draws the world's attention."

"Yes, and for good reason."

"Yes, it's rather unusual to have something like that set in stone, so vividly and honestly depicted in stone. Although some of the sexual organs, particularly male, carry a touch of exaggeration."

"My boyfriend, *ex-boyfriend*, snickered at it."

"The diarrhea was no blessing, but I carry pills for it, so I took a pill and I got better pretty quickly. But still, I was dehydrated and tired, so I stuck around Khajuraho for four nights. If it weren't for the diarrhea, I probably wouldn't have stayed four nights. So I didn't have anything to do except to drink Pepsi and visit those temples, you know, they're here and there, spread out over an area, and I'd look at the temples, and I'd look at the people who arrived to look at the temples. You know, it's a tourist attraction, but it certainly isn't your run-of-the-mill attraction."

"Run-of-the-mill?"

"It means regular, or nothing special, nothing unusual."

Herta nods, and Wade knows that she is adding this to her English vocabulary, which is ever-growing.

"Naturally a lot of budget travelers came to look at the erotic art, but there were other people as well, so-called regular tourists who arrived by air-conditioned bus, middle-aged people from Europe or North America, men and women both."

"Did you see anyone snicker?" Herta asks.

"No, I didn't see anyone snicker. For the most part, people looked at it and kept a straight face. Naturally there were smiles now and then, but nothing out of the ordinary, certainly no hilarity that I saw."

"Yes, probably if you had seen me, you'd have seen me like that, too."

"No doubt."

"Except when my boyfriend chuckled in a childish way, then you might have seen me frown."

"Yes, I might have noticed that. You didn't make a scene, though, did you?"

"No."

"So I might not have thought about your boyfriend's snickering for too long, or about your frowning for too long."

"What did you think about at Khajuraho?"

"I thought about a lot of things, one of which was how everyone was walking away with those erotic images in their heads, and maybe back in their hotel rooms some people might have giggled or talked about those images, or maybe even tried a few of them out. But more important, those images would be in people's minds for them to do whatever they wanted with those images, for there are no restrictions on what you can do in your mind."

"That is correct. But what if I want to explore this beyond my mind and my boyfriend makes that impossible because he wants to be the boss, you know, always in charge? That's discouraging."

"So he was kind of macho."

"Yeah, kind of that, but I think the real problem was that he wasn't creative. He was closed to things, so even though this would be fun for him too, he was closed to it, particularly if I suggested that those temple carvings were showing us a spiritual aspect of sex. But he couldn't get past the *dirty* aspect. To him, looking at that erotic art was like looking at a dirty magazine."

"I see."

"What I think is really good about Khajuraho is that it's a tourist spot," Herta says, "so it's okay for men and *women*, no matter their lifestyle, to go and look at it. It's on the itinerary: Delhi, Taj Mahal, Varanasi, Khajuraho."

Wade smiles.

"I think Khajuraho will free people," Herta says.

"Well, don't you think some people will be afraid of that, or think that it's evil? I mean, another thing I thought about when I saw those temples was that it's surprising that they haven't been destroyed—Christian evangelists, Muslims, whoever."

"They're sacred. That's why they haven't been destroyed."

Wade reaches for a coconut chickie.

"They may be sacred," says Wade, "but I don't think that's why they haven't been destroyed. I think they got lucky."

"Lucky?"

"Yeah."

"Do you think what we've been doing is lucky? You know, this kind of sex?"

"I think it's a lot of things, but, yeah, I feel lucky."

"You mean you don't think there are reasons for it?"

"I think there are reasons for it, but we can go on and on about reasons. Actually, reasons are infinite, and in the end, with the confluence of time and place and particulars, we are left with coincidence."

"Coincidence?"

"There are reasons for things," Wade says, "but reasons don't necessarily negate coincidence, nor does coincidence erase reasons. I mean, like you showing up in my room that first time. Of course you saw me the day before at the well, but you could have been somewhere else at that time, or I could have been somewhere else at that time. So what was it that brought us together? There are a lot of reasons, reasons why you looked for me the next day, and reasons why you were able to find me, and reasons why I happened to be sick and laid up instead of on my bicycle traversing the Deccan Plateau, which was where I had planned to be. In this respect, we live in a mysterious world, for there are reasons, but there are other things too, which are mysterious, and which are kind of linked to coincidence."

"What's the difference between mysterious and spiritual?"

"I think it simply depends on the individual. In my opinion, spiritual connotes something higher, something supernatural, whereas mysterious connotes a sense of wonder or astonishment with regards to phenomena—which is this world. Mysterious doesn't have to go beyond phenomena, and it can be rather inclusive, such as to include mundane phenomena, everyday events. Coincidence, in my opinion, is mysterious because we can't explain it. So in that sense, it is like magic, because you realize that it doesn't have to be that way—yet it is."

Herta picks up her bottle of Pepsi from the floor and sips.

"We didn't have to meet," Wade says. "But we did. The proof of mystery and coincidence lies in experience, personal experience, for how can we dispute experience? Experience is us. We own it. We live it.

"I use the word 'lucky' because of the fantasy-like sexual exploration that you've introduced, and that, for whatever reasons, I am a part of. It doesn't have to be. Yet it is."

Wade puts the chickie in his mouth and chews.

Herta says, "What Khajuraho is about, and what we are about, and what all sexual activity is about—is to deliver semen and to receive it. This is genetic and it can carry pleasure. And it can bring babies. But we are very smart, smart from a long time ago. Khajuraho proves that. For we can exploit the *pleasure* aspect of sex. We can twist it and pervert it, and the line between perversion and dancing is kind of strange. We don't even need love. I didn't see love at Khajuraho. Yet I saw something that stirred my insides. Perhaps deep, perhaps dark, perhaps scary. Or perhaps . . . a new aspect.

"With my boyfriend . . . My boyfriend and I had already established certain habits. We couldn't get out of those habits. I needed someone else."

Wade stops chewing. Herta raises her bottle of pop and sips.

Reaching up and setting the bottle on the table, Herta says, "Let us take a shower, Wade, and then have cheese and bread, with a candle on the table and no lights and the shutters open. The night will surround us. After that, in the moonlight, with the candle out, we can explore more positions, which might involve the mouth and sexual organs."

Wade is looking at her.

"And you know what else I was thinking, Wade?"

"No. What else?"

"Perhaps we could meet some people, another couple for example, while we are traveling around. It is possible. We might meet some people who would be open to sharing these activities with us."

It was after they had showered, and after their dinner of cheese and bread, and after incense was lit, and after they furthered their Khajuraho-like poses, which because of Wade's condition lasted and lasted, for it was his fourth go-around that day . . . It was after all that and after they had settled on their respective beds, moonlight streaming in through the screened-windows with the prospect of sleep at hand that Herta said, "Wade, what happens when we reach Cape Comorin?"

She immediately had his attention once again, but in a different way. And so, he assembled a response and verbalized it in that moonlit room with the gentle sounds of insects outside chirping in the trees and bushes.

"In the Punjab, where I began this, that question was so far off that it didn't require my thoughts, and that was a major part of why I set my sights on Cape Comorin, for it was a destination that was so far away that I didn't need to think about its outcome. But now, as I've progressed south, that question has begun to grow, and I'm certain that it will continue to grow as we venture on, which in the end will put us on a beach at the southern tip of India. And I imagine that I'll look out at the sea and wonder what to do next."

It is another off-day, meaning that they have a day without long-distance cycling, which was what they had the day before, but it quickly becomes apparent that it's not the same as the day before. There are, though, similarities, such as Wade's waking to the sounds of birds as opposed to the sounds of chanting and the aroma of incense. Wade is up before Herta, which in itself is unusual, so unusual in fact that Wade notes it as a "first," for he realizes that she has always gotten up before him.

Wade's groin area is sore, and as he examines his penis in the bathroom he is relieved to find that his skin has not been abraded, for any kind of skin abrasion in India is cause for concern, infection via washing and bathing a real threat, water teeming with bacteria. It is Herta's hand pulling at Wade's organ that initiates the feeling of chafing as opposed to stimulation, for at times it's like she is yanking weeds from the ground, and Wade's told her to take it easy, and she's backed off, but then, as if instinctual or habitual, she has a tendency to return to it. So Wade's had to repeat himself, "Go lightly there, honey," which causes her to look down, as if to study the situation, and then to say, "Like this?" "Yes, like that."

Of course it works the other way as well, Herta issuing instructions, Wade complying with those directives. Actually, that's the predominate mode of pedagogy, Herta instructing, Wade responding.

When he leaves the bathroom he finds Herta sitting on her bed cross-legged. She is naked and Wade wonders if this is a prelude. They exchange "good mornings," but these pronouncements convey neither enthusiasm nor apathy. They are courtesies, the civilities of a couple, but as the day progresses, beginning with Herta reaching over to a chair where her green-cloth wrap sits in a heap, it becomes more and more apparent that they are not merely "a couple," but rather a "couple traveling together," and it is after a breakfast of cheese and bread, and after washing clothes and hanging them up to dry, and after sitting on the porch with a bottle of Pepsi, and after Herta retreats to her bed with a copy of *Siddhartha*, in German, thus getting the real word without translation, her third reading, or so she has said, that the issue of boredom becomes evident as Herta stands up and puts her book down on the table and begins to pace. She says, "Maybe we should have lunch or something, or maybe sex?"

The day has heated up and humidity is noticeable. The ceiling fan is on, second speed, and Wade is in a chair catching the draft from the fan while reading a paperback book that he picked up in a trade while in Goa, a common practice among travelers, swapping books, which has led Wade into readings that he might not have done otherwise. At present, he is reading *The Godfather*, by Mario Puzo, which would seem disjunctive for someone traveling in India, but this doesn't bother him, and maybe this is because there's hardly any choice. He picks up what he can. As it turns out, *The Godfather* is interesting, and it's a thick book, so it'll last him a while. But now he lowers the book, for Herta has made her boredom an issue that she is drawing attention to, an issue that Wade is familiar with, for it is an issue he has dealt with time and time again with himself.

"Eat or sex or bicycle to town," Wade says.

Herta stops pacing and looks at him, irritation in her stance and in her expression and in her eyes.

Wade says, "What do people do with all the dead time that prolonged travel creates? Play cards, read books, smoke hash. If there's a beach nearby, go to the beach."

Herta places a hand on her hip.

"For me," Wade says, "the bicycle solved this problem in a major way. Some people, though, would find pedaling boring, particularly a lot of pedaling, but for me it works—physical exercise, sweat, scenery passing by, weather, and the ever-present next place. Yet, even with pedaling, there is still boredom from time to time when I stop pedaling."

Herta is looking at him, hand remaining on her hip.

"But . . . to be bored while alone is different than to be bored with someone else," Wade says. "Two people traveling together, no matter if they are the same sex or the opposite, tend to get on one another's nerves when things get boring or tough. With one person the issues are the same, but it's not exuberated with this back-and-forth that occurs between two people. When you're alone there is only yourself and your situation to deal with."

Wade pauses. Herta stands, looking at him.

"A couple, for example," Wade picks up, "husband and wife, boyfriend/girlfriend, two people living someplace, a house, an apartment, don't face the same things that two people traveling together face. People living someplace have jobs or school or movies or TV or friends, or any number of things that might very well be missing when traveling. And as for a vacation, like two weeks off from some job with spending money in your pocket, it isn't the same thing as wandering around India without a time-frame. It's simply not the same boogie. In a sense, there isn't enough time for serious boredom to set in when you're on vacation, and there isn't the oddness of situation that can create a nothing-to-do feeling, which is what some-times happens while wandering around."

Herta says, "You are delivering a lecture."

Wade hears this, and then there is this delay, like some sort of nothingness, before blood rushes into his face. Herta has touched a sensitive spot, a spot with two sides, both sensitive. Foremost is that Wade now hears himself, hears what he has just said, a mini-lecture of sorts. And then in back of this he very much knows that he can sound didactic at times, and he doesn't like to hear or see himself in this way. It is this, among other things, that serves an impetus for his preferring reticence.

"I thought this was going to be exciting," Herta says.

"Well," begins Wade, "how about yesterday?"

"Yesterday was pleasant. But tomorrow we're going to be bicycling. We're going to leave this place, which is kind of good because now there's nothing to do. It is like we did it all yesterday. But then tomorrow we are going to be pedaling again, like the two days before we arrived here."

"That's right."

Herta looks at Wade. And that's all there is. They have reached a dead-end. Outside the day has fallen into its midday lull, lethargic and heavy.

Herta's hand comes away from her hip as she walks over to a window and closes the shutters. After this she moves on to the next window. Wade dog-ears the page in his book and stands up and sets the book down and steps over to a window and closes its shutters. The room has four windows. Herta closes the shutters of the fourth window, which darkens the room to the extent that Wade turns on a table lamp.

Herta goes to the chair Wade was sitting on and sits down. The lamp is nearby and it puts a tawny hue on Herta. She unknots the green cloth that's tied at the back of her neck, arms raised as she does this, and as the cloth falls to the sides of the chair there is her skin in that yellowish-brown light. She begins to use words and phrases that she has elicited from Wade beginning from when they were together in the palm-frond room. This diction is a translation of formal words into their less formal counterparts, and since Herta is an accomplished linguist who has since practiced and played with this acquired lingo she not only understands the meanings but the textures of these expressions. As it is, she uses this argot as foreplay that reaches across the room to entangle Wade.

The scene and the language complement one another because there is nothing else in the room to look at except Herta as she sits on a chair lazily stimulating herself, vernacular rolling from her throat like caramel.

She sometimes pauses to shiver, and, oddly, what fleets through Wade's mind even as he's getting hard is that this is one aspect that was missing at Khajuraho, for those stone figures were anchored in pure silence, except when there was a wind that haunted them.

Wade lowers his gym shorts and drops them on the bed next to where he is standing, which leaves him naked, but since he isn't within the radius of the lamp's light he stands in darkness and watches and listens to Herta, who now senses, as if some scent were alive in the room, that Wade is naked and that he is watching and listening, and so Herta talks to him as if he were a phantom, lurking. This seems to put her in another spot, and Wade sees her eyes swim.

When he walks across the room barefoot to enter the lamp's yellowy light Herta's slow monologue ceases while she places her hands on her thighs. A glint is on her flesh, maybe perspiration, or maybe something else, for it's like a vibrant glaze. She seems crazy. But then, with Wade standing slightly to her right and placing a hand on the nape of her neck where he feels the dampness of downy hair, she rolls her eyes upward to look at Wade's face as she says, in what might be described as a normal voice, "We must go very slowly, Wade, for when this ends there will be nothing to do."

They are sitting at the table and they are eating bread and cheese, white wedges of processed cheese, and instead of Pepsi-Cola they have orange soda pop that is no cooler than the Pepsi they've been drinking, room temperature. The table lamp remains lit, and the shutters of the room remain closed, and the ceiling fan continues at speed two. Also, Wade and Herta remain without clothes. It might be said that they are relaxing in the afterglow of prolonged sexual activity, for they both seem to be at peace.

"If we were in love, this would not be possible. But since we are not in love, anything is possible. More and more, I feel that this is the age we are entering."

It is Herta who issues these assertions.

"When you say 'age,'" asks Wade, "do you mean our ages, like how old we are, or do you mean the time we are living in, you know, the era?"

"Both."

CHAPTER 7

She meanders around the house late at night, two or three in the morning. He hears her. He's in his bedroom, sometimes sleeping and sometimes not, and when he's sleeping he'll wake to the sounds of slippers on the floor outside his bedroom door. He's come out of his room at times and has gone to the kitchen to see her going through the cupboards as if she were looking for something but not knowing what. The refrigerator as well undergoes this same scrutiny. Or he finds her in the service porch lifting the lid on the washing machine and looking in and then closing the lid. She does the same with the dryer. She never starts either machine.

He's asked her why she's walking around and what she's looking for.

"Oh, I don't know."

Between the stove and the refrigerator in the kitchen there is a small table and on that table he has placed a piece of framed pegboard that has the contours of a square, one-by-two pieces of wood the framing, which elevates the pegboard. In the pegboard he has drilled holes that are large enough to accommodate small Dixie cups, a drill bit that he uses on doors to install deadbolts employed. There are twenty-one holes, and they are arranged in seven rows, three holes to a row. At the top of each three-hole row he has written a day of the week beginning on the left side with Sunday in abbreviation, "Sun," thick black marker utilized. The abbreviated days continue across the board, "Sun" to "Sat," just like on a wall calendar. Also, on the far left, in the area that might be considered a wide left margin, he has written, "Morning," "Noon," "Night," each term corresponding to one of the three holes that are arranged vertically, a top-to-bottom sequence. At the top of the board, for purposes of reference and reminder, he has written, "Pill Board."

Next to the Pill Board there is an alarm clock. But the alarm is never engaged. It's only the face of the clock and its hands that are important.

He has gone through all the little plastic bottles of pills that were in the kitchen cupboard and he has separated and thrown out anything that was no longer current, of which there was plenty.

He now has a little notepad that usually resides in the top, right drawer of the desk in his bedroom. He removes the notepad from the drawer and takes it with him when he and his mother go to Dr. Green's office, which is where he sometimes uses the notepad to note changes in medication. The notepad also leaves the desk drawer when he goes to the kitchen to select pills for the Dixie cups. Of course there are instructions about dosage and times of consumption on the plastic bottles of pills, but those instructions are often superseded at the instruction of Dr. Green.

Theoretically, all his mother has to do is go to the Pill Board and lift a Dixie cup out of its hole, a cup that corresponds to the present day and time, which should be the next pill-containing cup of a familiar calendar sequence, and get a glass of water and take the pills that are in the Dixie cup. The empty Dixie cup can either be thrown away or put back in the hole that it came from, which would then leave either an empty hole or an empty Dixie cup at that place.

Also, with regards to "theoretically," this system should eliminate and/or answer such questions as, "Did I take my pills?" and/or "What pills should I take?" and/or "Is it time to take a pill?" and/or "Didn't I just take my pills?"

But—"Never take two cups with pills at the same time, Mom. If you miss taking your morning pills, for example, and it's noontime, only take the noontime pills. Leave the morning pills where they are. Just leave them in their cup. Never double-up on pills."

These were the instructions Dr. Green issued when Wade asked about this, but of course Dr. Green's instruction were terse.

The Pill Board-slash-Dixie cup-slash-notepad creations were Wade's ideas and handiwork that he had worked up because, at times, even he had gotten mixed up about dosage and about what his mother had taken and what she hadn't taken.

After a couple of weeks, Wade understood that the Pill Board was working out pretty well. In addition, Wade noticed that Dr. Green's curtness eased up a bit when he saw Wade getting out a pen and a notepad, as if maybe pen and paper merited a modicum of consideration.

A fleeting thought occurred to Wade one day when he was setting up the pills, and it was that the Pill Board was a good idea, perhaps even a marketable idea. Wade could build these things one after the other, no problem, and he imagined any number of people could use something like this. An enterprising person might be able to make some money off this. But then that's where his thinking got stuck, for Wade didn't think of himself as "enterprising." He felt that he was too old for "enterprising." And then, following through with this thought, he understood that he had never been "enterprising."

There are these little cans, albeit made of mostly paper, very strong paper and with some sort of a waterproof coating on the inside. These short, squat cans have a viscous nutritional drink in them that comes in a variety of flavors. Paula likes strawberry and vanilla best, so Wade stocks up on those. He buys them at the supermarket or at his mother's pharmacy, but at either place they are expensive, although of late the pharmacy has offered Wade a discount if he buys them by the case. Dr. Green recommended this supplement, a supplement that a lot of old people drink, as Wade has discovered via conversation with the pharmacist, who is a man of about Wade's age and who is accommodating.

The pharmacist's native language is English, but, as Wade has observed, he is fluent enough in Spanish to communicate with Spanish-speaking customers. The pharmacist has an assistant, who is a fairly young man and whose first language seems to be Spanish, for the assistant's pronunciation and Latino way of speaking seem to be right-on as indicated by the pharmacy's Spanish-speaking customers, for they seem completely at ease when talking with the assistant. Of course the assistant can speak English, but Wade suspects that it's his second language because it is accented, yet easily understood. Wade likes the accent. Both the pharmacist and his assistant try to save Wade money by recommending this or that, generic products for example whenever they can be substituted for brand products, or the nutritional drink by the case. It's a small pharmacy that's privately owned by the pharmacist.

Not a chain operation, not a mammoth drugstore. Wade doesn't mind going there, which is fortunate because he has to go there often.

Paula is supposed to take walks around the backyard, and Wade is supposed to assist her in this, Paula holding Wade's arm as she walks. The purpose is exercise. Sometimes they walk during the day, sometimes at night. But there are times when Paula doesn't want to walk at all. She simply refuses. She says that she's tired or doesn't feel well or that it's too hot. Wade can do nothing but acquiesce to this, for what else is there to do—drag his mother out of the house and into the backyard?

But Paula does go out to the backyard every morning, sometimes early, sometimes late, to throw seed for the birds, handfuls of wild bird seed that's kept in a small plastic barrel on the patio, barrel with a tight-fitting lid so that the squirrels don't get into it because the squirrels that come to the yard like the sunflower seeds that are part of the bird mix.

The squirrels, though, are not to be denied, for they, too, are Paula's friends, and so there are large bags of raw peanuts, unsalted and unroasted, that are kept in a closet in the service porch, and from an opened bag Paula extracts a handful of goobers and tosses those to the squirrels, an activity that is triggered with their arrival and with Paula noticing their arrival, which she usually notices from the kitchen window. Sometimes it's one squirrel on a solo venture, while at other times it's two squirrels that show up, and whenever a squirrel or two arrives, with Paula going out the backdoor with a fistful of peanuts, a blue jay appears. What peanuts the squirrels don't eat on the spot they bury in the yard, which is why the blue jay perches on a power line and waits and watches, for when a squirrel hops away from its cache the blue jay will come down from the power line to unearth the buried peanut and then to either eat it or rebury it at a location of its preference somewhere else in the yard.

Wade's been watching this business with the blue jay and the squirrels with some interest, interest enough to have purchased an Audubon field guide. Technically the blue jay is not a blue jay. It is a western scrub jay, but to look at it there is a lot of blue, along with some gray and black. There's no crest on its head, but its sounds are loud and its character is humorous and cocky. Wade has coaxed the jay down to land on the side table next to the chair that Wade often sits in on the patio, peanut held up for the jay to see, which the jay acknowledges with squawking, after which Wade places the goober on the low wooden table. The jay then comes down and lands on the table, Wade's elbow inches away. The jay will then cock its head this way and that to look up at Wade's face and then to look at the peanut before snatching the peanut up in its beak and giving it a shake to make sure the shell isn't empty. Assured that it has a real prize, the jay will then fly off.

The squirrels that visit the yard are predominately gray in color but have some black areas and brown areas in their fur as well, bodies about ten inches in length, big fluffy tails nearly that length, too. They are eastern gray squirrels according to Wade's Audubon field guide, and Wade has coaxed them over to where he sits in his patio chair, peanuts in their shells the enticement, and he has gotten one of the young squirrels to take peanuts from his hand, the squirrel's little front paws producing a scratchy feeling on Wade's palm.

There are days, one after the other, when Wade has no work. At other times he works every day for a couple of weeks without let up. It all depends on the telephone and the nature of each job, and since he calls himself a housepainter slash handyman his work is varied, and this is primarily due to "handyman," which has Wade building shelves, hanging framed paintings on walls, fixing sprinklers, assembling patio furniture, clearing back and front yards of weeds, and so forth.

He works alone, and after nine months of this he traded in the Pontiac and bought a pickup truck. The Pontiac trade-in brought in next to nothing. In essence, the dealer was taking the car off his hands.

He put a low camper shell over the bed of the pickup truck, shell no higher than the truck's cab.

The outlay for the truck was considerable because he paid in cash, or more precisely a bank check. He took money from one of his mother's accounts and termed it a "loan," for he was determined to pay it back, and indeed he has set to work on that. A portion of everything he makes is funneled back into that specific account. He didn't tell his mother about this because that might confuse her, confuse her more. She doesn't know what accounts she has nor what their respective balances are. But of course Wade does, and what his mother's financial situation amounts to doesn't make her rich, but there is a bit of a cushion in the bank.

The new pickup truck also meant higher insurance premiums, which further taxed Wade's earnings. But, as expected, the pickup truck made his work easier, and it expanded the vistas of his jobs, so that now, for example, he can make trips to the dump, regular dump and "green" dump, as well as to recycling centers and hazardous waste places. So it's not just yard trimmings (trees, bushes, weeds) that he hauls away. It's all kinds of junk—old paint cans, rotten lumber, broken furniture, lengths of galvanized pipe, box springs and mattresses, outgrown bicycles and tricycles, moldy carpeting, boxes of aerosol cans, dormant doghouses, cracked crockery, discarded kitchen appliances, and etcetera. This stuff comes primarily from backyards and garages.

On a rickety bicycle that Wade picked up for nothing because it was part of what someone wanted to clear out of his garage, Wade pedals four suburban blocks to a Mexican food restaurant that has a bar. Sitting down on a barstool, he asks for a bottle of Dos Equis. It's a U-shaped bar and there are tables as well as a few booths. It's Friday and Wade has caught the tail end of happy hour. He soon understands that the happy-hour attraction isn't so much the barely reduced price of drinks as it is the free food that's on a table, heating appliances keeping some of the more exclusive foods warm (taquitos, wedges of quesadilla, miniature tacos, refried beans).

Wade feels fortunate for having gotten a stool at the bar because there's a good crowd in the barroom, men and women, all of whom appear to have come from work—office workers who are dressed casually, postal workers from a nearby post office, and tradespeople. Everyone is in a clique, which is understandable, but Wade isn't in a clique. He's there alone, which leaves him with nothing to do but to sip his beer and maybe play Keno and look around, but not to stare. Gazing at his bottle of beer is another option, which also introduces the option of daydreaming in a pensive sort of way.

When happy hour ends, almost everyone clears out as soon as he finishes the drink he's working on. The free food disappears, and the barroom becomes quiet because there is no music and no chance of music because there isn't a jukebox. The Keno games, though, continue on a

TV screen, wall-mounted TV, mute and with no humans appearing in the broadcast. It's all automated, and it's mostly numbers.

In order to facilitate some interaction with someone, namely the female bartender, Wade fills out a Keno card and gives it to the bartender along with some money. The bartender, whom Wade has studied and eavesdropped on, is bilingual, Spanish and English, but with Wade she doesn't exercise either one of those languages. Her transactions with Wade, including when she places the Keno ticket on the bar in front of him after she's put it through a machine, are wordless. And when Wade first sat down and asked for a bottle of Dos Equis her response was to nod and get the bottle of beer. But . . . when she brought him his bottle of beer, she did state a price, in English.

The bartender is wearing cream-colored pants that are made of some soft elastic-type material that really shows off the contours of everything in the garment, and Wade has noticed any number of men at the bar looking at those pants when the bartender's back is turned.

So maybe the bartender is tired of men looking at her, or maybe she's tired of her job, or maybe she's dissatisfied with her wages, or maybe everyone who comes to this bar during happy hour on a Friday is chintzy when it comes to tipping. So maybe she's pissed off and doesn't want to award anyone any words beyond those that are absolutely necessary.

Then again, the bartender might be emphatically married and doesn't want to encourage anything to disturb that. On the other hand, maybe life at home isn't so good and maybe she's brought "isn't-so-good" to work. Or maybe she is introverted and shy, and is the happiest person in the world.

Wade gets the bartender's attention by raising his empty bottle and she comes over to stand in front of Wade. She's late twenties or early thirties. Her face is pretty. Wade says, "Another Dos Equis and a shot of vodka. Whatever you have in the well is fine." This time when she brings him his drinks she doesn't state a price because Wade has some bills on the bar. She selects a few of those bills and walks away.

Wade leaves the bar without winning anything at Keno and without seeing the bartender smile, and as he bicycles home he wonders if he, himself, smiled while he was in that barroom.

Wade tries the bar a couple more times, but not during happy hour. He pedals those four stucco-house-lined blocks after he's given his mother her dinner, and on each occasion he has a couple of beers and a couple of shots of vodka while sitting at the bar, but as with his happy-hour visit he sits on a barstool and watches Keno, conversation of any sort absent.

So he stops going to that bar, which means that he doesn't go to any bars, for he does not want to operate a motor vehicle with alcohol active in his system. As it is, that bar, the bar in the Mexican food restaurant, is the only bar within reasonable bicycling distance from Wade's house, which is really his mother's house.

He sometimes sits in his room at night with a can of beer and a couple of inches of vodka in a water glass. At other times he sits out on the slab of concrete that's in the backyard and that's termed a patio, sipping beer and vodka. This, too, the patio locale imbibing, is usually at night, which means that he sits in the dark with the sounds of the neighborhood at his ears—car alarms, sirens, dogs barking, neighbors with loud TVs, helicopters with searchlights, thumping music from backyard parties, and air-planes taking off or landing from a runway that's three blocks away. But now and then he'll sit out there on the patio real late at night on a weekday, one or two in the a.m., and it'll be almost quiet.

But it's not only alcohol that he drinks in his room or on the patio. He drinks tea and coffee as well, but these tend to be daytime beverages.

There is a clock radio in his room, which is left over from his early youth, for he remembers listening to that radio and waking up to it when he was in high school. It's not a battery-powered device. It's plug-in, and it still works well, and it still brings in a lot of stations, because in that respect nothing has changed. This is the house Wade grew up in, and it's located in the eastern sector of the San Fernando Valley, which is part of Los Angeles, and beyond that part of Southern California, which is part of a megalopolis that stretches from the Mexican border to Santa Barbara. Therefore, as in his youth and even more so now, this represents a huge market. Thus, there is no shortage of stations, and of those stations nearly every interest group is spoken for.

Wade sits on a chair, framing wood, seat and back woven rush. The clock radio is to his left on a low table that Wade made with two-by-fours and plywood, a bedside table, and of course there is his bed on the other side of the table. He has his can of beer and/or glass of vodka in hand or on the table. The volume of the music coming from the radio is low, and the station is either a country-&-western station or a jazz station.

There's a small lamp on the table next to the clock radio, lamp with a forty-watt bulb, and the light from the lamp just reaches the wall that Wade faces, which is a wall on the other side of his small bedroom. A desk is against that wall, the desk that he used when he was in elementary school and junior high school and high school, and even for a while when he was going to junior college, which people now call community college, and in that linguistic regard junior high school is now "middle school."

Above the desk and tacked to the wall there is a new addition to the room and its furnishings, and it is a poster that Wade picked up since returning home. He bought the poster at a poster shop in a humongous mall. The poster looks like a good-quality print of an oil painting, but it is actually a print of a pastel, pastel on paper, by Edgar Degas, and it is entitled, *Waiting*.

Two women, one seemingly middle-aged, the other young, are sitting on a backless wooden bench that is indoors, indoors indicated by a plain wall in back of the women and by a wooden floor at their feet. The young woman is in a ballerina's outfit. The older woman is dressed in black, including a black hat, and there is a collapsed black umbrella loosely in the woman's one hand, umbrella angled downward toward the floor. The ballerina is bent forward and she has a hand on her ankle, and it is because she is bent forward while looking down at her ankle that her face can't be seen. The older woman's face is partially in view, the brim of her hat shrouding the upper half of her face, thus leaving the lower half of her face (nose, mouth, and chin) in view, and of that view a no-expression expression registers on that middle-aged woman's face. It is the expression of "waiting."

It is this poster, with the weak light from the lamp just reaching it, that Wade looks at while sipping beer and vodka in his bedroom.

Stacked boxes containing watercolors and graphite drawings and colored pencil drawings are in one corner of the bedroom. Wade sent these boxes home now and then from abroad, and, having alerted his mother by letter as to the handling of these boxes, the boxes were not opened. Paula simply stacked them in the bedroom as they arrived over the years. There are fifteen boxes in all, and thus far Wade hasn't opened any of them.

Also, regarding "thus far," Wade hasn't done any drawings or sketches or studies, much less any watercolors, since arriving home. He explains this to himself by saying that he feels uninspired.

CHAPTER 8

It is a long stretch of flat roadway through terrain that is dry and in need of trees, shoulder of the road dusty with orange silt that lifts in the draft of passing trucks, but there aren't many trucks and traffic in general is sparse. It is hot, and the sun dwells in a lightly hazed sky that is whitish blue, tires of their bicycles gummy on the macadam that runs beneath their moving shadows while they pedal side by side as if in the ease of companionship.

Up ahead and on their left and set back from the road's shoulder there is a tree and in the tree's shadow there appears activity, and near that activity a pile of large rocks sits in the sunshine, and since Wade and Herta are traveling on the left side of the road, as does all traffic in India, they will pass very near that activity, and in this way discover its nature.

Between Herta and Wade there is no conversation because they are too tired for conversation. Rivulets of sweat gather airborne dust to streak their arms and legs and necks with reddish slime. Their legs move as if on automatic, yet at the same time there is this continuous pushing feeling even though they are not on an incline, nor is there a headwind.

The heat, the soft blacktop, the heaviness of their bicycles, and the repetitive scrub that punctuates the land and that doesn't even yield a crow seem to be conspiring against them. But they "push on," and of that there have been reoccurring discussions that lapse into arguments.

But now, activity distinguishes itself from the monotony of the land, and as they near that activity there are sounds that are not the sounds of this landscape, for this landscape has no sounds. It is a windless day. A little more pedaling is needed in order to get close enough for their eyes to delineate detail that will yield information that their minds will assemble with the prospect of identifying what is going on. And when they understand that, they will understand those sounds, for of themselves those noises are unique, unique in the sense of "first experience." And so, it is the desire for "understanding" that occupies their cognition.

They are in saris of indelicate fabric, colors varied, yet singular for the dusty hue that they share. With age, too, variation registers, ten years old or thereabouts to fifty years old, or maybe sixty years old, and of this upper age bracket there are deep wrinkles on dark complexions that camouflage ten years here or there, middle age and old age shifting under a veil of weathered skin, bare feet black and leather-like, hands indelibly creased. They are on their haunches, and, as might be deduced from their clothing, they are all female. About thirty-five of them, each with a ball-peen hammer that is reducing a large stone to a cluster of small stones, and now that Herta and Wade are near the group it is clear that there is this other pile of rocks that is developing from the pile of large rocks that sits in the sun. The pile of small stones is in the sun, too, but that pile isn't as noticeable as the pile of large stones because it's not piled up so much. This might change, but for now the small stones form a flattish pile.

Both Herta and Wade stop pedaling so as to coast by these women who are all pinging away at rocks, and of course it is that sound that was unidentifiable, but now it is very much understood, and at the same time they understand the nature of this labor, for the women are creating gravel, the sort of gravel that might be mixed with tar to produce asphalt for the paving of a road. What is imaginable is a truck pulling up, a dump truck perhaps, and then the gravel getting shoveled into the bed of the truck, which is probably how the large rocks arrived, via truck, perhaps a dump truck.

The women keep pinging away as they look at Herta and Wade gliding by, and of Herta and Wade there are sunglasses and khaki shorts and floral-print shirts, and so the women look at Herta and Wade with what might be the same astonishment with which Herta and Wade look at the women, and nothing in this exchange of information changes until Herta and Wade thrust with their legs and start pedaling, which puts distance between them and the women, who are wisely in the shade of that green-leaf tree.

The bridge flows with moderate traffic, while the river below the bridge flows with clean water. It is the stones that can been seen at the bottom of that river that confirm its clarity, along with what is not in the river, such as raw sewage and the murk of mud. But it is the elephants, one large, one small, mother and child perhaps, that are in the river's shallows and are lying on their sides with a skinny teenager at each animal with a long-handled wash brush that cause Wade and Herta to stop on the bridge, for the elephants are getting a scrub, and the way those two elephants are so relaxed suggests that they are enjoying it.

It is a wide bridge with a pedestrian walkway, bridge seemingly new, a public works project that serves the people. Wade and Herta dismount and jump a low curb with their bikes, which puts them on the walkway. They lean their bicycles against the bridge's steel railing. Unencumbered, they rest their forearms on the railing and look down at the elephants.

They saw no hotels, and so Wade consulted his map and found that there was a train station, and any kind of train station meant a waiting room, or at least someplace to wait, which meant someplace to sleep. They left the main road, where there was a sign indicating the station, and after ten yards the pavement of the train-station road gave out onto dirt, and not long after that there was an open sewer that ran down the middle of the unpaved road, a trench in the dirt. Lining the dirt road were mud-brick structures with half-naked children and rail-thin men standing in doorways, and as Herta and Wade walked their bikes along that dank avenue the men and children stared at them. Garbage and wood smoke scented the air.

The waiting room was an open-air affair with a corrugated aluminum awning and with a chain-link fence surrounding a slab of concrete on three sides, the fourth side facing the tracks. For furniture, there were some wooden benches. A sign, scripted in English, declared "Waiting Room," and next to the waiting room there was the station office, again another sign, "Station Office," which was where tickets were sold by a uniformed employee who locked up the station office and left a half hour after Wade and Herta's arrival. On his way out that dark-skinned man smiled and nodded to Wade and Herta as he walked by the waiting room.

A light bulb, a wire cage enclosing it, was fastened to one of the rafters of the awning, and fortunately, as if providing a measure of security, the bulb shone throughout the night, and it allowed Wade and Herta light enough to read by. It could also be said of that sixty-watt bulb that it kept the insect population busy in a never-ending cloud that hovered around that incandescent glow. A bat, working at the periphery of the awning in a jerky way, took advantage of stray bugs. Surprisingly, Wade and Herta found that mosquitos weren't a serious menace, but of course mosquitos had other habitat that was more accommodating, such as an open sewer with standing water on that thick-aired street that led to the station.

In the opposite direction from the station office, a concrete outhouse stood in the dark at the end of the platform, flashlight required in order to prevent mishap. As Wade and Herta discovered, the interior of that restroom was prime locale for spiders and web-spinning.

In general, though, everything was fine until a young man, late teens/early twenties, showed up, a friendly chap who wanted to bring them chai and who wanted to exercise his broken English. And that was the problem: friendly and generous with chai. Wade had heard from several people, travelers and Indians alike, that there had been incidents of foreigners drinking tea laced with poison, robbery the objective, modus operandi always the same: someone friendly and offering chai, free chai. Wade had heard about this when he was in the Punjab, but he had also heard that these crimes had made the news, which prompted some people to speculate that copy-catting was going on, for such cases had since popped up here and there at different places in the country.

So Wade had to say no to the chai even though a glass of tea would have been nice, and beyond this he had to tell

Herta to say "no," while communicating the reason for this. Meanwhile, some other young men and boys had begun to gather to gawk at Herta and Wade, and since there was nowhere to go Wade and Herta had to sit through this while waiting for time and boredom to wear these bothersome people out, friendly chai man included. To help this along Wade opened his paperback edition of *The Godfather* and started reading while ignoring the friendly chai man and the others. Wade told Herta to employ the same tactic, and she did, *Siddhartha* forthcoming. Fortunately the friendly chai man's listening comprehension of English was as weak as his speaking, and so he couldn't understand Herta and Wade's exchanges. As it turned out, Wade and Herta got a lot of reading done because it took two and a half hours before they were finally left alone.

The morning was long, and now it is noon and they coast into a town/village where there isn't any green and where shade is scant, as is activity. But they are hungry, and there is no telling when opportunity beyond this cluster of one-story structures will arise again, so they dismount and walk their bikes. An occasional car passes, horn blaring. No people are about. There is a tractor parked on the road's shoulder. There is a dog that walks crookedly. And then, to their right and across the street, there is an open doorway on a low building, no windows and no sign, but compared to everything else there is a glimmer of potential, which might involve food.

They park their bicycles near the open doorway and chain the bikes together and step into a shadowed room by crossing a raised threshold, a four-by-four piece of worn wood that separates outside dirt from inside dirt, and in addition to spatial delineation there is also the dirt's composition that is declared, for outside, where the shoulder of the road runs, the dirt is loose and powdery, whereas inside the dirt is packed hard and slightly moist. Of color, the dirt outside is a light orange, while inside the dirt has an oxblood hue.

Low wooden tables with squat wooden stools are along two walls, six tables in all. Against another wall there is a regular-height table that is somewhat large, pots and other things on the table. Next to the table, a man sits on a low stool, his one elbow propped upward on the table's edge. The man is wearing a green-and-beige-stripped *lungi* and a pair of sandals, belly and chest bare, belly protruding. He is smoking a beedi while gazing at the shadowed room, a room that gets most of its light from the open doorway, but there are a couple of square holes in the walls, holes high up and about the size of a softball, and they, too, contribute light, but its quality is different than what comes from the doorway, for the light from the holes is distinctly rayed and it is angled downward, one hole on each wall, four holes in total, none of which have glass or screens or shutters.

Compared to outside the room is cool, and it takes a few moments of eye-adjustment before its interior is clearly visible. The man doesn't stir, and if he's looked at Wade and Herta, it's not apparent. Wade looks at the man and says, "Food?"

The man rises to his feet laboriously and picks up a couple of cut banana leaves from a stack on the table, leaves cut to the shape of a large rectangle. Regarding a verbal reply to Wade's inquiry, there isn't any, but the banana leaves and the pots on the table are enough for Wade to say to Herta, "Let's sit down," and with this Wade selects a couple of stools that will allow for a view out the doorway. This will enable Wade and Herta "to keep an eye" on their bicycles, which is better security than the chain that's threaded through the spokes.

The man comes to their table and places a banana leaf in front of Wade and Herta respectively. He does this with one hand, for the beedi is still in the other hand, but after the banana leaves are in place the man steps over to the doorway and inhales on the beedi and then flips it out onto the dirt outside to the left of Wade and Herta's bicycles. The beedi smolders on the orange dirt, which would have been of no significance except that a crow immediately swoops down to land on the ground and to investigate the beedi, crow cocking its head this way and that to have a good look, which attracts two more crows, and suddenly there are three birds surrounding the beedi, and then one of them takes a stab at the beedi with its beak, which sends that smoldering nub skittering, and that's the way it goes, beaks stabbing, beedi flipping, until one of the birds picks the beedi up with its beak and swallows it, presumably after it's been extinguished. Wade sits with the understanding that this is a routine of sorts, the man flipping his beedi butts out the doorway and the crows coming down to eat the tobacco after its lit end is out.

The man approaches their table with a tin cup in each hand. He sets one cup down near Herta's leaf and the other next to Wade's, and then the man goes back to the food table to stand. In each tin cup there is water.

Wade says to Herta, "We're supposed to pour some water on the leaf and push the water around with our fingers, right-hand fingers. This is to supposedly wash the leaf. After the washing, you pick the leaf up and shake the water off it while holding the leaf out over the floor."

Herta says, "Okay." Her face is red from the day's heat and from her efforts on the bicycle. In the past few days, it's become apparent that Herta's face has slimmed, and so has her body. She is losing weight.

"But," Wade says, "the water isn't going to do the leaf much good in terms of hygiene, because it's the water that's the main problem."

"Okay," Herta replies, "so we don't wash the leaf. But what's the leaf for?"

"The leaf is a plate. He's going to put food on it."

Herta looks at Wade.

"Don't worry. The leaves are disposable. They're only used once," Wade says, and leans and points beyond Herta to where there's a sink with a hole in the wall above the sink. "There's probably a cow outside," Wade says. "We'll put our leaves through that hole when we're done eating, and we'll wash our hands at the sink. The cow outside will eat the banana leaves."

"Oh."

"But the thing is," Wade says, "I think he," and here Wade gestures with his chin toward the man, "is waiting for us to wash our leaves before he serves us the food."

"I'm hungry. What's the solution?"

"There is no satisfactory solution," Wade says. "There is only custom and unhygienic water."

"Are we just going to sit here?"

"These leaves probably already got a dousing of water when they were cut. I've seen women cutting banana leaves at the sides of restaurants, and the leaves are dusty, and the women want to make the leaves look good, so they dipped them in a bucket of water and gave them a shake before taking them into the restaurant."

"I'm hungry."

"Let's wash the leaves and hope that the food isn't too hot, because sometimes it is."

They "wash" their banana leaves, and the man comes over and serves them. The food turns out to be a large helping of white rice ladled from a bucket. To go along with this, the man spoons eight dollops of runny vegetables onto each banana leaf, little puddles with space between each puddle so that they don't blend. The runny vegetables have come from separate tin cups, eight tin cups on an aluminum tray that the man holds with his stubby fingers, each cup with its own silver spoon.

Wade grabs some rice with the fingers of the right hand and dips the rice in one of the sauces. This then goes into his mouth, where his premonition about hot and spicy turns out to be the case. He dips another gob of rice into a different runny-vegetable sauce, but this, as it turns out, tastes the same as the previous sauce-laden rice, hot chili overwhelming any sort of vegetable flavor. Hurriedly, while hoping for relief because his mouth is on fire, Wade works his way through the eight dollops, but finds that all the sauces taste the same.

Herta and Wade start sweating and hiccupping, and then they're jamming plain white rice into their mouths in an attempt to neutralize the hot spices.

True to form, when Wade and Herta go to the sink with their food-dirty banana leaves, there's a cow's head on the other side of the hole where a chute slants down. The cow's tongue is quick to pick up the leaves once they are sitting on the chute.

The price of the meal is one rupee each, which comes to eleven cents in U.S. currency, two meals for twenty-two cents. Outside, while still hiccupping, Wade tells Herta, "I think we got ripped off."

They mount their bikes and push on, and, as if it were a miracle, ten minutes outside of town there's an old woman sitting on a square cloth in the shade of a tree, and in front of the woman there is a pile of bananas.

Bananas are the safest food in India. No washing, no cutting, no tampering with contents. In addition, they are extremely cheap, and they are gentle on the stomach. Regarding banana peels, both crows and cows love them.

Wade and Herta are in the shade of that tree, eating bananas and tossing the peels.

A sign announces a town that is off to the left of the main road and indicates a road that leads to the town. In a sense, the main road is a bypass, which is very unusual, but this section of the main road is in good condition, smooth and wide, which indicates that it's new, and of all things it has a paved shoulder that is bicycle-friendly. But it's not only bicycles that utilize the shoulder, for oxen carts piled high with hay also use the shoulder, as do motorbikes and sari-clad women who walk with copper water pots balanced on their heads.

Since Wade and Herta stocked up on provisions in the previous town, and since the weather is good thanks to some clouds and a breeze that translates into a light tailwind, they are going to continue on and skip the town. But then Herta's rear tire goes flat just before the junction for the town.

Wade carries tube-changing tools along with two new inner tubes, but, as he discovered early on in his journey, taking a wheel off his bicycle requires a lot of time and work, for the bike isn't equipped with quick-release hubs. Actually, the engineering and construction of his and Herta's bicycles, as well as all the bicycles in India, is antiquated. But, regarding punctures, a quick fix is possible, and it's easy, easy for its ubiquity, because almost anywhere within a reasonable distance along any moderately traveled road there is a skinny man at the side of the road, squatting down on his haunches with a few tools and a basin of water, and this man has one job, and it is to repair punctured inner tubes on bicycles. The beauty of this convenience is two-fold: one, it is cheap; and two, it is quick, for the repair is made without removing the wheel from the bicycle. The tube is simply slipped out of the tire and then inflated and moved through a basin of water to locate the puncture, which is then patched after the air is let out of the tube. Some more pumps with a hand pump inflate the tube in order to check the patch, and then the air is let out before sliding the repaired tube into the tire and putting the tire back onto its rim, whereupon the tire is inflated. It's a ten-minute operation that costs pennies.

And so Wade and Herta walk their bicycles along the road that leads to the town, for it is certain that there'll be an inner-tube-repair man in town, and since the town is nearby this is the surest way to get the flat fixed in a hurry. And sure enough, almost as soon as the buildings of the town begin there is a park, and along the park's periphery, where the road goes by, there are a couple of men squatting, a basin of water in front of each man.

The town seems to be somewhat prosperous, for active commerce is underway. The park looks pleasant, and the streets are clean.

Herta parks her limp bicycle in front of a repairman, who immediately sets to work. There are some big trees in the park, and Wade looks at how their leaves shimmer in the breeze. Herta lights a beedi.

Some young men walking by stop to look at Wade and Herta. Wade glances at the men, who are slim and in their late-teens, and who are dressed cleanly and neatly. Again, moderate prosperity is implied, but now, because of these young men, other people begin to gather to see what the attraction is. Suddenly, Herta is saying, "What the fuck are you looking at?" This surprises Wade. There is of course the language, but there is also volume and its intent, which is anger, and which seems to have materialized from out of nowhere.

Wade doubts that the growing crowd understands the language, but because of the volume and intent of Herta's voice there is interest among the bystanders, which then serves to draw more people, and in reaction to this there is Herta waving her arms and saying, "Fuck off!" which comes across as a shriek. People begin crossing the street from a sidewalk that is lined with shops. They join the crowd, which swells that population to about a hundred people.

As gently as he can, Wade says to Herta, "Take it easy. We'll be out of here very soon." But Herta is in no mood for instruction or advice. She drops the beedi on the ground and starts screaming, a conveyance of panic.

Fortunately, the repairman ignores both Herta and the crowd while concentrating on repairing the inner tube, and of this Wade is thankful, because the sooner the tire is fixed, the sooner they can get away from this, and the sooner they get away from this, the sooner it will stop, and what needs to stop is this back-and-forth between Herta and the crowd, for the crowd is growing proportionately in relation to Herta's hysterics. She has become a spectacle and everyone wants to see it. And now, while continuing to scream, she starts swinging her arms back and forth.

The tire is repaired and Wade pays the man, and the man smiles, mouth purple with betel nut.

Herta and Wade can't mount their bicycles because of the pressing crowd. So they walk their bikes through the crowd, which has swelled to about three hundred people. Cars and trucks have stopped because of the crowd in the street, horns blaring. As Wade and Herta advance, the crowd parts in front of them as if they were celebrities of an odd sort, Herta yelling, Wade leading the way, Herta right in back of Wade. Finally they are at the edge of the crowd, where they mount their bikes and start pedaling.

"Let's go," Wade says, while standing up on the pedals of his bicycle to put more energy into the wheels, Herta mimicking this, and then Wade glancing back to see a half dozen teenagers mounting bicycles with the obvious intent of giving chase. "We're going to have company," Wade says. "Just keep pedaling. They'll drop off after a while." Herta looks back and says, "Fuck!"

The concrete levees on either side of a shallow river are smooth and white, and they angle downward in a gentle slope. Stretched out on the levees are saris that are drying in the sunshine. There are women at the riverbank beating water-soaked saris on flat rocks, whips of water coming off the saris as the women swing them down from over their heads, but it is the saris that are drying on the concrete levees that provide the pageant, for each sari is individual for its coloring, and so the levees are like rainbows that follow the course of the river.

The road's wide dirt shoulder has widely-spaced young trees that appear to have been planted recently. The trees are dusty and thin, yet there is shade, and it is in the meek shade of one of those trees that Herta and Wade sit on a bench, sipping chai. Other people on other benches are drinking chai, too. The chai wallah is a skinny man with betel-nut-stained teeth and lips, and his thriving open-air business is midst that gathering of wooden benches. The nearby roadway is moderately busy with traffic that keeps a light mist of dust churning.

A boy is circulating amongst the benches, a wooden tray held horizontally at the height of the boy's belly. A canvas strap, slanting down from around the boy's neck, is fastened to the extended corners of the tray, so as to keep the tray comfortably horizontal. On the tray there are colorful pictures that are each about the size of a postcard, but they are not postcards. They are pictures of Hindu deities. Herta takes an interest in the boy's wares, and the boy notices and comes over.

The boy is about ten years old, and while looking at Herta the boy smiles, teeth white, and perhaps more so because of the boy's dark skin. The boy's hair is short and black, and it is dusty. He is barefoot, and he stands patiently while Herta shuffles through the pictures with her hands. The pictures are made of thin paper.

Herta selects three pictures and sets them on the bench next to herself and gets out a coin purse and extracts a folded, single rupee note, which she then unfolds and hands to the boy, who continues to smile, except now his smile dims as he looks at the bill that's in his hand, but then Herta waves the boy off to indicate that the transaction has been completed. After a moment the boy understands, which is indicated when his smile is renewed doubly, for at the front of his tray, which is lipped with thin slats of wood so as to keep the pictures from sliding off, while a couple of stones sit on the pictures as paperweights, it is written: *5 – 1 R.* So it would seem that five pictures are gotten for one rupee. But, as it is, Herta is satisfied with three pictures for one rupee.

Herta says, "Good boy," but it's not clear if the boy understands this. But the boy does understand Herta's smile, for the boy is all smiles in return. The boy walks away after a prolonged moment or two, whereupon he goes over to stand at the base of one of the young trees. He leans against the tree's skinny trunk, and he continues to look at Herta.

Herta turns to Wade and says, while showing Wade one of the pictures, "Ganesh." With the next picture she holds up, she says, "Krishna." And with the third picture, she says, "Saraswati." Wade replies, "Good selection." Herta says, "Do you know what they mean?" Wade says, "Not exactly." Herta says, "I thought you knew everything about India." And this is what Wade has feared, and even though he has tried avoiding it, circumstances have initiated responses on his part that have come off as pedantic.

Wade sips his tea and looks over at the boy, who continues to lean against the tree while staring at Herta and Wade.

Herta, while showing Wade the pictures, says, "Ganesh: intellect, wisdom, learning, removal of obstacles. Krishna: lover, trickster, god-child. Sarasvati: music, arts, knowledge, nature. A true goddess."

Wade nods. Herta sips her tea, pictures held in her one hand. It's three-thirty in the afternoon, and even though the day's heat is noticeable, it has begun to abate. The town is medium size, and, as indicated by the crowd sipping chai, some of its workers, clerical and laborers both, are taking a break.

"I'm curious," says Wade. "Why did you stop chanting?"

"I stopped chanting because the bicycle has become the vehicle. The bicycle is the way, the means, the mantra. Chanting is no longer necessary."

Wade nods slowly while thinking about this.

"I want to put these on the bicycle," Herta says, and indicates the pictures.

Wade looks at the pictures and says, "On your bicycle? Where?"

"Oh, I don't know," Herta responds, and sets her glass of tea down on the bench and stands up and steps over to her bike and starts holding the pictures up against the sides of the cardboard box that's on the rear rack of her bike, box held in place with a couple of bungee cords. Herta's rolled-up sleeping bag is in the box. But, attaching the pictures to the box is a problem, which is immediately obvious.

And now here comes the boy, who un-loops the canvas strap from around his neck and hands the tray of pictures to Herta and then takes off running across the street. He dodges through traffic like a weasel, and then, after dashing across the shoulder on that side of the road, bounds up two concrete steps, where he pulls open a door to go through a doorway and disappear, door closing behind him.

Wade looks at the building and sees that it's a post office, and with this Wade smiles and looks at Herta, who is standing with the tray of pictures while looking across the street at the building that the boy has entered.

The boy emerges from the doorway with something in his one hand. Zigzag, he's crossed the street and comes up to Herta and shows her what he has in his hand. It's a small cardboard card with a glob of gray glue on it.

Wade stands up and comes over and takes the tray of pictures from Herta. The boy and Herta then start experimenting with where to place the pictures on the box that's on the rear rack of Herta's bicycle.

Ganesh gets pasted on the left side of the box, Krishna on the right side, and Sarasvati on the rear of the box, which strikes Wade as the most exalted position because any traffic coming up from the rear will see that picture.

Herta has diarrhea. Fortunately the room's toilet facilities are adequate—a porcelain, Asian-style toilet on the floor, an overhead tank with a chain that releases a gush of water, a small window for ventilation, and an electric light bulb for nighttime visitation. And the room itself isn't bad, either—screened windows, ceiling fan, two beds, a table, a couple of chairs, and a sink with a mirror above it. A cold-water shower is in a room that's separate from the toilet. It's a clean room, and there's a view of the town's main street from one of the windows, and since it is a relatively small town traffic noise dies down fairly early in the evening. The room is on the second floor. A restaurant is on the first floor, but the sounds of the restaurant don't invade the room. The town, Belur, isn't a bad place, for there are shops and a few restaurants. A shop across the street from Wade and Herta's hotel sells cold soft drinks.

The town's attraction is the Chennakeshava temple, which is part of a temple complex. Chennakeshava has stone sculptures and friezes, Hindu, that are in excellent condition. The sculptures are on exterior surfaces, while inside the temple there are elaborate pillars.

Wade looks at the temple and strolls through the grounds of the complex. It is quiet and there is a river nearby and there are palm trees as backdrop. Herta would appreciate this. But she's sick. Maybe tomorrow, though, or even later today, she could be on the mend, for Wade has given her some pills for the diarrhea, and with himself Wade has found that the pills work pretty quickly. But he has to couch this with a footnote, for intestinal problems can range from a mild case of the trots to amoebic dysentery, and amoebic dysentery would call for antibiotics, which Wade carries as well, tetracycline. In India almost any drug can be purchased at a pharmacy, prescription not necessary. Thus, self-medication becomes an option—or a necessity.

It was early in the morning at first light, a misty gray at the windows, that Wade heard the toilet flushing and then saw Herta returning to her bed. No more than fifteen minutes later she was at it again. Wade suspected problems, and confirmation wasn't long in coming, Herta getting out of bed and on her way to the toilet a third time.

"Do you have the shits?"

"Yes."

"Are you nauseous?"

"Nauseous?"

"Do you feel like vomiting?"

"No."

"Fever?"

"No."

"Okay. I have some pills."

He thinks about this while looking at stone deities, and he thinks about Herta requesting ginger, and about telling her that he forgot to bring the ginger that she gave him in Goa, which was a minor lie because he purposely forgot the ginger, which in essence negates "forgot." So then, as if to further himself from recrimination, he said that the Goa ginger was already old by the time they left and that it probably wouldn't have been any good. Wade then promised to go out and look for ginger in Belur as soon as the shops opened. He also mentioned that he hoped he could remember what ginger looked like. But to get things going right away, Wade suggested that Herta take a diarrhea pill, and to Wade's surprise she agreed, for he had anticipated that she'd want to handle this in an organic way. A few hours later Wade went out shopping, and when he returned he had a piece of raw ginger. In addition, he brought back a supply of cold soda pop and some crackers that resembled matzo.

Herta peeled the flaky skin off the ginger with a pocketknife and cut slices from the root and ate the slices, which caused Wade to wince because it didn't look appetizing. Wade wasn't sure what the benefits of ginger were, but he somehow felt that raw ginger was more of a laxative than a remedy for diarrhea, and so he had wondered about the ginger interfering with the pill, like maybe the ginger would reduce the effects of the diarrhea pill. And that's one of the problems with getting sick and trying to figure out what to do, speculation turning into a guessing game.

Given hindsight, Wade's dealing with his illness in Goa, which turned out to be hepatitis, was the correct course, but he had been tempted to start an antibiotics cycle, yet had somehow feared it, which was nothing more than a feeling or a hunch, at least before he knew what he was dealing with. And then, after looking at his chalk-colored stool and knowing that he had hepatitis, he knew not to take any medications, or he sort of knew, for that was what he had heard from other travelers—sit it out and douse it with glucose.

On another occasion, when Wade had just entered the state of Maharashtra, central India, and was down with a bad sore throat that had gone up into his ears, he put himself on a five-day tetracycline program, infection clearing up by the third day, but Wade continuing to take the pills because that's what he remembered from such treatment in America—complete the cycle. But it was guesswork, and it was dangerous, and he knew that antibiotics would clear his system of good bacteria along with the bad, which could leave him more susceptible to illness. But what choice did he have? His ears were killing him, and he had a fever, and he was dizzy.

Wade sits down on a stone step and looks around at the Chennakeshava temple complex, and he thinks about illness and about Herta. After she had taken the diarrhea pill and was lying down, Wade had tried reading *The Godfather*. But he was restless, yet he felt that he owed Herta his time and care for her having spent so much time at his bedside in Goa—her patience, her talking to him, her telling him stories, her going to the village and bringing back provisions. But Wade wasn't good at this sort of thing, caring for sick people, and he wondered about this. Perhaps some people were better at it than others, for it struck Wade that this wasn't his forte, and yet he was truly concerned for Herta. He wanted her to get well, and he feared that if she got seriously ill he wouldn't know what to do, or maybe he'd do the wrong thing. To be sick in India is no trifling matter, proper medical care hard to find, and/or far away.

But actually, it's more the issue of traveling and getting sick that looms as a basic problem. Wade, himself, getting sick is less frightening for him than Herta getting sick, because Wade feels that he travels with the understanding that if things go wrong he won't be hurting anyone but himself. But if things go wrong with Herta, he'd really feel bad. And what really frightens him is the possibility that Herta could get sick and die. Wade, of course, faces this with himself, and in this he'd either go missing or his death would be reported to the American embassy, in which case his mother would be notified—maybe. And so his mother would probably worry and/or grieve for a while, but Wade doesn't feel responsibility for that. And that's the thing, for he now feels a sense of responsibility regarding Herta, and it scares him.

He stands up and heads back to the hotel, and when he arrives he finds Herta sitting up in bed, reading *Siddhartha*. She looks up from the book and smiles.

CHAPTER 9

He's standing on a well-maintained front lawn of a single-story house in Studio City, and he has measured the exterior of the house, and now he is figuring out how many gallons of paint it will take to cover the stucco. In hand, he has a clipboard with a piece of paper on it, and to go along with this he has a pencil and a pocket-calculator. It's a good-weather day, four in the afternoon, mid-June, and the homeowner, Evelyn Walsh, is standing next to him. Evelyn has a couple of color charts that she's looking at.

The house, like other houses on the south side of Ventura Boulevard, is not a tract home. It is custom built, and if Wade were to go inside, he thinks he'd find three bedrooms, or maybe two bedrooms and a den.

Wade comes up with a price and writes it down and circles it. He shows this to Evelyn. He has already told her that he'll patch the cracks on the stucco and sand the wood and patch any blemishes he finds on the wood and apply a primer/sealer before painting the wood. As far as he can tell, the wood is in good shape and doesn't need to be replaced.

Evelyn looks at the price and says okay and asks when Wade can begin. Wade says he can begin the day after next. Evelyn nods and then shows Wade what color she has chosen for the stucco and what color for the wood. It's a straight-forward deal—no detached garage, no patio woodwork, no deck, no wheelchair ramp. It's not a new house, single-car garage indicating that, but, like with the lawn and flowerbeds, the house has been well-maintained.

So the house isn't any kind of an issue, and the location isn't a problem, for Evelyn's house is about fifteen or twenty minutes away by car from Wade's mother's house, but that fifteen or twenty minutes is cause for at least a fifty-thousand-dollar price difference, with regards to the same size house. Studio City is nice. In fact, Wade's been frequenting a Starbucks on Ventura Boulevard that's only a block and a half away from Evelyn's house. He likes to sit at an outdoor table at that Starbucks with a cup of coffee and watch people go by on the sidewalk. For Wade, this is a pleasant diversion from his mother's house and its neighborhood. In addition to people-watching, Wade also likes to eavesdrop on conversations at adjacent tables. Wade's worked on other houses in Studio City, and he's found the people he's worked for agreeable, perhaps because they are more interested in quality than economy, and for the most part they aren't on his back about getting the job in a nanosecond, which is a real plus, because Wade's not the fastest worker in the world, age coming to bear.

There's something about Evelyn that strikes Wade, but he's not sure what it is. She seems like a professional person, someone whose income is comfortable, but at the same time she's not ostentatious. There's a white Volvo wagon in the driveway, but that's hardly flamboyant. She's wearing a pair of loose jeans and a dark brown T-shirt that has Arches National Park in beige lettering above a pocket on the left side. Her feet are in huaraches, no socks. She is thin. Her forearms show evidence of sunshine. Her hair is very black and very short, and it's cut in a bowl-like style. There are no tattoos that Wade can see, but along her left ear there are four silver studs that glint. She's not wearing glasses, and she's not wearing makeup, except for a light red color on her lips. Her eyes are hazel, eyebrows black and not penciled on. Crow's feet seem to be threatening, but this may be because she is squinting because of the sunshine. Wade detects a sense of sadness about her, yet she doesn't speak that way. Her speech is normal, but then again it's a little abnormal for Southern California because everyone in Los Angeles speaks TV-fast, which is to say that Evelyn doesn't speak that way. Her words are not rushed. Wade guesses early forties, but of course that's only a guess. Thus far, no man, nor anyone else, has been mentioned. The backyard shows no signs of a pet, but that doesn't necessarily rule out a cat.

"How long will it take you to finish?"

"About a week."

So he finished Evelyn's house in a week and was paid, but he still thinks of her from time to time when he goes to that Starbucks on Ventura Boulevard that's near her house. He never did find out what she did for a living, or if there was a man in her life, or a pet, or any kind of serious sadness.

It rains one night. And Wade is in bed when he hears it, two in the morning, but he's not asleep. The windows in his bedroom are open and the rain is tapping on the awnings of the windows and on the dry leaves of the elm in the backyard, a gentle rain. No lightening, no thunder. It's the end of summer, mid-September, and so the rain is evidence of unusual weather because September is not a rainy month in Southern California.

He lies in bed and listens, and it makes him think of other places and other times, but of course his thoughts often retreat to that realm, rain or no rain. His dreams, too, involve said domain, and he wonders if this is nostalgia.

He'd like to ask other people about this, people like Art Perez or Art's wife, April, people who have spent their whole life in Southern California, for Wade wonders if they, too, think about the past in a nostalgic way. But he hasn't seen Art or April in over a year, and even if he did see them, it'd be hard to ask such a question because people don't talk about such things, or so Wade feels, for everyone seems to be talking about more down-to-earth things, such as career or entertainment or current events that appear on TV in the form of news, and, like with television and its presentation of news, all the immediate issues that people talk about are only touched on, short clips of speech and abbreviated composition and shortcut-opinion, and whether this is because of habit or avoidance or a lack of true interest Wade can't tell. If it were only young people, such as those Wade's eavesdropped on at Starbucks, Wade could assume that these truncated subjects and sentences and opinions were a form of cool speech, which is under-standable given the combination of youth and recent technology. But it's middle-aged people as well, and people who are edging beyond middle-aged, too, everyone using TV-speak. It's epidemic, and somehow Wade got left behind. Even going to a movie theater to see a movie is a challenge for him—booming sound, quick speech, scenes flicking in rapidity without allowing any scene to develop. After three films he gave up on going to the movies.

Pitter-patter, pitter-patter, the sound of rain, and it takes him to far-off places that register as a different epoch. These recollections seem to have a life of their own, for they are vivid, and they run without encouragement, and they are emotionally moving. Wade sometimes feels that this is a form of capturing those experiences in a unique way, for it's as if hindsight was enabling him to see those times in a fuller, more detailed way. He has stepped back, so there is an expanded backdrop against which these events take place. When they were happening it was all so immediate that it was hard to understand them. They were simply there in front of him. And then he was in them—absorbed.

Such events and experiences roll in his mind as living memories, and he has begun to equate them with getting lost, like getting lost in a painting or a piece of music or a novel, fictive, yet somehow real. He's in it, and not in it. The two aspects of experience that are needed for understanding.

A strange twist has begun, for his current life, his real-time life, sometimes seems to be unreal, as if he were living a fiction. It's not the same as his memory-fiction, but there are carryovers. In his present life he often sees himself as a persona, and he eavesdrops on his own conversations. He is a voyeur looking at himself in a mirror that is not so different than memory.

He has begun to attend AA meetings, open meetings. He attends them now and then at his choosing. He has gone over to an office in the West Valley and has picked up a little booklet that lists meetings, days and times. Throughout Southern California, and in the Valley alone, to Wade's astonishment, there is a meeting going on, often a couple of them simultaneously, at almost any hour between early morning and late at night every day of the week.

He has turned down the advances of a "friend," for he fears a "sponsor-" relationship. Wade is not a group-type person. He is not a "joiner." He's afraid of being "tied."

To attend these open meetings, even in a listening capacity, he's felt obligated to stand up, like the other new attendees, and say, "My name is Wade, and I'm an alcoholic." But it's more than obligation that's at work, for what Wade is saying is not a lie. He's telling the truth. And this allows him to participate, for he is telling the group he is one of them. Wade's participation consists mostly of listening, and listening has told him that a lot of people regurgitate experiences, which are memories, and AA supplies a venue where those memories are verbalized in front of others. To see this unfold is to witness those memories coming alive, which can be painful. Emotions on display are not unusual at these meetings.

Wade is still drinking, but he is drinking with less regularity.

Hangovers have gotten to be a problem, and he views this as another manifestation of age biting at his heels.

He's in the cafeteria of a hospital in Van Nuys, mid-San Fernando Valley. There are only three people in the cafeteria besides himself, and one of them is posted at a cash register. On the table in front of him there is a cup of coffee that sits idly. He is gazing at the sunlight that's on the linoleum floor next to the table where he's sitting, late-afternoon rays slanting in through a window.

"Hello, Wade."

He looks up and sees a woman standing on the other side of the table. Her face is familiar, and while responding "Hello," his mind is scuttling for identification, which turns out to be halfway successful, for he places her, but he can't get the name.

"You painted my house about a year ago."

"Yes, I remember, in Studio City."

"That's right."

"Thank you for the referrals."

"Well, you did a good job, and my friends have told me that they were pleased with your work, too."

He smiles a half-smile, a hesitant smile, a crooked smile. "Would you care to have a seat?" He gestures to the chair opposite him.

She sits down, and, like Wade, she has a coffee cup, but her cup is full and steaming, whereas Wade's cup is not steaming.

"I'm sorry. I've forgotten your name."

"Evelyn."

"Oh, yes. Now that I've heard it, I remember."

Evelyn sips her coffee. Wade sips his coffee.

"My mother fell and hurt her back," Evelyn says. "She's in the rehabilitation wing upstairs."

"Really? My mother is in the rehabilitation ward, too. It wasn't her back this time, though. Last year it was. Last year she fell and hurt her back. This time it was a potassium deficiency, and it caused her to hallucinate. She was seeing streams of ants on the walls. But there were no ants."

Wade pauses to raise a hand. "Potassium," he says. "It's everywhere: bananas, sweet potato, zucchini, canned tuna, cantaloupe, broccoli, chicken breast, leafy vegetables. And to imagine that not getting enough of it can cause hallucinations." His hand comes down.

"I see. But why the rehabilitation wing, if it was a potassium deficiency?"

"She's not in good shape. She has all kinds of problems. Rehabilitation allows her to stay in the hospital a little longer. You know, it all has to be justified for Medicare.

So, with the assistance of a therapist she's doing hand exercises with some putty. She's also walking around in the hallway behind a walker. A therapist accompanies her."

Evelyn sips her coffee. Wade sips his coffee.

"I think I'm going to put my mother in a care facility," Evelyn says.

"Oh?" says Wade. "Did you speak with Ms. Stevenson?"

"Yes. Just now, actually. Her advice seems sound. My mother lives alone, and, as Ms. Stevenson pointed out, the elderly have a tendency to fall and hurt themselves. It's dangerous for them to be home alone. Also, my mother's house is in Sun Valley, which isn't the nicest of neighborhoods. I'm worried about that, too."

Wade nods. "Yes, that's what Ms. Stevenson told me last year. You see, I live with my mother, and I'm away during the day, working. But . . . my mother didn't want to go to a care facility, so that didn't happen. Of course I'm going to have to talk to Ms. Stevenson this time, too. It's part of the protocol. And the decision this time isn't going to be any easier than last time. Ms. Stevenson told me last year that in situations like this I'm the one to make decisions. I have power of attorney."

"I see."

"I came home two and a half years ago from abroad to take care of my mother because she was old and sick."

Evelyn nods, and then sips her coffee. Wade sips his coffee.

"It's funny you should mention Sun Valley," Wade says, "because that's where my mother's house is."

"Really? Is that where you grew up?"

"Yes."

"In that case, we grew up in the same neighborhood."

Wade nods. And then he says, "But I got a feeling it wasn't at the same time. I mean, I don't think we met at school or anything."

Evelyn smiles, and raises her cup of coffee and sips. After swallowing, she says, "What were you doing abroad? Military, multinational company?"

"No, no military, no big company. Travel—third-rate accommodation, short-term entertainment, low-paying jobs."

"I see."

"I guess you could say I was trying to prolong youth."

"Prolong youth?" Evelyn says, a smile teasing her complexion.

"Yeah."

"Well, that doesn't seem too bad—trying to prolong youth."

"Yes. But then age started catching up with me."

Evelyn's expression indicates that she finds this interesting, or perhaps entertaining. She says, "Yes, it has a tendency to do that."

They sip their coffees, and on Evelyn's face something like curiosity lingers, while on Wade's face there is a tinge of interest as he looks at Evelyn's face, and then at her yellow blouse that has little white buttons down its center.

"Well," Evelyn says, "I'd better get back upstairs. It was nice talking to you."

"Yes, nice talking to you, too."

She stands up and walks to where she sets her cup down on a wide sill of an open window, kitchen on the other side of the window. Turning away from the window, she walks across the cafeteria, a modest gait, flower-print pattern on her skirt that comes to below her knees, black sneakers on her feet. Wade's eyes follow her, while his mind tells him all kinds of things, such as Evelyn's awareness of Wade's eyes. But she doesn't turn to look at him.

While his mother is in the hospital, he starts turning the backyard into a chaparral garden. This requires the removal of the elm and some bushes and then the lawn. The purpose is to transform a water-thirsty yard into a non-water-thirsty yard. Or, viewed another way, return that small parcel of land to what it used to be before people started using imported water to fulfill suburbanite paradigms, for the San Fernando Valley in its natural state, like most of Southern California, is semi-arid, chaparral landscape dominant.

There is a cat that sits in the shade of a wall and watches him as he works, a calico that he found out on the front lawn one day, a young cat, which Wade then took around the neighborhood to ask people if they had lost a cat. But no one had, so the cat became Wade and his mother's pet. The cat's name is Linda, but Wade calls her Buddha.

It's seven in the morning and he's working in the yard and the cat turns and looks at Wade's cellphone because the cellphone, which is sitting on a brick, is buzzing and jiggling. Wade, understanding that only his mother and the hospital have his cellphone number, walks over and picks up the device with apprehension.

When he arrives at the hospital he goes to his mother's room and he stands at her bedside and looks down at her face, sunlight slanting in through the mini-blinds of a window nearby. He stands for a few long moments and then he places the back of his hand on his mother's cheek. He feels the softness of that cheek and the littleness of her face. The room is quiet, for the other bed in the room is vacant.

After he's through with this, he goes to the nurses' station and starts filling out forms, which is when he learns that his mother's death was due to congestive heart failure.

On the way home from the hospital he stops at a liquor store and picks up a six-pack of beer and a pint of vodka, and for the next two weeks, while he works on the backyard, he drinks at night and wakes up the next morning with a hangover that gnaws at him throughout the day while he labors in the sun.

At an office in Burbank he picked up his mother's ashes ten days after her death. The ashes are in a sealed tin box that now sits on top of his mother's dresser in her bedroom.

The telephone rings now and then, and if he answers it he takes people's names and their phone numbers, and he tells them that he is currently busy and that he'll call them when he is no longer busy. But more often than not he lets the answering machine take a message.

And so it is ten in the morning, and he's standing in the kitchen with a cup of coffee when he hears the telephone ring. He lets the answering machine click in, and after his message and a beep, he hears a voice and a name and he steps into the dining room and picks up the receiver.

"Hello, Evelyn. This is Wade."

He sometimes thinks about how these things work, particularly the advent of chance, coincidence, and randomness. He thinks about these things while sipping coffee and while looking out the kitchen window at his chaparral backyard, a combination of drought-tolerant plants, gritty dirt, and pastel bricks. Or he thinks about them while lying in bed before getting to sleep. But more significantly, he has begun to talk to Evelyn about these things, and she has begun to talk to him about these things, for these things involve what Wade and Evelyn are wrapped up in, which is two people finding one another and clicking.

She called him because she wanted her mother's house painted, the interior. She was going to sell the house and was clearing it out. Her realtor-friend, Don Vinn, who was going to handle the sale, told her that it would sell quicker if it were painted. Evelyn's mother was tucked into an upscale care facility in Van Nuys, which translated into a mini-apartment in a somewhat lavish complex—registered nurse on duty, twenty-four-hour supervision, meals either in one's room or downstairs in a dining room, organized games and outings, exercise room, outdoor garden, and entertainment choices: DVD night, bingo night, and so forth. It seemed that Evelyn's mother was content there. Evelyn had been visiting daily. The house, only a few blocks from Wade's house, was a burden— utilities (water bill in particular), property tax, gardener, and the threat of break-in. Evelyn had consulted her mother, and this was what they had decided: sell the house, and in the event that Evelyn's mother grew to dislike the care facility she could move in with Evelyn, for Evelyn lived alone in her house in Studio City. This sequence of events was rather rapid, and purposely so, because Evelyn wanted to wrap things up before school began in the fall, or actually late summer, for she was an art instructor at a college in the Valley.

After Wade finished painting the interior of the house, the house went on market and someone made an offer within a week. Don Vinn had liked Wade's work, and promised to start pushing work Wade's way, people readying their houses to put on the market, or new homeowners wanting work done.

But a more important consequence was Wade and Evelyn getting to know each other, not completely but somewhat. There was no direction or implied intent to this, such as when people go out on a date. It was simply two people spending time together on a common project, which happened to take place during the summer.

Framed photographs and drawings and watercolors and pastels were on the walls in every room, and as Evelyn took them down there remained a square or a rectangle that contrasted with the rest of the wall due to faded paint versus not-faded paint. The interior hadn't been painted in a long time.

Wade couldn't help but to look at the photos and drawings and watercolors and pastels, which were either the work of Evelyn's mother or Evelyn. So before these were carted over to Evelyn's house in Studio City to be stored in Evelyn's garage, they became subjects of conversation that naturally filled Wade in on Evelyn's background and her current employment.

They'd break for diet Dr. Pepper or bottled water or sports drink, and they'd look at a watercolor and Wade would ask about it and Evelyn would explain and comment. They'd be sweating, but fortunately the air was dry, and they'd be in shorts and T-shirts, T-shirts with the sleeves cut off at the shoulders, and they'd be standing and looking at a piece that was off the wall and leaning against a table leg. Evelyn would lean down to point something out with a finger, and Wade would be looking and listening while noting that Evelyn wasn't wearing a bra, which was a change from the first day when he went over, for he was pretty sure he would have noticed that if that had been the case. It was about five days into the project that he noticed—no bra.

Sometimes when they broke for lunch they'd go over to Wade's house that was around the corner and two blocks over, and in this way Evelyn became privy to Wade's lifestyle, which was sparse and plain. She met his cat, and she saw the chaparral garden that constituted the backyard, Wade explaining the logic of it.

But then something curious happened after about two weeks, project at Evelyn's mother's house nearing completion. Wade and Evelyn were at Wade's house having lunch—pita bread, cheddar cheese, feta cheese, olives, iced tea. She was on her way to the bathroom when she stopped, for the door to Wade's bedroom was open and she noticed a worktable in there with a certain look, and then when she came out of the bathroom she took a second look before continuing on into the living room where she stood with a hand on her hip and said, "You didn't tell me you draw and paint."

Wade lifted a shoulder and shrugged. He had stopped drinking, so the hangovers had stopped. His head was clear.

"I did watercolors and drawings and pastels to pass the time when I was abroad. I haven't done anything since returning to L.A. I went over to an arts supply store on Ventura Boulevard last week and picked up some materials, and . . . started fooling around."

"Do you mind if I have a look?"

"No, go ahead."

So she went to the bedroom and Wade followed her, where he then stood in the doorway to watch Evelyn go to the workbench that Wade had recently constructed out of two-by-fours and plywood. She looked at what he had been doing, which were studies on sheets of sketchbook paper. But there was one piece that was more serious, a watercolor in development, penciled outlines, watercolor filling in. He had laid down washes, but there were also areas where the paint was opaque. Hints of cubism and fracturing were at work, as were exaggeration and fantasy, but it wasn't abstract, for subject was evident: two people sweating in a room that was slightly atilt, windows with rays of sunlight, rays dashed with shades of color. Nudity seemed to be emerging. Evelyn picked the piece up to look at it at different angles. She set it down and said, "It's us, isn't it?"

"Well, kind of."

It was hot, for the air-conditioning unit in the dining room, the house's only source of cooling, wasn't on. But it wasn't as hot as other days because there were light clouds high in the sky, which brought the midday temperature down into the mid-eighties.

Evelyn shifted her weight from one foot to the other, huaraches on her feet, legs bare to where her safari shorts began, shorts loose at her thighs. She seemed to be thinking. She looked toward the window, which gave out onto a view of the backyard, chaparral yard—dryness, stillness, simplicity.

Her view returned to Wade, and he shifted his weight, and she said: "How do we do this?"

He moved his mouth, a side to side kind of thing, but he didn't say anything. Evelyn looked around the room. She stepped over and sat down on the edge of Wade's narrow bed. The room was a little cramped because of the newly constructed worktable.

Wade left the doorway and went to her and leaned down and lifted the bottom hem of her shirt up and over her head. She accommodated this by raising her thin arms. When the shirt was off, Wade dropped it on the bed and then reached down to fondle her breasts. After a few moments she said, "Do you have condoms?" "Yes." She looked up at his face, and he said, "I bought them the other day." This seemed to amuse her, a grin on her face, which persisted as she ran a hand up the inside of his thigh and into his shorts. A minute or so of this went by, and then Evelyn said, "I want to get my glass of iced tea. And why don't we bring that fan in here?" Wade smiled a crooked smile, which was how he always smiled, but now, as opposed to the other times, Evelyn asked him about it. "Why do you smile like that?" He answered, "I fell off a swing when I was four years old. A nerve got pinched. The left side of my face between my mouth and my eye is paralyzed. There's no movement there." Evelyn's hand, which was still up his shorts and was arousing him, stopped. She laughed, as if things were suddenly so simple, for maybe she had wondered about that smile's intent. But there was no intent.

She walked into the living room topless and she brought his and her glasses of iced tea back to the bedroom, while Wade set the fan up and turned it on, after which he opened a drawer on his desk, a small desk, a boy's desk, the desk he had used in his schooldays. From the drawer came a box of condoms, economy pack.

They started talking about all this—the cramped bedroom, the heat, the pint-size glasses of iced tea, the condensation on the glasses that they rubbed on one another's bodies like a couple of kids. Of course it was after they got to know each other better that they could discuss such things, and by then their time together in that bedroom with a fan blowing dry air at them had become "past," for that room on that particular day became part of what they could share, and so they talked about it within the parameters of memory.

But it was more than reminiscing, for "memory" became a vehicle into the present, and in recounting memories there was this amalgamation that took on various emotions, such as grief in the form of weeping or good times in the form of laughter, while on other occasions the telling of memories was like fantasy, which they brought into real-time by way of creations and ideas and inspirations that they tried out.

The beginning of all this was a couple of weeks after Evelyn's mother's house was finished and with escrow in the works, for it was then that Evelyn called Wade one afternoon, his cellphone buzzing, to ask him to come over to her house in Studio City because she wanted Wade to give her a price on turning her backyard into a chaparral garden. This was a breakthrough on a number of fronts, for they had been having sex at Wade's house, but never at Evelyn's, which was kind of curious since her house was more comfortable, but, as they later discussed and concluded, Wade's house had the history of that first time when they were solving the question of: "How do we do this?" And so Wade's house carried a pedigree of freedom born in simplicity, which got even simpler as he rid the house of his mother's things, furniture and clothing, and in the process converted his mother's bedroom into a studio by clearing everything out of that room and moving his worktable in there, while adding a yard-sale couch and coffee table, along with a full-length mirror that was movable due to casters.

With the makeover of Wade's house, Evelyn brought over a sketchpad and began sketching him, and he began sketching her, one or the other of them at the worktable while the other sat or reclined on the couch, iced tea and soda crackers on the coffee table, the two of them without clothes, full-length mirror employed for added perspective and sexual fantasy. It seemed that Wade's house was cause for nudity and sex, and what went along with this was that Evelyn's commuting to Wade's place allowed her the freedom of choice, whether to visit him or not, which was contingent on her feelings and her work schedule, for she was getting ready for the school year.

It was September when Wade went over to Evelyn's house in Studio City to talk about a chaparral garden. This in itself was a breakthrough of sorts, for it was clear that this would be a "paying job," for once the sex began at Wade's house the line between "favor" and "job" got blurred. The painting Wade did at Evelyn's mother's house was straightforward, "a paying job," but the hauling of things to the dump in Wade's pickup truck and to recycling centers and to Goodwill, and the yard sale that went on for a weekend, all fell within the bounds of "favor." So there was a lingering question: What would the future be, if work were called for? Fortunately, right on the phone, Evelyn said, "I want a price for it, Wade. No helping out, no favors. I have money. You need work. It's that simple."

The part about "I have money" would warrant a footnote, for part of why Evelyn had money to spend was tied to major revelations beyond "a paying job."

A Saturday, weather hot and dry, and Wade and Evelyn are in Evelyn's backyard, Wade with a tape measure and a clipboard. The clipboard has paperwork pertaining to what it cost Wade to turn his backyard into a semi-arid garden—square feet, price of bricks and plants, hours of labor invested.

After measuring and sketching a rough plan for the backyard, Wade and Evelyn go out to the front yard to look at that, but thus far the front yard is only in a "maybe" project.

After discussing the front yard and how a chaparral garden might look out there for everyone to see, Evelyn invites Wade into her house for "coffee." But . . . there is something to this, something more than "coffee," for Evelyn seems a bit apprehensive, and Wade senses that this might have to do with Wade never having been inside Evelyn's house.

So they go through the front door and Wade is in a small entranceway that is mostly designated by a door to a closet that's off to the left. A mere few steps and they are in the living room—off-white walls, hardwood floor, wooden furniture with pastel cushions, a fireplace, a large throw rug of Navajo design. The room is meant to be Western-casual, but its neatness and order cancel this out. The room looks unused.

Wade begins to take in details—a menorah on the mantel of the fireplace, while at the other end of the mantel a bronze Hindu deity with eight arms stands. A few framed watercolors are on the walls. Wooden end tables have table lamps that sport colorful ceramic bases and stiff yellow shades. At the windows there are oat-colored curtains that resemble canvas, the sort of canvas that's used for oil paintings.

Beyond the living room there is a room with a wide entrance that looks like a dining room, but instead of a table and chairs there is a black piano. A tall, small-paned window with an arch at the top, cut glass in the arch, allows for daylight to slant in and glint off the piano. The piano's large, triangular lid is lying flat, and on top of that glossy surface an American flag, folded to the contours of a fat triangle, sits.

Comprehension is at work in Wade's head, and at the same time he senses Evelyn shifting her weight, huaraches creaking. Wade's eyes go somewhere else—a framed poster/print, Van Gogh, *Irises*. His view returns to the flag.

"It's what you think it is."

"Oh, boy."

"My son was killed in Iraq."

CHAPTER 10

They've just passed through a sandalwood forest of stunted trees, and now they are gliding down a winding road that has no traffic, hills subsiding. In view there is a plain that stretches to a distant horizon. The road, like a black slash, is on that flat earth, and it runs toward a dull sky that merges with that far-off horizon like an evasive arc. A truck is on the road, but aside from that vehicle only the road and a tree and a small white structure interrupt the terrain.

"Easy going," Wade remarks.

"Good," Herta says. Her short, yellow-blonde hair, which has grown somewhat ragged, is flicking in the current of air produced in her bicycle's descent.

At the bottom of the hill their legs begin to work, temperature between warm and hot, air mildly humid. Scrub vegetation and rough-edged pebbles punctuate the landscape. Now and then there's a crow.

They drift off the road and onto an ashen-dirt shoulder, where they stop and straddle their bikes and brace them-selves. The truck sounds its horn and flies by, impact of the truck's draft hitting them, and then abating. They resume pedaling.

Their immediate itinerary has them progressing through southern Karnataka on a route nearing Mysore as if they were on course. But agenda is elusive, for each day's circumstance is enough to unravel their journey like a dream upon waking.

Because of its isolation the tree grows in their vision as if to measure their progress, limbs heavy, leaves broad, color dappled-green. The tree's shadow appears inky on the roadway, while above the road tattered foliage is sheared at the height of trucks.

"If it were like this all the way to Cape Comorin, I wouldn't mind it," Wade says, and leans back on the seat of his bicycle. "No hills, no wind, no rain, no traffic."

"It won't last," responds Herta. And to this, Wade doesn't issue a rejoinder because there is nothing to dispute.

They pedal on, and after a few minutes the tree further claims Wade's attention because there are hints of movement.

"Do you think there are bats in that tree?" Wade says. "It doesn't look like birds."

"Bats?" says Herta. "I hope not. That one we saw before was horrible. The whole tree crawling with those things."

Wade, eyes remaining on the tree, says, "Those are monkeys."

"Monkeys?" questions Herta.

In addition to in the tree, there are a few monkeys on the ground, and of those on the ground they now rise up to stand on two legs, but they don't look at Wade and Herta. They look in the opposite direction, and then they leap onto the tree's trunk and fly up into the leafy greenery, while from that greenery screams explode, silence of the landscape shattered.

Two dark-skinned men on bicycles are on the road from out of nowhere and they're coming to the tree from the opposing direction that Herta and Wade are. The torsos of the men are over the handlebars of their bicycles, legs pumping like jackhammers. The men reach the tree and dismount in a hurry, backs hunched, footsteps somehow cautious. One man goes to the roadway, while the other unties a bundle that's lashed to the rear rack of his bicycle.

The screams of the monkeys are onto the savanna as cries to a deaf world, for nothing stirs except that tree. It is panic serving itself, and it is not only vocal but visual as well. Monkeys are leaping and twisting and looking down from the highest limbs they can navigate, as if the tree has run out of itself in the sky. Beneath this, one man is looking up and down the roadway, the other unrolling a burlap bundle.

Wade stops pedaling and Herta coasts by and looks back at him.

"Wait a minute," Wade says. "Something's not right here."

Herta stops and straddles her bicycle, two feet on the road's asphalt. Wade has assumed the same stance. The shrieking of the monkeys continues. Wade swings a leg over the bar of his bike and then walks the bike forward to where Herta is, the two of them parallel on the road.

The one man separates a burlap sack from the bundle and drapes the sack over the rear rack of his bike. A second burlap sack comes off the bundle and goes over the rack as well. The man then pulls a double-barreled shotgun out from a third sack. That sack, too, goes over the rack of his bicycle. The man takes two shells from his shorts' pocket and breaks the breach of the rifle open and inserts the shells. He closes the rifle with a snap.

The man without the rifle is scanning the roadway, body bent in stealth. Wade and Herta are dismissed with a glance. Evidently these men have other concerns aside from why two Westerns on bicycles are out on this desolate stretch of road, and for that dismissal the scene sketches itself in a freakish way that imitates pornography, for suddenly Wade and Herta are voyeurs.

The man with the rifle sneaks around the tree, trying to catch the monkeys off guard, feet cautious, eyes darting. Large rocks, like black mounds, are at the base of the tree and demand a wide circumference. The man goes from one side of the tree to the other, body alert, movement secretive. The monkeys keep a limb between themselves and the rifle.

The armed man motions to his friend, and the friend picks up stones and throws them at the monkeys. The man's throwing motion is stiff-armed. The monkeys scream and look from one man to the other, but not a single monkey swings around to avoid the stones, and not a single stone hits a monkey. The man stops throwing stones.

The askew picture before Wade's eyes is about sixty yards away. Wade stands, mesmerized. Herta strikes a match and lights a beedi.

The two men come together, their heights short, their faces gaunt. The man without the rifle flings an arm up and dashes to the opposite side of the tree. The monkeys keep the tree between themselves and the man with the shotgun, and if it weren't for the terror in the monkeys' voices and the movement of their bodies the episode would fall into farce.

The man with the shotgun can't get a clean shot off, and it seems that he is unwilling to blast away. Perhaps it is his friend's concern with the road and what might be coming down that road that contributes to a hesitant trigger finger or maybe it's the cost of buckshot.

The tree is electric, monkeys shrieking, bodies tense, hair stiff, ligament and muscle like cord, while below two men in shorts and plaid shirts sneak around. It is fascinating before its image matures, before emotion springs from understanding.

And it continues, one man waving a rifle, his partner at the road on the lookout, tree charged with fear, locale imbibed with screaming.

And then it ends, and it ends in the same way as it began, for the source of that ending is a mystery. Its form, though, is the stock of the rifle coming away from the man's shoulder while the man's body sags. The rifle continues downward until it hangs at the end of the man's arm like a relic. The man shuffles over to his bicycle and breaks the rifle open. He takes the shells out and puts them in his pocket. He closes the rifle and slips it into a gunnysack.

A communiqué enters into the cries of the chimps. The man rolls the shotgun up with burlap and secures the bundle with rope to the rack of his bicycle. The two men get on their bicycles and pedal away laboriously in the direction from which they came. The monkeys watch. The tree is mute.

Wade looks at Herta. Herta inhales on her beedi.

Wade turns back and looks at the tree as if expecting something more, but there is nothing more, only the tree and the road and a small building beyond the tree.

"We've seen, and we've seen, and we've seen," says Wade. "And now we've seen some more."

Herta drops the nub of her beedi on the ground and rubs her shoe on it.

They begin pedaling, and when they are under the tree they stop and look up, leaves floppy, lower branches thick and worn. It is a huge tree, and in its shadow it is cool.

A dozen or so monkeys are relaxed and looking down, eyes hazel and blinking. The larger animals are the size of a cocker spaniel, skin and hair black. Babies cling to the undersides of mothers.

Blackened stones and the remains of incense and flowers are at the foot of the tree. Coconut rind lies in litter. A few monkeys begin to venture down.

"We'd better go," Wade says.

They pedal, and after thirty yards they come to the building. Two rough-planked doors are clapped shut with a length of steel. To one side of the structure a hand-pump rises from the ground, handle of the pump padlocked.

Wade and Herta park their bikes and walk to the base of the building's three steps, entire edifice whitewashed, except for its wooden doors. Above the doors there is a frieze of Hunman, half monkey, half human.

Wade yells, "Hello!" to the building, and at first there is nothing. But then a young man in sandals comes from around the building, body lithe and wrapped in beige cloth. His head is shaved. A smudge of yellowish paste the size of a thumbprint marks his brow above his nose. He walks up to Wade and Herta and stops. He smiles and says, "Hello."

"Hello," says Wade. And then, "I was wondering if we could get some water."

The man hesitates, but then says, "Yes."

"Is this a temple?" asks Herta.

"Yes," the man replies, arms and hands thin and smooth, face without blemish or weather. "Would you care to go inside?"

"Can we?" says Herta.

"Yes," the man says, English wrapped around a cadence that is common to the Indian subcontinent.

The young man goes up the steps and brings out a ring of keys. He unlocks a padlock and lifts the bar and opens one of the two doors.

The three of them go inside. There is only one room, and it isn't large, walls and ceiling white, floor concrete. To go beyond the entranceway would require the removal of shoes, but this isn't necessary because the shrine is easily seen from where they stand. There is a large painting of Hunman, fruit on an altar before the colorful image. Bluish-white light from small, rectangular windows high up on a wall floods the room.

"Hunman," Herta says.

"Yes," replies the man. "This is a monkey temple."

The three of them stand, mood ponderous.

"Didn't you hear the monkeys screaming just a while ago?" Wade asks.

"Monkeys screaming?" questions the young man, head at a tilt.

"Yes."

"The monkeys make a racket from time to time," says the man. "They live in the tree. The tree is their home. They quarrel. They are like humans."

Wade looks at him, looks at the man's smooth face, and the man accepts this without reaction. And that's what Wade is looking at—no reaction.

Stale incense scents the room's cool air. Wade's view returns to the shrine, and again the three of them stand, contemplation suggested.

They turn in unison as if some inner clock were at work, for there is no verbal decision, just their bodies turning away from the shrine, and the three of them step over a wooden threshold to go outside where the sun beats down.

Two monkeys are sitting on the ground, one picking lice from the back of the other. Herta and Wade walk to their bikes, while the man locks the doors of the temple. The monkeys approach Herta and Wade.

"Hold your hands out," instructs the young man. "Open your hands. Show you have no food."

Herta and Wade open their hands. The monkeys look and lose interest.

Wade gets two plastic water bottles from the basket of his bicycle. The monkeys come over to Wade, and Wade holds the bottles down. The monkeys put their small, black hands on the plastic, noses twitching. They turn away.

The young man removes the padlock from the pump and then backs up and stands with the lock in his hand. The monkeys run over to the pump. Herta and Wade go to the pump, and Herta holds a water bottle under the pump's spout while Wade pumps. After a number of pumps water gushes out and runs into the bottle and over the bottle and over Herta's hand. The monkeys have their little hands out and are gathering water from under the dripping plastic bottle. Wade raises his view and sees monkeys cascading down the trunk of the tree.

"We got to hurry," says Wade. "There's a ton of monkeys coming this way." Herta puts the other plastic bottle under the pump's spout while Wade pumps.

Herta and Wade get away from the pump just as the troop arrives. The larger monkeys have their way over the smaller ones, animals jockeying for position at the concrete square below the pump, a four-inch lip bordering the small slab. There are about a dozen monkeys, some scooping water with their hands, others with their muzzles down at the concrete. One monkey screams and the others jump back. After a moment the group returns tentatively, hands skimming water, eyes shooting glances at the one that screamed. The young Hindu walks through the crowd of primates and padlocks the pump.

"Thank you," Wade says.

The young man wags his head and then watches as Herta and Wade get on their bikes and pedal away. Wade glances back. Monkeys remain at the pump while exercising habits of hierarchy.

The road and its blacktop guide them through a hushed landscape, and in response to whatever thoughts they might have there is only their pedaling and the movement it produces. Thorny bushes colonize the area, and now and then a dirt track branches off through the chaparral en route to an unseen destination, which was where the shotgun-men must have come from.

After a while the road takes on a slight incline. In the western sky a smear of vapor casts shafts of pastel light, and with this the landscape softens, conventions of sunset beginning.

In the direction they are headed there appears a low cloud over the land, and it is strange for its shape and density. It has a greenish shade and it becomes even stranger as it twists and turns, and then as it banks to follow the road, and in this way it is no longer a cloud. It is a strewn flock of birds, and as it nears Herta and Wade the birds' clipped wingbeats and the color of their plumage become discernible, and so their naming arises: small, green parrots.

Wade and Herta stop in the middle of the road, and they watch as the birds approach, and then as the birds stream overhead, wings with a percussion of air, sky full of green as it races by in blunt-faced increments. After the initial overhead-vision there follows a din of squawking that is mixed with the sounds of airy wingbeats as the flock continues and continues until its numbers end, bird-noise passing and then fading as the choir of squawking goes into the distance along with the vision that it elicits.

Wade and Herta are twisted around, eyes stuck on that cloud of green, while in the vicinity of Wade and Herta silence has returned like a stilled visage.

The flock slows and gathers itself as it circles above the tree where the monkeys dwell, and of that tree its position is now understood from the vantage point that Wade and Herta command, for Wade and Herta are on slightly higher ground, thus it becomes apparent that the tree and the hand pump are lapping groundwater from where a vast basin drops to a faint nadir.

The horde of birds grows until the last birds arrive, and with this the assemblage lowers itself onto the tree where it settles like a migration coming to rest.

Tree, temple, sky, earth—all in pastels.

Wade and Herta turn and begin pedaling, but after a few minutes Herta brings her bicycle to a halt. Wade coasts ahead and looks back. Herta is straddling her bike, feet on the ground. Wade stops, and while looking back, he says, "What is it?"

Herta only stands, vision at someplace beyond Wade, or maybe at Wade. Wade turns his bike around and walks back to her.

"What is it?" he says.

She gazes past him at the road, or maybe at the horizon that the road crests in the distance, and as Wade waits for an answer there is this tangible silence of aloneness.

She looks at him, and she says, "I want to go home."

PART 2

CHAPTER 11

The room's utility more than anything else indicates that it's a man's bedroom, for there are few keepsakes, much less flowery wallpaper or bottles of perfume or snapshots lining the edge of a mirror. The bed is made, and there are no clothes in sight aside from a Lakers cap that's a little soiled and sweat-stained. The walls of the room are light brown, curtains beige and bunched to the sides of two windows. Sunlight from the windows illuminates the room. There's a desk with a laptop computer on it, laptop closed, and there's a digital clock on a bedside table. Framed photographs are absent and so are posters. There is a bookcase with books, and even from where Wade stands in the doorway he can tell that most of the books are textbooks.

They've come down a carpeted hall from the living room to where Evelyn opened a door to the bedroom. Not a lot had been said in the living room after Wade spotted the folded flag on top of the piano, which was when Evelyn told him in one brief sentence about her son, and with this they both had stood, neither one speaking, for it was as if this information had not only caught Wade unawares, but Evelyn, too. There seemed nothing to say, perhaps because whatever might be said would seem banal, or just plain stupid, as platitudes often are. But finally, Evelyn said, "Come. Let me show you his bedroom."

Wade enters the room as if to take in its feel. He goes over to where a boogie board is leaning against a wall. A pair of fins, Churchills, are on the floor next to the boogie board. He looks at these, and he sees a memory. The room is warm. The windows aren't open.

"When I asked you to paint the exterior of the house last year, it really wasn't the exterior I wanted painted. It was this room.

"But then I couldn't do it. I was going to clear the room out and have you paint it. Having you paint it would *make* me clear the room out. I was going to put the flag away, and I was going to erase this room. So then you came over, but I had changed my mind, and I couldn't very well divulge the reasons for this. Not to you, not then. You were a stranger. A housepainter. Someone who was coming over to give me a price on some painting. And in another sense, I couldn't have explained my change-of-mind to anyone. Not even to myself. I thought that I wanted to put this away, put it in the past, so I could move on. It was time to put it away. That's what I thought. And I still think that. But there's something else, something besides thought, and reasons and logic.

"So rather than sending you away after having asked you to come over to do some painting, and then me feeling embarrassed about that, I asked you to give me a price for the exterior."

Wade nods.

"It's so strange when I think about it," Evelyn says. "I mean... the exterior really didn't *need* painting. Of course it looks better with a fresh paint job. But actually, you painting the exterior was a mishap, a mishap that I could hardly feel bad about because of money. You see, I suddenly had a lot of unexpected money, and the reason for this was because my son was killed while in the military. If he had been married, his wife would have gotten that money. As it was, though, I received that money. A lot of money—along with the flag."

Evelyn shifts her weight, huaraches squeaking, a new pair in the process of getting broken in. Wade is standing next to the boogie board and he is looking at Evelyn, who is in the doorway.

"We've talked about coincidence," Evelyn says. "You know, how we came together, you and me. But all the while, I was thinking of how it went back further and in a more arcane way than we were talking about. But I couldn't tell you about that then, because by that time I wanted you to see me without the color of this history. I was tired of people looking at me through the lens of my son's death. I knew right away that you weren't seeing me that way. That was the erasure I was seeking. Or needing. With my friends and colleagues I was the mother of the boy killed in Iraq. It was time to move on, for that was about two years ago, his death I mean. I was tired of people feeling sorry for me. It felt like a weight.

"Of course this tied in with my wanting to take the flag off the piano and put it in a closet, and with wanting to clear out his room."

"Yes."

"So you see, I asked you to come over so that you could paint my son's bedroom, but then you painted the exterior of the house. And if it wasn't for that, we wouldn't have spoken to one another in the hospital cafeteria. And I wouldn't have called you to come over to paint my mother's house."

"Of course."

"And. If I had had you paint this room, I would have taken the flag off the piano before having you come in to give me a price on this room, the bedroom, because I wouldn't have wanted you to know the history of this room.

"So if things had happened that way, and we would have gotten together like we did, then I would have had the option of not ever mentioning my son's death, which would have constituted a lie of sorts, providing we continued to see each other. For how can you not talk about the past, or at least parts of it, when you find yourself building something with someone? It's like denying your thoughts. Or denying the other person your thoughts."

"Yes."

Evelyn begins a smile. "I don't mean a person has to be a blabbermouth. But… not to tell you about my son would constitute intrigue. A game of sorts. I'm too old for games. Particularly after this."

"Yes."

Evelyn shifts her weight.

"I've thought of so many things, as you can probably imagine. I mean, why not move the flag from the piano into this room? Why not, for example, put it on the bed in here?"

Wade nods.

"But then I thought that'd be like closing the whole thing off in this room, which would allow me to lock it away by keeping the door closed. It'd have its own room. A ghost lurking. I'd be afraid to open the door. It'd become a phobia."

"Yes."

"It'd become its own little museum, but without visitors.

"The flag on the piano shifts the focus, disperses the focus. This room is not frightening. How could it be? The flag on the piano forces me not to deny this room. This room..." She raises a hand. "This is me. This is a part of me."

Wade nods.

"This will never go away. At least not until I go away."

"Yes."

"But I don't want to keep crying over it, and I don't want people to keep seeing me in that light. And yet I don't want to hide this. I don't want to trick people, and I don't want to trick myself. There's a line here, a line between acknowledgment and overindulgence, a line between history and melodrama."

"Yes."

Evelyn's smile is gone. The hand that she raised has come down. Evelyn is looking at Wade. He shifts his weight.

Wade looks down at the boogie board. "We live...," he whispers, and trails off.

Evelyn cocks her head and looks at him anew, but he says nothing more. She watches him as he moistens his chapped lips with his tongue, a gesture of shyness maybe, as if he doesn't know what to do or what to say. Evelyn's smile returns.

"I went abroad, the first time—Europe, North Africa, Asia Minor, India—about a year and a half. I went away because I wanted to see something other than suburbia. And of course I did. And so, I came back, came back to Southern California. But not to the Valley. I was in a small apartment near Santa Monica Pier, a place with a sign out front: *Rooms for Rent – Men Only*. I was working in a warehouse. I had a bicycle, no car, and I was bodyboarding. Just like this." He gestures at the boogie board. "I loved it—the beach and the boogie board.

"There were a couple of relationships with women, one woman and then another, and 'the another,' the second woman, was because the first woman jilted me. She had two young kids, the first woman, and I was trying to fit in with that, you know, that lifestyle. But I had my own ideas about it, which weren't the same as hers. And in a sense, that's when I knew I had lost suburbia. So with the second woman I already knew that I was leaving. She of course was staying, staying to go to graduate school and to develop a career. Oddly, it was that first woman, a woman who I had met five years previous in high school and had dated, who had set my mind to thinking about going out in the world to find something beyond suburbia."

"So then you were gone for thirty-two years?"

"Yes."

They stand, their lives at a juncture.

"It was that in-between time, in between that first trip abroad and the second—the beach, the boogie board— Santa Monica, Ocean Park, Venice. Those waves and that feeling."

He shifts his weight. "And here it is. Your son's boogie board and a pair of Churchills. He's won my heart."

And again they stand, but now Wade sees Evelyn's lips begin to tremble, and he goes to her and puts his arms around her, her body shaking.

They are sitting at a table in the kitchen with cups of coffee. There's a window that gives out onto the backyard. The window is open, and the kitchen is warm, but it's not hot like outside.

"There are uniforms and some military photos in the closet," Evelyn says. "Some of his clothes are in there, too, his regular clothes, and of course there are clothes in that chest of drawers. I haven't gone through the chest of drawers, the same as I haven't gone through his desk or his laptop. I've thought about it. It's a temptation, but I've concluded that there might be things in those places that I shouldn't see, things that a mother shouldn't see, or maybe that anyone shouldn't see. I'm not saying that I'm suspicious. I'm just saying that even now I can't help but to respect his privacy."

They sip their coffees. The coffee at Evelyn's house isn't as strong as the coffee at Wade's house. A plate of muffins is on the table, but they haven't touched the muffins.

"It's a curious thing," Evelyn says. "I'm carrying on as if he were still here."

"Yes," Wade concurs. "But some people might say that you are respecting . . . his life."

"Yes, I thought of that. But does a person's life continue after they are dead?"

"The eternal question," Wade says.

"What do you think?"

"Philosophical or in a religious sense, I don't know. But," says Wade, "memory continues. Your memory of your son continues, and it continues. It'd be impossible for you not to remember your son, not to think about him. So then, in a sense, there he is. We tend to discount this because we can't physically touch memories. But common sense and psychology, and most importantly 'experience,' tell us that memories are there in our heads. They matter. They are part of what our lives are built on. Conscious and subconscious. Erase memory and what do you have? But that isn't so much a paradox, as is: Memories are a source of sanity, and insanity."

"I know," Evelyn responds, and raises her hand from the table to emphasize. Wade looks at her hand, fingers slim, no rings. Evelyn lowers the hand. They sip their coffees.

A framed poster/print is on the wall at the end of the kitchen. Wade looks at the picture and says, "Edward Hopper, *Automat*."

"Yes," Evelyn replies, while brightening. Her view is opposite Wade's, so her back is toward the picture. "Do you like Hopper's work?"

"Yes. But I don't really know Hopper so well. I had a calendar, a Hopper calendar, last year, and *Automat* was one of the pictures."

"He did *Automat* in 1927, oil on canvas. It's at the Des Moines Art Center in Iowa now. I've been tempted to go there just to see it. That poster's been on the wall in here for years, and just after I put it up I thought to take it down. But somehow I didn't. It's not what you would call a cheery picture—well-dressed woman alone in an automat at night, gazing at a cup of coffee.

"Hopper had been to Europe, but he didn't bring Europe back with him. Or at least he didn't put it in his work. Hopper tapped into America—its prosperity and its 'aloneness.' One can assume that this is what he saw and felt. Yet he was a successful artist, and he was presumably happily married. His wife was an attractive woman who promoted his work.

"I meant to take that poster down because it's not a *happy* picture. We usually want to make the kitchen a bright, happy place. But through all the years that it's been on that wall, the wall you look at when you enter the kitchen, I've found that it gave me strength, or something like strength. For every morning when I walked in here, I was a 'single mother' raising a son and pursuing a career. The son made me not so lonely, as did some men I dated, which was kind of tricky as the son got older. And both the son and the career made me busy, which was probably good. The career gave me money and benefits, benefits that are necessary, such as health insurance. So the career, by way of money and benefits and status and so on, gave me a sense of accomplishment and security. This house in Studio City also gave me a sense of accomplishment.

"So every morning when I came in here to make coffee, there was Hopper, which made me feel that my life wasn't an anomaly. Because underneath this upper-middle-class life, there is something else. Or maybe a lack of something else.

"With *Automat*, the question is: What is that woman thinking about? And that's the question with all of Hopper's people. What are they thinking about? What has happened to them, or not happened to them, that makes them reflective?"

Wade looks at the framed print.

"Hopper never answered that question," Evelyn says. "Which is more than okay for a couple of reasons, one of which is mystery. What is that woman thinking and why is she alone in an automat late at night, or seemingly late at night? That is the mystery, and mystery is one of the reasons we look at good art again and again. We look at it again and again, and we see more and more."

"Yes," Wade says, his view having returned to Evelyn. "But do we see more of the picture or more of what we're thinking?"

"Both."

Wade chuckles. "Yeah, I suppose that's true."

"That's the main reason I want to go to Iowa to see the original. I want to see if I can see 'more.' I already know that it will be different, because seeing it in a museum will be different than seeing it every day on my kitchen wall, reproduction withstanding."

"Of course."

They sip their coffees.

"So go to Iowa," says Wade. "I imagine it's no more than three or four hours from Los Angeles by airplane."

"Yes, well, I might. But actually, there's all kinds of places I want to go. I want to go to Vienna, for example, to see Klimt's work, and to get a feel for the place where he produced it."

Wade nods.

"Place," says Evelyn. "It's so important."

He goes home, and he can do nothing but think: a son, a single mother, Iraq, death, loss. The son's name is David, and the father is a blank because in those years, as Evelyn put it, "I was wild and not careful." She was twenty-two years old when she gave birth. "It could have been any one of several men." She didn't care to find out who it was because she didn't want to marry any of them. They disappeared quickly from her life, which underwent a major change with the advent of motherhood. And, as Evelyn told Wade with a chuckle, "Not that any of those men would have stepped forward to take responsibility. They were like me before pregnancy hit." And "like me" meant imitating a bohemian lifestyle, "as if that were a formula for art and creativity." She moved back in with her parents, the Sun Valley house, and received both emotional and financial support from her mother and father. Evelyn ruled out abortion on the same grounds as she had a husband—she didn't want it. Eighth month into her term she felt that her life was changing in ways that she couldn't have imagined. And so, while her son grew in her belly ideas grew in her head. She would go to graduate school and get a degree that would qualify her to teach at a college. This would turn an interest in art into a viable career while foregoing a life of "chance—a one-in-a-million chance of hitting it in the fickle marketplace of art." Her parents were in full accord, and after David was born "they loved him like they had loved me when I was a child." So the boy's early years were spent in the same house that Evelyn grew up in.

"Having that baby made me responsible, made me grow up, but at times it was so lonely and so hard. Yet what else was I to do? Be a bad mother? Again, like with the issues of a husband and abortion, there was no decision to make. It was simply there. The decision was there at the same time that the issue was there. I had to carry on. Fortunately, my loving that child and my interest in art, and my parents' support, made it possible—and rewarding."

CHAPTER 12

He hired Gil Sanchez, who lived one block over, to take down two trees in Evelyn's backyard. Gil had a big truck and chainsaws and block and tackle and temporary workers who assisted him. Gil's business card, on the English side, said: *Tree Surgeon.*

After Gil was through, Wade took out the lawn and the shrubs, thus clearing the ground. Pastel bricks, as meandering paths, were set down according to Evelyn's plan, which was based on what she had seen at Wade's, bricks breaking up the monotony of dirt and stones and plants, and giving the plot a "garden" feel. With the bricks in, Wade planted drought-resistant plants that he bought at the same nursery where he had bought the plants for his yard.

While working at Evelyn's he would sometimes see her, which was when she'd come out the backdoor with two cups of coffee. They'd sit at a patio table, aluminum awning overhead, concrete underfoot, and this would constitute a break for Wade.

But Wade was never invited back into the house. And so, in this respect, the conventions of their summer went unbroken. Wade's house was where they'd rendezvous for their "real" time together, late afternoons or at night or on weekends. Thus the casual freedom of their summertime fun continued. But in continuing it deepened, and it deepened in a number of respects. Artistically, more developed work evolved by way of watercolors, colored pencil, and pastels. Conversationally, their exchanges deepened via recollections of what had transpired in their respective lives. And sexually, their activities would some-times incorporate these other two aspects of their time together, namely: art and conversation.

In a sense, they had an on-and-off arrangement, which, on the one hand, set strict boundaries so as not to infringe on one another's money-paying jobs. Evelyn didn't bother Wade when he was working, and Wade didn't bother Evelyn when she was working. But when they were together at Wade's house, those boundaries came down. This very topic, "on-and-off arrangement," came up a couple of times in conversation at Wade's house.

"I now have two worlds," Evelyn said. "My world here, and my world not here."

They were in the studio, and Evelyn was on the couch posing naked, and Wade was drawing her, but then Evelyn picked up a sketchpad and started drawing Wade as well, for he was naked, too, while sitting at the corner of his worktable. And so Wade started a new sketch that featured Evelyn naked and sketching. In a way, they were mirroring each other, the two of them sketching nudes ... who were sketching.

"But don't we always live in different worlds?" Wade responded.

"Yes, I suppose we do. But this is a true day-and-night thing. For example, I spend time helping students with their drawings and watercolors. And I spend time doing my own sketching and drawing, and doing watercolors. Of course those are different—teaching art, and doing my own art. But here, at your house, something else occurs, something different. Of course that's understandable in a general way, but I'm now talking specifically about 'art.'"

"Sex," said Wade, "might account for that."

"Yes, sex is definitely part of it. But there are other things. I suppose you could say that this is synergism. But that doesn't quite get it. It's too cold of a term, too neat and tidy and scientific. I would prefer something like 'two different worlds.' Evidence of this is when I look at my work, my recent work. I see changes. So in a material sense, you could say that I'm carrying these changes out of this world, 'this world at your house' and into my regular world because I now have this new work sitting in my studio at home, and I sometimes work on those pieces."

She pauses. And then she continues.

"I have different thoughts now," Evelyn says, "thoughts that come up in my head, thoughts that materialize from out of nowhere. This can happen while I'm at school talking to colleagues or to students. Or it can happen when I'm at home alone. For example, I'm looking at a student's work and I'm having thoughts that I never had before. Of course I don't express those thoughts in critiquing a student's work, because I have to keep to the rules, rules of drawing or doing watercolors, which are good rules. But that is precisely part of the problem—rules. This gets really tricky, particularly when you get past sketching. I have a watercolor class this term, which automatically involves color, perspective, and of course technique."

"Sure."

"But, Wade, *you* are breaking a lot of the rules. So if you were in my class, I'd have to correct that, wouldn't I?"

"Yeah, I guess you would."

"But here, at your house, I don't need to correct that, nor anything else, rule-breaking or otherwise. I don't need to correct that because the results are too telling. It's obvious that you came to this in a completely different way than the 'rule way,' the 'school way.'"

Again, a pause, before Evelyn resumes.

"In a sense, it's all backwards. I mean, I'm the teacher. But as it is, I'm the one changing my work based on your work. It should be the other way around."

"Well, I've picked up some things from you," Wade says.

"Yes, I know. But those are only small things, whereas my work is changing radically."

"Is that good?"

"I don't know."

Wade looks at her, but he now looks at her with a thoughtful eye, or maybe a questioning eye, as opposed to an artist's eye, which he had been employing before.

"But I don't think it's all you and this house," Evelyn says. "I've thought about this, and I now feel that this change in my work has something to do with me getting over my son's death. For the first time in a long time there's some sense of excitement entering my work, some sense of 'new.' In other words, I'm moving on.

"When I visited my mother yesterday at the care facility, like I do most every day, I brought a watercolor with me that I did recently, a watercolor that I started in this room. You know, we both did it—the cat sleeping on the worktable. I showed it to my mother, and she looked at it for a long time. And then she said, 'I haven't seen this before.'"

Wade nods.

"But I'm not sure if this was good or bad. I'm not even sure if she liked it or not. I didn't ask her, which in itself is unusual, because, even now, as silly as this might seem, I almost always seek her approval. So, the good-or-bad part remains a mystery as does the liking-or-disliking part. Even I don't know if this new stuff is good or bad.

"And that's something I want to ask you about, Wade. What do you think of your own work, the work you're doing now, the work you've done recently?"

Wade's pencil has been stopped for the past few minutes. He now sets it down on the worktable.

"I started doing this in India to pass the time—time in hotel rooms, time in cafés, time in the waiting rooms of train stations. It took my mind off of all that time—time that had me thinking about my life."

Evelyn's pencil stopped when she began talking, but the pencil remains in her hand as she looks at Wade.

"Of course it's evolved," says Wade. "But basically, I still come back to the tip of the pencil moving on paper, image developing. My mind comes back to the pencil or the eraser or the chalk or the brush—my mind thinking and then coming back to the tip of the pencil at the paper. In a sense, it's an in-and-out process. 'In' is my mind thinking. 'Out' is graphite going onto paper. And then in another respect, there is a back-and-forth process, which is my mind going back and forth between the image on the paper and the subject I'm trying to bring to life, which might be physically in front of me or imaginatively in my mind. Or both. It's interesting. Both the in-and-out process and the back-and-forth process help to alleviate the mental chatter that spins off of tedium."

"You mean, it's therapeutic as opposed to 'art?'"

"I suppose."

She looks at him.

"But it's also intriguing," Wade says, "and along those lines I experiment with technique and materials and composition. In addition, this...hobby of mine facilitates a closer look at what surrounds me, or what's in front of me, and/or what I'm feeling."

"Yes, but most people who get into this want to create 'art.' They want to be artists, so they go to a school to learn how to create art and be artists."

"That's fine."

"But that's not you."

"Of course not. How can it be?"

There are times, late at night, when she's lying in his long arms and the room is dimly lit and the clock radio next to his bed plays softly, a country-and-western station, that she begins to talk.

"It was emptiness. Vacuumed out. I think it was the finality that was so shocking and that caused the pain to repeat and repeat and repeat. There'd be a fond memory, but then there'd be the thought of his death, so the good memories, all those good memories turned into loss. But below this, in that deep 'me' place, that basic 'me' place, there was nothing. And that's when insanity hovered, because I couldn't find 'me.' I couldn't locate myself.

"It wasn't loneliness, but of course it was that, too. It was below the loneliness and below the sorrow that there was nothing. I didn't know who I was. And the thought that I would never find myself seemed a real possibility.

"I had lost my son and I understood that that was devastating and I understood that 'devastating' was understandable or acceptable or normal. Who wouldn't be devastated? I understood that, so it wasn't as though my thinking process had stopped. And it wasn't as though I didn't feel sorrow and grief for my son, who had lost his life at such a young age."

She pauses.

"All I could think to do was to go through the motions of what my life used to be. His death was during the summer, so I had to decide whether or not to teach the classes I was scheduled to teach in the fall semester. I didn't need the money, and a leave of absence would have been understandable. But I decided to go ahead and teach those classes with the idea of imitating my life, my outward life. The idea was that maybe this would be a way of rebuilding, or rediscovering my insides. A way of finding 'me.'

"For the longest time I felt that I was faking it. I felt I was faking my life. Oddly, the quality of my work, my teaching, was as good as before, perhaps even better. The person my students saw was okay. And there again, I felt some falsity, like I was fooling people. In effect, I was lying. But if I would've expressed the truth, I couldn't have done my job. I couldn't have done anything.

"And there were days, days at home, when that was the case—I couldn't do anything."

"But," says Wade, "that wasn't the case when I met you, when I came over and gave you a price for the exterior, was it?"

"No. I was halfway back by then. But of course it's hard to give it a percentile, because it comes and goes. Advancement comes in little pieces. You think you're getting better, but then it hits you again. But, yes, I was finding my way by the time you did the exterior."

"I saw something, some sadness, or lost-ness."

"Well, you would have, wouldn't you?"

Late afternoon, a Saturday. A dish with some fruit on it is on the worktable. They're doing still life.

"What happened with Herta?"

"We went to the train station in Mysore, and she got on a train that would take her to Bangalore. From

Bangalore there was a train to Bombay. It was called Bombay in those days. Bombay had an international airport. She would get on a flight to Germany."

"That simple."

"In a sense, yes." He chuckles. "But she left me her bicycle. So I had two bicycles, but only one body. Walking back to the hotel from the train station, that's what I thought about—the extra bicycle. Of course it wasn't a major problem, but nevertheless that's what I thought about while walking away from the train station.

"It was around noon and it was getting hot, and as I was nearing my hotel I ran into Arkansas, a fellow I had gotten to know in Goa. He was from Arkansas, and he had an Arkansas accent, so everyone called him Arkansas. He had been all over—a year in Morocco, and then all over Africa, and then six months in Pakistan, a year and a half teaching English in Iran, and then India. Amazingly he was levelheaded, which wasn't the case with lot of people who had traveled like that. A lot of people got whacked out. But not Arkansas. He was levelheaded, and he was well-read, and it was a pleasure talking with him. He knew all the Hindu deities, what they stood for and their histories and stories, yet he wasn't all mushy in the head over that stuff.

"So there we were, standing in the street, laughing, and it was like, 'Hey, man, what the fuck are you doing here?' We went to his room, which was in a hotel just across the small square from my hotel, and we started smoking chillums, one after another. He had some hash, but he also had this big bag of Kerala weed.

"I wound up trading Herta's bicycle for half of that weed, which came to about a half kilo. We weren't going to bicycle together, because he wanted to cut straight across, an easterly direction, to Pondicherry, and then go up along the coast to Mahabalipuram, whereas I was headed south. But I think it was more than that. I think it was that we each wanted to travel alone.

"At first, in Goa, Arkansas had a girlfriend. She was from Oregon, and they had met in Iran. She cut her foot walking across a stream one day. So she went to a doctor in Panjim, and he bandaged her foot and gave her a handful of antibiotics and a pair of crutches. But then the next day, the other foot, the foot that wasn't cut, swelled up to the size of a football, which really freaked her out. She took an overnight bus to Bombay, and in Bombay she would get on a plane and fly back to America. She had had enough. And besides, 'She wanted to return to school, graduate school,' was what Arkansas told me in Goa. And then in Mysore, while we were smoking chillums, he told me how he had been really stuck on Linda, the woman from Oregon, and how he had felt really bad for about a month after she left. I think he told me this because I had just told him about Herta."

"He tried a semester at Valley College. He got mostly Cs. He was bored and he wasn't enthused. He told me: 'I want to do something real.' So he enlisted in the Marine Corps."

He pedals. He sweats. He goes up into the Kunda Hills. There are monkeys the size of German shepherds swinging in the trees. There are elephants. He stays in windowless rooms and smokes beedies that he's stuffed with Kerala weed. He comes out of the hills and parallels a train line, a fairly easy route, which, after a few days, takes him into Madurai, where he finds deep, rich coffee that's brewed and sold everywhere. Finally, real coffee, five cents (U.S.) a cup.

Madurai is a temple town, and from his hotel room, which has windows and a ceiling fan and a cold-water shower and a boy at the end of the open hallway who fetches hot coffee and anything else he might want, he hears melodic bells in the late afternoon, and this tells him that an elephant, beautifully decorated, is being led into a temple that's a few blocks away. He knows this because he's gone out to follow the elephant into the temple, a large structure that has mandala-like colored chalk illustrations on its concrete floor.

Perhaps it's the coffee, or maybe the temples, pure Hindu, no Mughal influence, or maybe it's the abundance and variety of fresh fruit, or maybe the fragrant flower stalls, or the spice shops, or the dark-skinned people who tend to be lithe. He finds himself liking Madurai without effort.

He thinks about terminating his trip. Madurai—why go any farther? He's in the south of India, the deep south. He's gone from north to south, and while he weighs the issue of continuing, five days slip by, so if he's going to continue, he had better get going soon because he feels himself getting sucked in, for his trip is catching up with him. He's tired of the bicycle. He's tired of pedaling. But then he understands that boredom is setting in, and so is loneliness. So he gets on his bicycle and starts pedaling because he deems pedaling a remedy for boredom and loneliness.

"But couldn't it have been that you had set a goal?" Evelyn asks.

"Set a goal?"

"Yes. Cape Comorin. Isn't that what you told me? The southern tip of India, where the three seas of India converge."

"Yes. But my life was already a sequence of giving up, of abandoning goals."

Sometimes she comes over directly from school. She has a key to his house. If he's not home, she waits for him. She goes into his studio and sits at his worktable and sketches, or works on a watercolor or a pastel. She has her palette there, the same as he has his palette there. She's brought over materials, but her materials and his materials have gotten mixed together, so there's no sense of *his* materials and *her* materials. There are no oils or acrylics in his studio because he doesn't work with those mediums, and in keeping with this she hasn't brought oil paints or acrylics to his studio. She reserves that work for her studio at her house in Studio City. She has some clothes at his house that she sometimes changes into. But on occasion she simply sheds her clothes and sits naked at the corner of his worktable and looks at herself in the full-length mirror and does a sketch, which might turn into a finished drawing or a watercolor or a pastel, or maybe even an oil painting. Or maybe even a combination of such, a fractured piece with a collage-like impression. And she's even begun to make sketches of Wade and herself engaging in various sexual postures, and the thought has struck her that the Herta stories have influenced her. And of late, they're not just sketches or studies, for some have become finished pieces that naturally incorporate color, and here, too, her methods and Wade's methods have mixed. In a sense, she has borrowed from his stories, which, at the same time, have her borrowing from his perspective. This is terribly interesting, for it represents exploration, invention, experimentation. In a word, it is "new." There is an edge to it, an edge that sometimes frightens her, an edge that she gauges as dangerous, for even while finding renewed excitement and interest in her work she sometimes wonders where this is leading. She feels sort of groundless, for she doesn't know where this is going—her time in his studio and her time with him. And she's certain that he doesn't know, either. But that, precisely that, along with their ages and lifestyles, is the difference between her and him, for Wade is practiced at not knowing what's coming next, but she isn't.

The road south from Madurai runs through lowlands, lush and green, rice paddies and coconut palms, an easy route, and near the end of this, where the Indian Peninsula expires, the road skirts just to the east of the Western Ghats as those hills terminate. It is mid-May, and the monsoon is approaching.

He arrives at Cape Comorin to find two-foot waves rolling in, and if the Bay of Bengal and the Indian Ocean and the Arabian Sea differ in color or peculiarities, he doesn't see it. He sees only grayish ocean.

It is three in the afternoon, and the sky, like the sea, is mildly gray. He stands next to his bicycle, looking at the ocean and at nearby temples. Visitors are strolling the seaside, men in slacks, women in saris.

A boy with a galvanized bucket comes up to Wade, bottled drinks in the bucket, but no ice or water. Wade selects a bottle of pop and the boy uncaps it and sticks a paper straw in the bottle and hands Wade the bottle in exchange for some money. The first sip tells Wade that he has selected a pleasing lime-flavored drink that is almost cool. The boy, after distancing himself by about ten feet, squats on his haunches and stares at Wade. When Wade's done with the drink, he motions with the empty bottle and the boy comes over and takes the bottle. The boy, while smiling, says, "Thank you," in English, and Wade says, "You're welcome," in return, and in the next few days Wade will discover that quite a few of the local people speak English, which in India often suggests education and a degree of prosperity.

Daytime temperatures are in the low thirties, Celsius, but three days after Wade's arrival rain starts and the temperature comes down. As with the rest of India, the monsoon brings relief from the heat, but in most of the Indian subcontinent the pre-monsoon heat is a lot more severe than low thirties, Celsius.

Wade has found inexpensive accommodation in what is termed a "guesthouse," and he has found an open-air café that serves cold beer. The café is away from the seashore, for the seaside is deemed holy, which automatically rules out bikinis, nude bathing, and alcohol.

There are other travelers in the café, but they are clustered in small groups of three or four, and they don't talk to Wade. No matter, though, for Wade is content with sipping cool beer and chewing peanuts. When it rains, he watches it fall from the sky and from the edges of the palm-frond awning that's over the patio-restaurant.

"And if things could have stayed like that," he tells Evelyn, "you know, the contentment of those first four or five days, I would have never left, for the issue of subsistence was pretty much solved when the owner of the guesthouse asked me to tutor his two children, a boy and a girl, who were in grammar school. Free rent in exchange for English lessons, two forty-five-minute lessons each day except Sunday, one lesson for the boy, the other for the girl, who was older. They had materials, textbooks and readers. Their father, the guesthouse owner, was particularly keen on American English, which surprised me because British English was favored in India, at least then it was."

"Sounds good."

"It was. The kids were nice, and they were precocious. We became friends. They were always smiling and laughing, that sort of thing. 'Hi, Wade. How's it going?' But of course their father wanted them to call me Mr. Wade."

Evelyn laughs.

"But those lessons only took up an hour and a half of my time, which left me with all this other time.

"It didn't rain all the time, but it rained often, and it rained every day. I still had some of that Kerala weed, so I'd be smoking beedies with weed rolled up in them, and sometimes I drank beer at the café. All the other travelers had cleared out, probably because of the rain."

Wade pauses. And then he says, "I was supposed to be happy, but I wasn't."

"I understand," Evelyn says.

"It was in that open-air café, I had my journal, and I'd be writing in it, and then I was making these little sketches at the sides of pages, and that was how the drawing started. Also, I remembered this woman I had traveled with in Greece for a couple of weeks in the Peloponnesus. She was into drawing and watercolors, and what pedaling was to me drawing was to her, a way of stopping the mind's insistent chatter by coming back to graphite on paper, or a brush on paper. We had talked about this, my pedaling, her drawing and doing watercolors. So there I was in southern India, making these little sketches in my journal while understanding that I couldn't get back on the bicycle. The bicycle was unfeasible. No way was I going to get back on that bicycle."

"Yes."

"So I took a local bus to Nagercoil, a large town that was nearby, and I bought some supplies—paper, colored pencils, watercolors."

"Of course." Evelyn is grinning, as if amused.

"So that kind of worked for a while. I started drinking coffee instead of beer. Big savings in the money department." He pauses. "But then..."

"Yes?"

"There was this combination of boredom and antsiness, and need of direction that had me searching for something to do. I had all this energy, this excessive energy, and on top of that there was loneliness."

"Loneliness. Yes."

"Also, my visa was long expired, a problem that I hoped would be overlooked at the border, or perhaps solved with some money, a little gift, baksheesh, tucked into the pages of my passport. So in essence, I was inventing reasons to leave, as if my visa were suddenly so important. But in actuality, the real culprit was that after about two months a sense of desperation had set in. I had to do something."

"So you left?"

"Yes."

She nods.

"I gave the bicycle to those two children."

There are obligations associated with her job aside from contact hours in the classroom, such as office hours for students and faculty meetings and paperwork, but there are also departmental gatherings that are social in nature yet somewhat obligatory. At the same time, these social occasions sometimes yield contacts and networking, which in the art world, at no matter what level, are vital for getting one's work in front of people—gallery owners, potential buyers, reviewers.

This is what she sometimes tells him when they are in the studio, sketching or relaxing on the couch. There are even times when she tells him these things, as if thinking aloud, while they are lying on his narrow bed with the clock radio playing softly, and with the room's lighting at a cozy amber, and with their sexual needs having been satisfied.

"Do you enjoy these obligations?" he asks.

"Yes and no. When David was young and active and in need of my attention, I detested the meetings and paperwork and parties and dinners, because they made me too busy. But then he got older, and with that he gained more independence, which allowed me more of a social life, not that I wasn't seeing men when David was young, because I was, and that required impinging on my parents even more than I already was, you know, babysitting on a Friday or Saturday night. They never complained, but I felt guilty about that. But then David got older, and my job situation firmed up, and I bought the Studio City house, so then these social activities with my colleagues and their friends and acquaintances served as a social outlet apart from dating, which had become a little tiresome because I was tired of the men I had been seeing.

"But there was more to it than that, because by that time I had a body of work that I wanted to show. Some of the people I knew were having shows at galleries, and that seemed really exciting, and I wanted to do that, too. These things not only add to your commercial résumé, but contribute to your academic curriculum vitae as well. Of course I had a portfolio, and as it turned out I secured a show at a gallery in Westwood.

"And so there was the opening, and the talking to people, and the three reviews that were in the local papers, and the sale of about half the pieces, and the expansion of networking, which promised more exposure—more shows, more hubbub, more sales, more of a *name*. How could it not have gone to my head? How could it not have been exciting?

"David was just entering high school then, and that gave me more time, and more and more time would be forthcoming as he got older. Yeah, I had two more shows, one in Westwood and one in West Hollywood. But things didn't really take off. There was no progression. Those three shows were all kind of at the same level. My work wasn't advancing, and neither was my 'name.' It seemed that things had stalled, had flattened out. It seemed that I couldn't go any further. The excitement waned, and suddenly I felt middle-aged, middle-aged in my work and middle-aged in my life. Of course I was middle-aged. So it really wasn't the actual years so much as it was ... It was more that it hit me, and with this I began to ponder my station in life.

"What had started out as a challenge, a goal, and 'the right thing to do,' mixed with a lot of struggle, was followed by a sense of security and accomplishment and mild success that suggested more success, which meant that things would continue to advance, and with this the feeling of upscale and upbeat would continue. That's what I thought, and that's what I felt. But then middle age and flatness set in, and so did reflection. It was at this juncture that my son told me, 'I want to do something real. I am going to join the Marine Corps.'"

She pauses, and then continues.

"I had missed something, because for me David wanting to join the Marines had come from out of nowhere. Perhaps I had missed this ... something, because of how busy I had been, and how I was so taken up with myself, for success, as mild and insignificant as mine was, had gone to my head. So maybe I had missed the obvious, or what seemed to be obvious from hindsight. And that's just the thing—hindsight. For even if I had been paying attention, wouldn't I have been taken by surprise, anyway? After all, I think we lose our children sometime around middle school, for by the time they enter high school they're pretty much gone. They have their own lives, and a lot of that is secret.

"Yeah, I knew he was going to the beach and body-boarding, and, yeah, I presumed that this was cutting into his studies, at high school and then at Valley College. He had a killer tan and muscles. There must have been girlfriends, but we never discussed that, just like we never discussed my boyfriends. We lived in the same house, but he had his interests, and I had mine. We rarely sat down to a meal together. We were friends. We got along. There were no big fights or anything like that, at least not after he entered high school. He was considerate of me, and I reciprocated by allowing him his life. He seemed mature, even though not a good student. We had this positive mother-son relationship, which meant respecting each other's privacy, each other's lives, but it also meant that he didn't know me, and I didn't know him."

CHAPTER 13

"There are these things that we don't forget, things that happen for no apparent reason, like they're suddenly there and we're in the middle of them."

"Yes."

"I was on a train headed north and it was the middle of the night and the train stops at this no-nothing station and then there's the conductor with these people and the conductor is motioning these people into the cubicle where I and this other man are sitting. There are four of these people, two men and two women, but one of the women is a teenager, and she is slight of frame and very white, complexion smooth. The men and the other woman are middle-aged and their faces and arms are weathered."

"I see."

"So now there are six people in the open compartment, three-and-three facing each other, just like all the other open compartments, these small wooden cubicles. But the conductor ushering these people was unusual, for 'usual' was people finding their own seats."

A pause.

"It didn't take me long to find out the nature of 'unusual,' because the teenage girl warranted this consideration. She was in a pastel green sari and she was delicately beautiful, but it was more than that. She was wearing elegant sunglasses, gold wire-rimmed sunglasses, and the middle-aged woman was guiding the girl's direction, guiding the girl with her hands and with words, but of course I couldn't understand the words, but I could see the woman's weathered hands on the girl's forearm and hip. The woman seated the girl next to me and the woman sat down across from the girl. I had an aisle seat, and across from me was one of the men. The other man was on the other side of the girl, which put him next to the open window, with the man who had been in the cubicle with me from before seated at the other window seat."

"Got it."

"The train had been traveling for some time, so the aisle of the carriage was littered with tobacco nubs and greasy food wrappers. It was hot and humid, but when the train was moving air circulated because all the windows were open, which was good in that way, but not so good when the train was stopped at a station because then the mosquitoes would come in. Of course the mosquitoes would get swept out once the train started moving again."

"Yes."

"Prior to this group's arrival people had been sleeping, and I had smoked a couple of beedies with marijuana rolled up in the beedies, but since the leaf of a beedi is harsh tobacco the smell of the weed was masked and no one noticed—standard procedure for long train rides through the night.

"But now everyone in the car was awake and they were trying to get a look at the girl seated next to me. The train was now moving, and the newcomers were talking among themselves in whispered voices as if to claim modesty."

"Was the teenage girl talking?"

"No, not really. Only a word or two at the beginning in response to the middle-aged woman.

"So anyway, people finally got bored with looking and started falling asleep again, and then the people in my compartment, the newcomers and the man from before, started nodding off too."

"But not you."

"No, not me. And as I soon found out, not the girl seated next to me, either."

"Oh?"

"It began with her right hand, the hand that was next to me, moving from her lap to my leg, the side of my bare thigh. I was wearing khaki shorts. I think it was the hair on my leg that surprised and startled her, for she jerked her hand back. Her fingers touching my leg were very light. I could see her hand, and I remained absolutely still. And then, after a few long moments, her fingers returned to my leg, and there were these light finger-touches moving all so quickly and delicately around a small area. But then her hand and fingers started branching out to investigate other areas of the leg."

"You're kidding."

"No. Her hand moved along my thigh to my knee, where there was no hair, which she investigated with her fingers, and then her hand moved below the knee to where my leg hair started again. All the while the pads of her fingers were tapping quickly and softly. Her hand came back up to the original area on my thigh and then returned to her lap. I sensed that she was waiting for reprimand, but everyone was sleeping, everyone but me and her, and I said nothing while remaining motionless."

"Of course."

"I thought the exploration and fact-finding were over. But that turned out not to be the case. Her hand returned to my leg, and then it went and found my forearm, my left forearm, where her fingers found more body hair, which was bleached by the sun, like the hair on my legs, but of course coloration wasn't an issue. Her hand and fingers went down to my wrist and then onto my hand and around my fingers. After that she slowly retraced a path up my arm to my shirt, which didn't seem to interest her much, but nevertheless her hand and fingers went over the contours of my shoulder before proceeding on to where the shirt was open, which was where her fingers investigated my bare collarbone and then got tangled in my chest hair."

"Unbelievable."

"Next, there was my neck and jawline, and then my face—my lips, my cheeks, my eyes, and my moustache, which she really touched and measured with her fingers. I had a big, bushy moustache at that time. I closed my eyes when her fingers were tapping nearby and when they went over my eyebrows."

"Yes."

"From my face her hand went back down, a retracing of its pathfinding venture, until it was back at my thigh, where it had all begun, and where she then removed her hand from my leg. Her hand went back to her lap."

"And that was it?"

"Yes and no. After about twenty minutes the conductor and an assistant entered the car at the far end and started waking people one compartment at a time, the conductor checking and punching tickets. When the conductor got to our cubicle I looked up at him and said, 'My ticket?' And with the sound of my voice and its language the girl next to me jumped. The conductor said, 'Yes, your ticket,' in English. But I had my head turned and was looking at the girl, whose face was folded with fright, like maybe she had no idea of who was sitting next to her in the middle of the night on a train in central India. The woman sitting across from the girl reached over to comfort the girl and to talk to her in a reassuring voice, a soothing voice. I gave the conductor my ticket and he punched it and gave it back to me, and the man across from me gave the conductor four tickets and the window-seated man gave his ticket to the conductor, tickets punched and returned, whereupon the conductor and his uniformed assistant left the carriage."

"Yes."

"It took about fifteen or twenty minutes before the girl's body relaxed next to mine. About thirty minutes after that the train stopped at a deserted station and the girl and her companions got off, conductor assisting. And then the train was moving again, and maybe twenty minutes later the first gray shades of morning began.

"And so there I was, with that graying sky and the rhythm of the train, and with a hundred thousand finger touches lingering."

"When my son was a baby, the way he touched my breasts with his little hands while he was feeding, it made me feel motherly, so motherly. It defined me, and I was perfectly content with this. He, too, was content.

"I couldn't help thinking, 'Where did he learn this?' He was too young to learn anything. It was simply part of him, and when I felt it, I was 'mother.'

"Where did it come from?

"But of course this is different from the touching you're talking about."

They are in the studio, Wade's house. They are doing studies of hands—big hands, small hands, old hands, warty hands, veined hands, twisted hands. Their renditions don't have to be perfectly realistic to convey "hand."

As Evelyn pointed out, "*Ukiyo-e*, Japanese woodblock prints, have people with hands and fingers that are strange, yet they are 'hands,' and they are interesting."

Halloween has come and gone, and of that ritual Wade was at his house in Sun Valley and Evelyn was at her house in Studio City, for they didn't want to leave one of the houses dark and vacant with kids coming around and trick-or-treating because that would have been discourteous, and it might have invited vandalism. Or so they reasoned.

Yet on the backburner there might have been other things at play, as if maybe Halloween were to establish a way of handling traditions, for Thanksgiving was on the horizon. And now it is rapidly approaching.

"Thanksgiving," Evelyn begins, thus initiating a shift in conversation. "It'd just be you and me and my mother at the table, wouldn't it? Your house or my house, and none of us would be eating all that much, certainly not the sort of eating that a Thanksgiving spread warrants."

She smiles at this, and Wade nods in concurrence, as if to express understanding for what now seems to be coming.

"And besides," Evelyn says, "conversation would be stilted. We certainly couldn't talk like we talk when there's just the two of us."

"Of course."

"My friend, Erin, and her husband, Tom, have invited me over, and Erin said I should bring my mother. Erin and Tom's mothers are going to be there, along with a lot of other people. A real family gathering, so there'll be that atmosphere."

"Of course."

And with this "of course" Wade smiles, which causes Evelyn to smile, a renewed smile, which is different from her previous smile, and during these smiles of theirs there is a pause in their exchange. The pause is terminated by way of action as opposed to speech, Evelyn leaning forward and putting her pencil and sketchpad down on the coffee table and then getting up from the couch and stepping over to Wade, who is seated at the worktable.

It is late afternoon, the Sunday before Thanksgiving, sun in the western sky warming the room, November in Southern California, marvelous weather prevailing. While leaning over Wade's shoulder from behind, Evelyn puts a braless breast, which is beneath a loose cotton shirt, on Wade's shoulder and reaches around and begins unbuttoning his shirt, her hands assuming a one-button-at-a-time descent. She whispers little whisperings near his ear about her hands and about Wade's hands, the raised veins on the back of Wade's hands and what they reminded her of. It is how they do things, how conversations morph into physical expression, fluidity at work in these transitions, yet, because of frankness, these shifts can produce abruptness and surprise that incorporate inventiveness.

As Evelyn's hands trail from one button to the next, Wade says, "There was this other blind person, a man in Peshawar, who I spent a lot of time with. He would put a hand on my forearm for guidance when we went out for a walk, which was completely different from the girl on the train. That man only used his hand once for information. We were standing in his apartment, and he told me to take his hand and to put it on top of my head. He wanted to see how tall I was."

Evelyn's hand is now at the bottom button.

"He didn't want any other information?"

"Well, he did, but not information via his hands. You see, we spoke the same language, English, but his variety was British."

"I see."

"But there was one other thing. I think the girl on the train was born blind, whereas the man in Peshawar had lost his eyesight when he was fifty years old."

"Yes, that might make a difference. Was he fifty when you met him?"

"No, he was about ten years beyond that."

All of Wade's shirt-buttons are undone. Evelyn steps around and says, "Okay. Now my buttons."

Wade starts in on her buttons.

"What was his name?"

"His name?"

"The blind man."

"James. His name was James."

As he moved north so did the monsoon. When he arrived in Delhi rain was falling from a dark sky, thirty-four degrees Celsius, ninety-three degrees Fahrenheit. The streets were runny with mud, particularly in Old Delhi, which was where he found lodging in a cheap hotel, Red Fort not far away. His business, though, was in New Delhi—American Express and a couple of embassies for visas. He figured he had enough money to make it back to Europe via the overland route. Thus he'd be heading west, and for the most part retracing the route that had gotten him to India. Greece was what he had his sights on. He had worked construction on Corfu two years before and he was pretty sure he could find work on Corfu again. But there was also Iran, where there were jobs teaching English, Tehran primarily, or so he had heard from reliable sources, such as Arkansas. He would check on that while heading west, and if he landed work in Iran there'd be no reason to continue on to Greece, for teaching English in Iran paid a lot more than construction in Greece.

These were his plans. And so after five wet days in Delhi, he boarded a train that took him to Amritsar, where the weather was about the same as in Delhi. Like everyone else heading west, he crossed the border near Wagah, which everyone called the Wagah Crossing, for it was the only recognized border crossing between India and Pakistan. Thirty-two kilometers beyond Wagah via bus, he arrived in Lahore, which was getting the monsoon, too, and getting the same sort of heat as on the Indian side of the border, mid-nineties Fahrenheit. He moved on after a couple of nights in Lahore, train service to Islamabad/Rawalpindi well-traveled, which was also the case between Islamabad and Peshawar. In Peshawar, though, the weather changed, at least as far as precipitation, for there was no monsoon, but there was some rain on occasion, yet nothing like Islamabad/Rawalpindi and Lahore and Amritsar and Delhi. Peshawar was semi-arid as opposed to subtropical.

"So, was it comfortable?" Evelyn asks.

"Days about ninety-five degrees, nights about eighty degrees. This was August."

"I don't imagine there was air-conditioning."

"Not where I stayed. And not at places where I hung out."

"Hung out?"

"The Afghan border isn't far away. Pakistan's tribal regions are to the northwest and southwest of Peshawar along that Afghan border, which is mountainous. Peshawar was, and probably still is, interesting, although now it is probably dangerous, particularly for Westerners."

"It wasn't dangerous then?"

"Yes and no. But not the kind of danger like now. That area of the world was relatively stable then. But 'stable' doesn't mean not poor. 'Stable' means 'no war.' The Shah left Iran in early '79, Khomeini coming to power, which swung Iran from pro-Western to anti-Western, and that pretty much brought the overland route between Europe and India to a close. And then in late '79 Soviet troops rolled into Afghanistan, which resulted in a civil war. Pakistan's western border areas were, and remain, deeply affected by the events in Afghanistan, events that have made the border area dangerous."

"When did you arrive in Peshawar, you know, on this trip?"

"August 1975."

"How long did you stay?"

"Two years."

He is in an overstuffed armchair in the living room, and he's reading a book, lamp on a side table to his right. The cat is asleep on the couch. A cup of hot tea, milk and sugar stirred in, is also on the side table. A chill is in the air, the first of the season, a hint of autumn briskness. Wade has the heater in the living room on.

Wade has spent the day prepping the interior of a small beauty parlor that's a few blocks away from his house. In the next three days he'll put on a coat of primer/sealer and a coat of paint and put everything back to the way it was so that on Monday morning Karen Davis can walk in and start refurbishing people's hair, elderly women mostly.

It's an unusually quiet evening, Thanksgiving festivities having wound down, everyone too full on turkey for gunplay or loud music. Dogs as well are quiet. Perhaps they, too, are digesting food, or maybe they are gnawing on bones. Even the nightly chorus of car alarms is sedated, as are low-flying police helicopters with searchlights. Sirens, too, are on hiatus, squad cars, ambulances, fire trucks. Wade takes notice: the neighborhood is tranquil. Perhaps everyone is out shopping.

He hears the squeak of the screen door as it opens, and then he hears a familiar knock, knuckles tapping lightly. She has a key to the door, but she only uses it if he's not at home or if he's asleep, and in the case of asleep there's no chance of a horrible accident because Wade doesn't possess a handgun or a rifle. On occasion, she's entered the house and slipped into his bed, but of course, having woken to the sounds of her undressing in the dark, he's awake by the time she snuggles up to him.

He puts his book down and stands up and opens the front door. She steps in and walks past him. He shuts the door and turns to see her pacing, and it's the combination of the pacing and the energized half-angry look on her face that gets his attention. Her clothing, too, is noticeably different than usual, a thick-knit beige sweater and a brushed charcoal skirt. Black pumps are on her feet, heels low. She's had her hair cut since last Sunday, hair shiny and very short. She seems alive. She seems younger than forty-three.

"We so look forward to these holidays," she says, "but it is actually memory that we are responding to."

She has stopped pacing and is looking at him. He is standing near the front door. The cat is now awake and is sitting on its haunches. Evelyn's diction is very clear, a reflection of her demeanor.

"This holiday is stilted and mannered, and if it weren't for young kids at the table, it would be lifeless, as almost every exercise in tradition is. Yet we do it every year, and the lead-up to it is fraught with anticipation, for we are remembering something from our childhood."

She pauses for breath. Wade has begun a smile. The cat remains statuesque.

"Unfortunately, today's event at Erin and Tom's, in Pacific Palisades, just off Sunset Boulevard, featured no children. We, adults, talked about the weather and the price of gasoline and about the latest movies, none of which I had seen. My mother sat, staring at her food. I had to help her eat. She's getting old, or perhaps she was nervous. After all, she didn't know anyone. At the care facility, in her room or downstairs in the dining room, she eats just fine."

Wade is smiling, a crooked expression.

"The food was wonderful, everything you'd expect, everything you remembered. But it didn't taste the same as when I was a kid. Memory has a way of playing tricks. As I was eating I had this feeling that the meal was a photocopy, a facsimile, a rote following of image and presentation, substance lacking. I had never felt this before, but I felt it today, and it undermined my appetite. It was like I was eating on stage, and that we were all actors."

Wade chuckles.

"It goes without saying that there was no talk at the dinner table, or pre-dinner table, that hinted at politics, for that might have brought Iraq and Afghanistan into the picture, and indeed it was a 'picture,' everyone taking photos with their cellphones of the food laid out on the table, which was a really big table. I think Erin had alerted everyone, you know, about my son's death. She probably told them to stay clear of 'war.' She probably told them that we were going to have 'a nice Thanksgiving.' And we did. It was so 'nice' that even with the stuffing on my fork dripping with gravy, as soon as I put it in my mouth it was dry, like week-old sponge cake. I drank a lot of water with my food."

The cat settles back down to resume sleeping.

"Very sophisticated people—a lawyer, a physician, a couple of TV people, a movie person, and some people in the music industry, one of whom is Erin's husband, Tom. Erin, of course, is a colleague of mine, Art History, modern art her forte, very knowledgeable. I love talking with her, but of course those conversations aren't at a large table with everyone doing 'a nice Thanksgiving.'"

Wade nods, and says, "Would you like a cup of tea, hot tea?"

"Yes."

Wade steps over and picks up his cup and walks past Evelyn and through the dining room. He slides open the door to the kitchen. The kitchen is cold. Evelyn has followed him. She assumes a hand-on-the-hip stance in the kitchen doorway.

"There was this woman there. She was with her 'partner,' male partner. She has a gallery in Ocean Park, next to Venice. Her name is Della Karr. She gave me her business card. I think that was part of the reason Erin invited me."

"You mean to meet Della?"

"Yes."

"That seems good."

Evelyn nods.

They return to the warm living room with their mugs of tea. Evelyn sits in an overstuffed armchair that's to Wade's left and that's next to the floor heater.

"There were bottles of wine on the table, but no one really drank much of it. Bottled water from Italy, poured into a stemmed glass, was popular."

Wade nods. He has told Evelyn that he sometimes goes to AA meetings, open meetings, and he's told her some of the stories he's heard there. Evelyn's not like Wade, no real problem with alcohol, but she has said that she hasn't had anything to drink since her son's death because she's afraid that it will make her maudlin.

"At some point during dinner, I started thinking about the Herta stories you told me. Actually, it wasn't so much that I was thinking about them; it was more like pieces came to mind, images and such, and certain things you told me Herta said. So it was like I had this secret, this eroticism that was sporadically punctuating this dull activity I was participating in. I somehow felt that this helped me survive the occasion. And on the drive home, over the hill, with my mother sitting silently in the passenger seat with her own thoughts, the Herta thing arose again in my mind. We didn't turn the radio on. I just drove, and I think we were both relieved to get to the care facility in Van Nuys. It had been a long day for her, too."

"Of course."

"It was after I dropped my mother off that I understood that I couldn't go home. I had too much energy to go home to that empty house. But it wasn't until I dropped her off that I had that energy, for dropping her off was the end of Thanksgiving, and something pent up was released, or maybe it was more of a feeling that I was set free, obligations fulfilled. I'm sure my mother went up to her room and felt set free, too."

Wade nods.

"And maybe all those people at that dinner today, Erin and Tom and Della, and everybody else is feeling that right now as well."

"Probably."

"But you, you sidestepped all this, didn't you, Wade?"

PART 3

CHAPTER 14

His forehead was thickly wrinkled like a bulldog's, and the rest of his face was in accordance—cheeks fleshy, jawline hanging, neck an outsized wattle. His lips were blubbery and his mouth wide, and in that mouth gapped teeth were neatly indexed along pink gums, tooth enamel yellowed like aged ivory. He was big-boned and barrel-chested, and his skull was very large. Stringy gray and black hair drifted over the dome of his head, scalp in evidence. His arms, particularly the forearms, had muscle wedged between bone and fat. But his legs were different, not necessarily skinny, more like common or average, and the same could be said for his feet, except that his feet were rather wide.

There was weakness in his legs, and why this was even he couldn't explain, except to say, "I've spent much of my life sitting." Another possible explanation was that he was top-heavy. Sometimes he needed the help of a cane in getting to his feet. Around the apartment, or "flat," he employed a four-footed aluminum cane with a horizontal handle, very stable and very obedient, the way it could stand on its own. He called it his "faithful dog." Outside, though, on the street, he used a regular wooden cane with a curved handle. As for a white cane with a red tip, which was given to him at a hospital, he used that only once years ago, for he discovered that it drew street urchins that stuck their "thieving hands into my pockets."

For clothing, he always wore *shalwar kameez*, awake or sleeping, but when sleeping he forwent the *shalwar* because he didn't like to sleep with pants on even though the *shalwar* were baggy and loose like pajamas. In bed he only wore the *kameez*, a long loose shirt, and during warm or hot weather it was often the case as well, only the *kameez*, while sitting or moving about his modest apartment, or "flat" as he called it, for the style of *kameez* that he favored came to his knees when standing, not an uncommon length, but one that required selection because *kameez* came in different lengths. Regarding buttons down the center of the garment on the front-side, his *kameez* were a little uncommon because the buttons went full-length, collar to bottom hem, whereas most *kameez* have buttons only to mid-chest. But of course his *shalwar kameez* were custom-tailored, in that they were made to order, so the full-length buttons didn't present a special problem, and the same could be said for size, although, given the looseness of the garments, size on the ready-made market wouldn't have been an issue. But, as he put it: "Since custom-tailored and ready-made were about the same price, why not simply duplicate what's comfortable?" And that was how he did it; he'd send Wade down to the tailor with a pair of *shalwar kameez* that he liked (material, size, and buttons), and Wade would tell the tailor to copy it, as if the tailor didn't already know, for this had been going on since long before Wade's arrival. As for color, it hardly mattered to him in one sense, but it mattered to him in another sense. He'd tell Wade, "Pastels, tans or beiges, gray too is okay, but no bright white, and absolutely no loud colors of any sort. I don't want to be a walking joke, nor do I want to look feminine." This last part was in reference to *shalwar kameez* as both a male and female fashion, but the women's were often more stylish, brighter colors incorporated, yet not always. Many women, like almost all men, favored earthy colors of a pastel nature.

His efforts regarding anonymity, though, were somewhat fruitless, for the look of his face nullified obscurity.

When Fran first brought Wade to the "flat," with the intent of "introduction," what Wade encountered was a large man with a big white face, broad forehead thickly wrinkled horizontally, a bulldog look, wrinkles evidently perpetual, for they did not cease no matter what expression the mouth and the rest of the face assumed. Residing at the bottom edge of the forehead were eyebrows with errant, kinked hair, some of it gray, some of it black. But then, as if to create a total spectacle, beneath the eyebrows and dead center in that albino face, a pair of wraparound sunglasses were nestled like the optical lenses of an insect, or maybe a weird reptile.

The glasses were made of black plastic and they never ceased glinting, and even with their utility understood the impression of those sunglasses on that face was not lessened. Wade's eyes kept returning to that visage, for it continually fluctuated in Wade's mind, attributes repeatedly changing even though the face, technically speaking, hardly changed at all, mouth region the exception, but there, too, with the mouth, consistency of expression by way of set patterns was difficult to establish in the brain. Every time the mouth smiled, for example, it looked like a different smile. Wade came away with a different impression each time he looked at that face. It took a while before he realized that this was the reason his view kept returning to that phizog—on-going newness and complexity, which elicited investigation.

And then there was Fran with the introduction.

"James."

"Yes, my dear."

"I brought that fellow I was telling you about, the American. His name is Wade. Wade, say hello to James."

"James. I'm Wade."

"Indeed. Well, let us have a handshake."

James extended his hand and Wade shook it, a somewhat soft hand, but with muscle beneath the bulk.

James was sitting in a wood-framed chair that had the look of age, a nice wood, walnut perhaps. The chair's seat and back were wicker, and there was a hinged extension attached to the end of the seat that functioned like a patio lounge chair so that James could elevate his legs if he so desired. The chair's right arm was missing, which allowed James to swing his body out in that direction to stand up, four-footed cane at the ready. On the chair's left side, the side with an armrest, there was a side table, a tasteful piece of furniture, quality wood employed.

Surveying the room, Wade saw this same sort of taste that looked to be left over from when the British departed in 1947. Wade had seen this any number of times in public buildings, train stations and post offices, in both Pakistan and India, architecture and furniture, British colonialism revisited.

The room had French doors that opened outward and were open, a narrow balcony beyond, balcony with a gingerbread outer face that overlooked a somewhat busy street. On the interior side of the French doors, there were accordion jalousies, which mostly covered the balcony doorway, a gap between where right and left jalousies came together. The jalousies' wooden slats were angled, sunlight pleasantly reduced. The hinged frames of the jalousies, when folded back, would lie flush to the walls on either side of the French doors. Looking at this, Wade saw utility and taste in collaboration.

James had a British accent, so with the three of them in that throwback room there were three varieties of English, for Fran was from Ireland, lilt very much in evidence.

James said, "If you'd be so kind, Wade, I'd very much appreciate you reading something for me."

"Sure."

"On one of the shelves over there," and here he indicated with his arm/hand a wall in back and to the right, "*The Old Man and the Sea*, by Ernest Hemingway, a soft-cover edition, very thin. See if you can find it. I'd like you to read the first page to me. Fetch a chair from the table and set it down to my right, and a bit forward of me, and read the first page aloud. Do you think you could do that?"

"Yes."

Standing in front of the bookcase James had indicated, Wade saw that all the books were by American writers, four shelves by those from the United States or Canada, one shelf, the top shelf, by writers from Latin America, English translations. Since the Hemingway books were grouped together, Wade located *The Old Man and the Sea* easily. Looking at an adjacent bookcase, Wade saw books by British or Irish or Welsh or Scottish authors. The next bookcase over was mixed, French, German, Italian, and so forth, all in English translation. Glancing farther right, he saw a bookcase with scientific books.

Fran, standing near the jalousies and catching the movement of air from an overhead fan, wide blades rotating slowly, said, "You see, Wade, the man that was here up until last week was British, from Bath as a matter of fact, so he read Shakespeare, George Eliot, Virginia

Woolf and the like, and before him I did some reading, mostly Joyce, but there was some Beckett as well."

Wade walked over to a table that was in a corner and picked up a straight-back chair, and while doing this he spied a small kitchen through an open doorway. There was another doorway along that wall, but its door was closed. Wade guessed a bathroom, specifically a toilet, perhaps a shower as well. Between the two doorways there was a highboy, woodwork impressive. Also in the room, along with a wardrobe closet and couple of overstuffed armchairs and a couch and a liquor cabinet, was a bed, patchwork quilt for a bedcover. And there was a bukhari heater, which was near where Fran was standing. The bukhari seemed a good model, wood-box nearby, but no wood; winter was a long ways off. It was a large room, floorboards worn. A few Baluch rugs were on the floor.

Placing the chair where James had indicated, Wade sat down and opened the novel to the first page and began to read aloud. The page had two paragraphs.

It was late afternoon and the sun was approaching the horizon and the call to afternoon prayer, *Asr*, had already concluded. It was hot, but not as hot as it had been earlier. The room was quiet even though a street hummed two floors down. James's apartment was on the third floor, the top floor of the building.

When Wade concluded, he looked up and saw that James's head was atilt. A brief interlude ensued, in which Wade felt the ceiling fan's gentle breath.

"Yes," James said, head straightening. "That'll do. That'll do just fine."

"Wade's from California," Fran said. "Los Angeles."

"Los Angeles?" questioned James. "I would have expected a more rapid clip."

"I grew up in a mixed neighborhood," Wade offered. "A lot of Hispanic people, and people from Nebraska, Oklahoma, Colorado, South Dakota."

"I see. So there's a slowness to your delivery. I like that. It serves clarity."

"He has a crooked mouth when he smiles or laughs," Fran said.

"Well now. I don't hear a speech impediment."

"No," Fran said. "I only mention it because that might also account for the slowness."

James nodded, a slow, measured movement. "So we're talking about a bit of a defect."

"You might call it that," Fran responded. "But it's expressive. Yet at times the expression is evasive."

"Does it put people off?"

"You mean women?"

"Yes."

"No. Actually, I think it invites interest."

Again, James nodded, and again thought was indicated.

"I told him that women sometimes come here to see you, and that sometimes there was filming."

"Good. So you understand that, do you, Wade?"

"Yes."

"Can you operate a typewriter?"

"Yes."

"So typing wouldn't be a problem. How about dictation?"

"I can't take shorthand."

"No. We're not interested in shorthand. Just write down what I say in longhand on a pad of paper, and then type it up."

"No problem."

"No problem," James enunciated. "I like that. 'No problem.' An American inflection—a cowboy image."

And now James laughed, and the laughter went all over his face, flesh jiggling, except for the wrinkled forehead, which remained steadfast.

"Fran," said James. "Does Wade know about the pharmaceuticals?"

"Yes. Wade knows about the pharmaceuticals, and he's not adverse to them in the least."

The frantic efforts that accompany the end of a term are over, students evaluated, paperwork submitted. Christmas is approaching.

It's been over two weeks since she's visited, and when she knocked on the front door she felt something like nervousness rippling her body. She wasn't sure why this was. His pickup truck was in the driveway, which meant that he was at home. It was ten in the morning and the day was warming up, a Saturday. People would be out Christmas shopping.

He opened the door and she saw a smile begin on his face, a crooked smile. A cup was in his hand. When she stepped past him she smelled coffee.

They were quick to go to the kitchen to take advantage of the still-steaming grounds in the Melitta cone, leftover water in the kettle instantly brought back to a boil, and as they stood waiting for the drip to finish in Evelyn's cup, Evelyn remarked: "Setting and place." Wade looked at her, and she continued, "A room or a place—it brings something back. It reminds us of something. I experienced this just now, coming to your front door, knocking, and then coming in. Odd, that this should already be happening."

"Yes," Wade says, "there is this connectedness, this interweaving, this looping—memory and setting, setting and memory. What surprises me, though, is how far back this can go, and how vivid it can be at times."

"Yes."

"Let's sit out on the patio," Wade says.

"Okay."

They go out the backdoor, cat following them, and they sit down on a couple of molded-plastic chairs, low wooden table between them, their cups of coffee set on the table or held in hand. The patio is a slab of concrete, and beyond that there is the chaparral garden. A red-throated hummingbird is at one of the plants in the garden, small red flowers in bloom.

"What weather," Evelyn remarks. The cat sits on its haunches in front of them, looking at the hummingbird.

An interlude of silence ensues, perhaps in appreciation of the seventy-degree temperature and the blue sky and the dry air. They sip their coffees.

"I once went to this place in the desert," Evelyn begins, "in the vicinity of Pearblossom, you know, just outside the Valley here. There was a mobile home, a doublewide, set on a parcel of land. We reached it by way of a dirt road that came off of a graded dirt road where a couple of mailboxes were. I went there with Lloyd, this fellow that I was kind of seeing. I had a part-time teaching position then. David was five, or maybe six years old, a Saturday, my mother looking after David. Lloyd wanted me to see something, and he had given me a brief description of it. So, since I knew roughly what was coming, I was kind of nervous or apprehensive. After Lloyd parked the car, and when we were walking up to the steps of the doublewide, everything struck me as very vivid. It was a day like today, and of course it was the desert, a scrub desert, so there were plants, and I saw a couple of hummingbirds."

Wade nods.

"And then Lloyd and I were at the front door on a wooden landing, but the front door was open, so we were looking through the screen door, and there was a fat woman standing there, looking at us and smiling. She was naked, but, as I said, Lloyd had forewarned me, so I knew that the man and woman who lived there were nudists, or as some people say, naturists."

Evelyn sips her coffee. Wade sips his. The hummingbird is gone from the yard.

"So the woman opens the screen door, and she says, 'Well, come on in.' I can remember this clearly because there was a twang to her voice. I'd say she was in her mid-forties.

"Her neck and forearms and face were reddish, but the rest of her body was white, which meant that she had been out in the sun, but with her clothes on. Her hair was yellowish blonde, and there were bobby pins in her hair to keep it kind of up, or arranged."

"Yes. I got the picture."

"So we stepped in, and that put us in the living room, which was larger than I had expected. It was clean and bright. The windows were open and the curtains were pulled back. There was a man standing by a couch. He, too, was overweight and white, and he was naked. His hair was short, a crew cut. The man was wearing glasses, bifocals. I could tell by the lenses.

"As I said, everything was very vivid. It was like my senses were on high alert, and I think this was part of it, for there was this sense of drama that I was creating, or maybe that all of us were creating. I don't think I would have had this sense of drama if I hadn't known what was coming, you know, Lloyd filling me in on the sequence of events in a general way. If I hadn't been forewarned, then the events that unfolded wouldn't have had drama. Instead, there'd have been surprise and shock, which would have colored the whole thing in a very different way."

"Yes."

"So, it was like going on stage to act in a play. I roughly knew what was going to happen, so there was that anticipation. Or maybe it was like I was part of the audience. I knew I was going to see a play, so I was anticipating that, which kind of created a drama sort of thing before the play began."

"Yes."

"Her name was Vicky, and his name was Randall, and don't ask me why, but their names struck me as strange. During the introductions, with Vicky and Randall standing there naked, and Lloyd and I clothed, I couldn't help to think that Vicky and Randall were fictitious names. But after the...event, while in Lloyd's car and on our way back to the Valley, I asked about that, and Lloyd said, 'No. Vicky and Randall are their real names.'"

"What names would you have given them?"

"I've thought about that, and the only thing I can conclude is that any names would have been strange, given my state of mind at the time."

"Yes."

"Lloyd and I were offered a seat on a sofa, a light brown sofa. Directly across from us there was an identical sofa, and between the two sofas there was a glass-topped coffee table."

"Let me guess. Randall and Vicky sat on the other sofa, facing you."

"Yes. But first 'tea' was served via a silver tray with real nice cups and saucers. Vicky tended to that, while Randall placed a bowl of cookies on the coffee table. So it was like, I was sitting there, watching this—the tea service and the cookies. I mean, there was a silver creamer and sugar in a small silver bowl with a hinged lid, and the cookies were these small butter cookies."

Wade is smiling. Evelyn sips her coffee.

"We start talking, you know, like we're going to have this conversation. It begins with chitchat about the weather and the drive out, and about how pleased Vicky and Randall are that Lloyd brought someone new, because Vicky and Randall like meeting new people. Actually, I'm like Lloyd's ticket for a revisit. Lloyd was out there before with another woman, which turned out fine because she didn't freak out or anything. But this other woman wasn't up for a repeat, and the qualification for visiting Vicky and Randall was that it had to be a 'couple' who visited, a man and a woman. In other words, Lloyd couldn't bring another guy or a bunch of guys or come alone."

"Yeah."

"Anyway, during the course of this chitchat, Lloyd and I are casually informed that if we want to take our clothes off, that's okay, but if we prefer to remain clothed, that's okay, too. Fortunately, Vicky and Randall didn't break conversation to wait for a reply, which meant that they weren't forcing the issue. Vicky went on to add that anytime during the course of 'tea,' if either Lloyd or I, or both of us, wanted to go 'natural,' then that was fine. 'Just place your clothes over there on one of the armchairs.'"

Wade smiles.

"All this is steeped in this conversation, which continues, and pretty soon we're talking about Lloyd's art, which is avant-garde, and then we're talking about my art, and the strange thing was, I begin to lose myself in the conversation, like maybe I've gotten used to having tea with two people who are naked."

Evelyn pauses. Wade sips his coffee.

"Here again," Evelyn resumes, "I've thought about this, thought about how this particular conversation was necessary, and how it was managed and fashioned to be pertinent to what Lloyd and I were interested in, and how there was maybe a tipping point that Vicky sensed or understood, like she knew when I was into the conversation, so that when she casually reached over and started playing with Randall's fat penis, there was this shock and surprise, even though I knew this was coming. But at the same time, I had to kind of treat this with a sort of nonchalance, because everyone else was treating it like that. In other words, the etiquette of the situation dictated this. My mind, though, was reeling in all sorts of directions. This, of course, was part of the deal, part of the package.

"And then there was the reverse side of this, which was Vicky and Randall's side, you know, instead of having a mirror to look at for example, Vicky and Randall had me and Lloyd to look at."

Wade nods.

"Lloyd had told me that he wanted to see if it'd be the same, you know, the same for him this time as compared to the previous time."

"Was it?"

"The scenario was the same, but for Lloyd the experience wasn't the same. This is what he told me when we were driving back to the Valley. One of the things that surprised him was that he wasn't used to it in the least, but at the same time it wasn't the same sort of in-your-face hit that he had experienced the first time. So while it wasn't as blatantly shocking, it nevertheless struck him as a new experience. What also surprised him was that Vicky and Randall could pull this off with genuine interest and a true sense of spontaneity, for they had done this any number of times with different couples. And here Lloyd pointed out what Vicky had said: 'It's not exactly performance art, for there is too much of an exhibitionist hue to it, and it's not exactly pure voyeurism on the part of our guests, because they are too close to this, thus they are somehow involved. Pornography might apply, but Randall and I feel that this goes beyond pornography. For the sake of reference, we call it an *event*.'"

Wade smiles. "That's almost philosophical. When did she say this?"

"Well, that's another thing. She said this after her hand had coaxed Randall to an enormous erection that she proceeded to climb on top of while facing us. That's when she said it, while on Randall's lap and facing us, and it was like she was continuing the conversation."

Wade nods.

"It was like she was playing with that same thing that I was going through," Evelyn says, "a division of feeling and thought."

"Yes."

"Vicky was somehow more of a mystery than Randall, and maybe this was because Vicky talked more than Randall, or maybe it was because she had this twang in her voice that Randall didn't have. At times I thought Vicky was very uneducated, yet at other times I thought she was very educated."

"What did you do when she was facing you, when she was sitting on Randall's lap and talking?"

"I reached for a cookie."

Wade smiles.

"And I realized at that moment that the cookie was a stabilizing agent, which it further served when I stuck it in my mouth and started chewing."

"Yes."

"The physicality of our world is so important because our minds can overwhelm us. The physical world brings us back."

"Yes."

"When she got off of him to pick up a cookie from the bowl, there was Randall's engorged organ, glistening. He had slid down on the sofa a bit to accommodate Vicky's hand and then her body. He still had his glasses on, which was another thing, because when Vicky was playing with him with her hand he'd sometimes look down at this, his glasses accentuating this, and then, with Vicky standing and picking up a cookie from the bowl, he was again angling the angle of those bifocals to look at himself, and it was as if he were finding something new about his body."

Wade nods.

"Vicky put the cookie in Randall's mouth and he chewed, and then Vicky got back on him, but this time with her back to us."

"Did the conversation continue?"

"Yes and no. She tried to talk, but the rush of the event was overtaking her. While twisting her head around to look at us, she stumbled on her speech. Her words got caught and her sentences got broken off."

Evelyn looks down at her coffee cup.

"This was not an act."

"We could get a small tree, a very small tree, just to put that pine scent in the house," she said.

"Of course."

"And we could put a turkey in the oven. Your oven works, doesn't it?"

"Yes."

"We could do other things, too. Candied yams, mashed potatoes, cranberry sauce. All the usual things."

"Sure."

"And we could have a few small gifts that are wrapped, and we could open them before dinner."

"Okay. But you have to tell me what your mother likes."

"We'll go shopping together, and I could buy her something, and you could buy her something, and I could help you out with that."

"Good idea."

"I know it's not going to be wonderful, but it will be something, some sort of Christmas. I think that's important."

"Yes, of course."

"Otherwise she'd just be there in the care facility. They'll be having something, but a lot of people will be going away with their families for Christmas Eve or Christmas Day, or both, so I think she'd feel kind of left out if I didn't take her out for Christmas. I'm going to go over there and spend Christmas Eve in her room, bring some food and watch a movie on her TV. They have a library of DVDs downstairs."

"Sounds like a good plan."

"And then I'll come over here Christmas morning and we can prepare the meal, and I'll go and pick her up and bring her back here."

"Fine."

Having come in from the patio, where Evelyn had told the Vicky and Randall story, they are now in the studio, and they are somewhat spent. For when they first came into the studio they placed the full-length mirror in front of the couch where they both then sat naked after putting cheese and bread on the coffee table. Evelyn then started a conversation while looking at the mirror, Wade looking at the mirror as well. Evelyn started stimulating Wade with her hand, conversation continuing, a conversation about art. Wade slid down on the couch a bit. A condom was unfurled and then Evelyn mounted him so that she faced the mirror, conversation continuing, Wade peering around Evelyn to look at the mirror. And then there was Evelyn getting off of Wade's lap to fetch a piece of cheese and to put it in Wade's mouth, and then Evelyn looking at Wade and then at the mirror, and then getting back on Wade, but instead of facing Wade as Vicky had done in facing Randall, Evelyn faced the mirror, finale forthcoming.

They had talked about this afterwards, which was cause for mirth. This was after Wade had gone to the kitchen for glasses of iced tea, and what Evelyn had said was, "Well, of course it's not the same, but I've had this in my mind. It's strange how these things can dwell in your mind, and how you can think about them from time to time, even years later."

Wade had nodded, and then he asked Evelyn if she had lost some weight, and she said that she had.

"Any reason for that?" Wade asked.

"I think it's because I've been working a lot in my own studio. I'm sometimes up late at night. I have this energy that's going into my work. I'm trying to take advantage of that."

"You look different now, very slim."

Evelyn then stood up to look at herself in the mirror as if to evaluate this, for they were both still naked. She didn't say anything, but after sitting back down she said, "When I stood up to get the cheese and then looked at you, you looked different. Particularly when I looked at you in the mirror. And perhaps this was what I was after—same person, but different."

It was after this exchange that their conversation moved on to Christmas, which was Evelyn's province. And so now she says, "I was kind of nervous about asking you about this."

She sips her iced tea. The studio is warm.

"You know," says Wade, "I somehow thought you were Jewish."

"I am, technically. My mother is Jewish, my father was Catholic. So we did a Hanukah thing, and then a Christmas thing. The Christmas thing was a bigger thing, though. And I think it was a bigger thing because it's a bigger thing in the United States as compared to Hanukah. We weren't really religious. Christmas was a custom, a tradition, a holiday, and it was terribly exciting for me as a child. My parents did it for me, and now I have that memory."

Wade nods.

"And of course my mother has this, too—a memory, which elicits expectation annually."

There was loneliness from all that train travel, and from southern India, and from Herta's having left him. It was always this way after having spent time with a woman—abandonment. That was the feeling even though he might have instigated the split, as if fault were important, which it wasn't. What was important, though, was "loss," as opposed to blame. From Mysore to Cape Comorin he had the bicycle, which provided pedaling, a meditative salve that eased his loneliness, for it occupied his body and mind. But at the southern tip of India he dismounted, and he was immediately aware of it.

A crowd of people, disembarking and disembarked, is moving over blackened concrete as if suffering from heat and a long train ride, which is probably the case. It's a varied population, young and old, dresses and burkas, slacks and *shalwar kameez*. He is part of this population, his sandals shuffling on blackened concrete. He carries a small burgundy-colored suitcase that is mostly filled with a folded, thin sleeping bag, which, according to a tag concerning materials and flammability, was made in Czechoslovakia, an Iron Curtain product that he picked up along with rudimentary art supplies in Nagercoil before leaving southern India.

Pigeons are cooing from the rafters of the overhang that shades the platform. There is an opening through a chain-link fence and people are exiting through that opening. He is moving toward that opening himself, but his step is slower than that of the crowd, for he wants the crowd to thin so that he can get his bearings upon leaving the station once he is through that portal in the fence. He needs to stand in front of the train station and look around in order to remember the street that will lead him to a hotel that he stayed in before, twice before.

So he has drifted to the rear of the crowd, and he can see along the course of the platform. He notices a woman sitting on a bench, a green wooden bench that is away from the train and near the chain-link fence, but well short of the fence's exit. She has a beedi between her fingers and she is wearing a loose brown skirt that comes to her shins, sandals on her feet. A light brown *kameez* covers her torso. Her hair is brown, and it falls to her shoulders, no wave or curl. Her complexion is confusing, for there seems to be weather on her skin, yet there is some kind of paleness, as if maybe she were the product of both day and night. She is medium in build, but there is a hint of slimness. There seems to be muscle on her frame. She is perhaps in her thirties, but age is vague. Her eyes are brown, and they are fastened on Wade.

He drifts along, but now it's more like being drawn, and this puts him in front of the woman, which is where he stops. She looks at him frankly, an up-and-down scrutiny, as he stands with his small, burgundy-colored suitcase.

"I think we might have met," Wade says.

"Yes, I believe so. But where?"

It's her voice, the lilt of her voice that brings it back.

"Paleohora, Crete. September or October, two years ago."

"I'm beginning to get it."

"You sang Danny Boy one night in that café that had an upright piano. A thin man was playing the piano. You sang Danny Boy twice, but the second rendition was different than the first. Both were really good, but the second one was deeply stirring."

She's listening.

"I ran into you several days later, in the daytime. It was in that same café, but the café was empty. We sat at a table. You had retsina. I had beer. And you started weeping after telling me about the suffering of this world."

She brings her hand up, beedi going to her lips. She lowers the hand and exhales slowly.

"That retsina was causing me problems."

Wade begins a smile, and she looks at this with interest.

"Now I remember," she says.

"Your name's Fran, isn't it?"

"Yes. And your name?"

"Wade."

"Wade," she pronounces, but that's all.

Wade glances around. His eyes come back to her.

"What are you doing here?" Wade asks.

"I'm selling morphine tablets."

CHAPTER 15

"We thought about moving, but we never did," Clara says. "It was just too cheap. Property taxes were nothing. We kept saying, 'Next year,' but we never moved, and am I glad we didn't, because it allowed us to save money. Jack and I were from the Fairfax area, not far from Fairfax High School. When we were first married Jack was working for a small film lab on Santa Monica Boulevard, but then he got a job with Disney, here in the Valley, so we moved out here."

They are in the dining room, which is small, but certainly adequate for the three of them. Wade didn't even need to put an extra leaf in the table, a heavy piece of furniture, tablecloth covering it. The small Christmas tree is in the living room, and when they were sitting in there before dinner the cat crawled up on Clara's lap and fell asleep. Wade had remarked, "I've never seen her fall asleep on someone's lap." Clara was pleased, and she said that the one thing she missed at the care facility was that you couldn't keep a pet. Clara is a small, thin woman, frail perhaps, and this reminds Wade of his mother, but unlike Wade's mother Clara isn't suffering from dementia.

Right from the beginning, upon entrance, Clara was talkative, and this put a smile on Evelyn's face. Perhaps it was the neighborhood, for Clara had commented about that right away when addressing Wade. "You're only blocks away from my house," which of course was the house that had been recently sold, escrow closing in October. Or maybe it was Wade's house per se that put her at ease, for Clara had remarked, "This might be in the same tract. Was this house built in 1950?" And Wade had answered, "Yes." And so Wade couldn't help to think that Clara was relaxed, which contrasted with what Evelyn had said about Thanksgiving in Pacific Palisades.

At the dinner table Clara went on to tell Wade that Jack, Clara's deceased husband, had worked on some of the Disney animated movies, the first of which was *Lady and the Tramp*, Jack having been an illustrator, a talent that he couldn't exercise at that small lab on Santa Monica Boulevard. Clara, too, had worked for Disney, but in the capacity of "a secretary," as Clara put it.

Of course on the "tour of the house," as Wade had termed it with a chuckle, the studio that Clara was shown was neat and tidy, all of Wade and Evelyn's work having been put away, thus out of sight. Clara had asked, "Are you an artist, too, Wade?" The "too" evidently alluding to Evelyn. "No," Wade said. "I'm a housepainter slash handyman." "Oh, that's very hands-on," Clara said, and with this the three of them had chuckled.

The gifts, which were opened before dinner, four gifts in all, two for Clara, one for Wade, and one for Evelyn, were all from Santa Claus—articles of clothing, very predictable and prompting smiles, along with "just what I need," or "just what I wanted."

The only moment of uncertainty occurred when "the tour of the house" came to Wade's bedroom, for Clara took an interest in the poster that was tacked to the wall above Wade's desk.

"I've seen this before," Clara said.

"It's at the Getty, Mom, the new Getty. But you might have seen it at the Norton Simon in Pasadena. It was over there before. It's jointly owned."

"Yes," Clara said, while still looking at the poster. "It's Degas, isn't it?"

"Yes," Evelyn replied. "*Waiting*. Pastel on paper."

Clara then turned to Wade, who was standing in the doorway. "Why did you choose this piece to put on your wall?"

"Well, I liked it. I saw it in a poster shop and I bought it and . . . " He trailed off.

"Yes, of course. I like it, too," Clara said. "Evelyn, what do you think of this?"

"It's a masterpiece."

"Yes. I've seen it in the museum, but now, in this room, it really strikes me. Odd, because it's usually the original that's so striking. In a museum, though, we see many pieces, so many great pieces, but in this room, there is only this one piece."

"Tea and biscuits" was what James would bark to send Wade to the kitchen, which was used mostly for brewing tea and the storage of nonperishable foodstuffs, fresh fruit and bread the exceptions. Tea was of the tea-bag variety unless James designated "a pot of brewed tea." Sweetened, condensed milk from a can was stirred in, ceramic mugs employed. James wasn't keen on "proper tea," as he expressed it. "Too many knickknacks, and I don't fancy those tiny cups." Regarding "biscuits," they were cookies or sometimes crackers, American English. If both cookies and crackers were in the "pantry," or "larder," Wade would ask: "Sweet variety or non-sweet variety, James?" The "pantry" consisted of a few open shelves in the kitchen.

Both British and American English flourished in the "flat," or "apartment," or "room" or "dwelling," although when Fran showed up there was also Irish English, which to the ear was the most pleasing, but at times Fran could get raunchy in terms of word choice.

On occasion there were "visitors" or "guests," and they spoke Pakistani English, and of them there were no females. As for females, or "ladies," who came to the "flat," their English, like everyone else's, was linked to nationality, which meant that most any kind of English could be spoken with the exception of Indian or Pakistani or Malay or Indonesian, for those nationalities of femininity didn't visit the flat.

And so, with tea and biscuits in place, conversation would begin.

"Lost the eyesight in a mishap at a lab south of here, a few kilometers outside of town. Consultation assignment. They were having difficulties with consistency. Often the case here, given irregularity of supply and scarcity of qualified chemists and lab technicians. A pesticides lab, attached to a makeshift factory. As it turned out, I unlidded a canister of methyl isocyanate that a spot of water had gotten into, and the resulting gas went up into my face, a mild dose so to speak, otherwise I would have been dead. The other man in the lab didn't lose his eyesight. Instead, he suffers from sinus, palate, and throat problems. He can't taste his food."

"Wow."

"They've since closed that facility, thank goodness."

"And when was this?" Wade asks. "The accident that is."

"Oh, going on ten years now."

"Why didn't you go back to England? Or did you?"

James shifts his weight in his wicker chair, and the wicker creaks.

"I was in the hospital, here in Peshawar. A London-trained doctor attending, but there was nothing to be done. They sedated me to ease the pain. Fortunately the pain subsided after two weeks, and by the third week there was no pain."

Wade nods, but then understands that this means nothing to James, so he says, "I see."

"But of course, there was the darkness that remained darkness."

The tea mug and the saucer with the biscuits, and everything else that Wade puts on the side table, have specific places. The furniture in the room, if moved, always needs to be returned to its usual place.

"I had been living in Peshawar for nearly five years when the accident occurred, and I was in this flat for those five years. My brother had come out just before I was discharged from the hospital. You see, it took time to contact him, time for someone to go to the flat and dig up my address book and then to go to the telephone exchange and ring up my brother. He of course had to arrange for time off from work, book a flight, and then take a train from Rawalpindi. Once in Peshawar, he had to make his way to the hospital. Mind you, it was his first time East."

James smiles at this and picks up his cup of tea and sips.

"So my brother, younger brother he is, says, 'We have to get you sorted out, don't we?' I said, 'Let's go to my flat.'"

James pauses, mug of tea in hand. It's ten in the morning and the day is heating up. On the street below, vendors are squawking, motorbikes popping, but in James's flat those sounds are muted, jalousie helping out with that.

"It was peculiar, Wade, for after a month in the hospital, returning to the flat felt like coming home. It was familiar and it was comforting. My brother slept on the couch. I slept in the bed. After a week, a routine of sorts developed. There were friends, who began dropping by. My brother, quite naturally, was in a hurry to return— London, family, job. An arrangement was made. One of my friends would look in on me, and there was the 'concierge' downstairs who had a telephone and could deliver messages. The 'concierge,' mind you, is not fluent in English, but what comes out of his mouth is under-standable. And already, several of my 'working associates' had dropped by with some questions regarding what could be substituted for a chemical that was in short supply. So instead of my venturing out for work, work was coming to me. Of course I couldn't read anything, but I could listen and offer advice. The terms of salary were the same as before my accident—an envelope with cash."

James sips his tea.

"I could have gone back to England, got a flat, or maybe lived in my brother's household, which was where my aged mother was living. I might have been able to secure work, but then again I might not have. Perhaps I would have been able to go down to the pub, a pint of beer, converse about football. And the weather? Winter in London is such a lovely time of year, Wade."

James smiles. A curious expression.

"Granted, if my brother would have showed up the first week of the accident, I would have been on an airplane headed for England, for my first instinct was to go home, to seek the comfort of family and friends. I was terribly frightened, you see. The darkness, the not knowing, the pain, the medications.

"But then time passed, and I got back to the flat here, and I spoke with my brother, who filled me in on so much, which served to remind me of what life in London was like, and on this I transposed my situation—fifty years old and blind.

"Once I was back here, in this flat, I realized that I still had spunk. I still had a life. I told my brother to put a record on the phonograph, and I sat with a cup of tea and listened to the music, a jazz piece, and it was so lovely. And when the phonograph wasn't employed there were the sounds from the street below, and the smell of roasting kebab wafting into the room occasionally, and the warmth of the day and the dry air.

"And then I thought of the *Other Place*, which has an upright piano. Of course I could still play that. All I'd need was to be led to it. So I told my brother to take me over there. I gave him directions, verbal directions. I told him we should go over at about ten at night, which is when the place always has some people. So we went over there, and I was given this welcome—the barman, the patrons, people who I knew and who had heard about my mishap. It was heartening.

"And, as is often my habit, I had taken a little sniff of meth, which would make for good beer-sipping and no hangover, and would add to conversation and to listening, and which would make the piano a lively instrument. Perhaps someone would get up and sing. Perhaps people would drop money into the tip jar. Perhaps I would run into a lady who I knew, or maybe a lady who had heard about me, for I sometimes made such acquaintances in there. It was possible, for even before the blindness I was considered somewhat of a freak, a sideshow attraction, and I thought to myself, 'Well, this might even add to that.'

"But I think, more than anything, it was the *welcome* that people gave me when I walked in with my brother, and it was a similar thing when I came back from the hospital to the flat here, the concierge downstairs greeting me, taking my hand and bringing it to his chest."

James sips his tea. Wade sips his tea.

"As for my brother, he was put off by the whole scene here—the chaos, the filth on the streets, the clientele at the *Other Place*, the cold-water shower, and of course when I told him to get me my supplies: the vial, the little mirror, the razorblade, the straw—very put off. I told him which cigar box they were in and where the box was on the shelf, and then he had to watch this, my preparing things blindly. But I wanted to try it blindly to see how it would go. Actually, that was what that whole week was about—trying things blindly, making adjustments. You see, I wanted to have a life. I wanted to stand on my own two feet again, so to speak."

James pauses.

"I told my brother to return to England. If at some point I changed my mind, I could have someone accompany me to Rawalpindi by train, go to the Islamabad Airport, and put me on a flight to London."

"So you never went back."

"No."

New Years has come and gone. The spring term is about to begin, so she is preparing for that. She comes over at night, and besides, Wade is in the midst of a chaparral garden in Toluca Lake, an upscale community just east of Studio City. This has him away from home during the day.

Wade could go into his bedroom and open a box among the unopened boxes that have remained stacked along a wall. He could get out any number of sketches, graphite drawings, colored pencil drawings, or watercolors of James to show Evelyn. He could even show her a Polaroid snapshot, although the quality of that photo might have deteriorated over the years. But he doesn't open any boxes, for Evelyn has agreed, or suggested, to work from verbal description, which is midst recollection, a form of storytelling. She has never worked in this capacity before, and Wade has never participated in such a project. Viewing Evelyn's depictions of his remembrances is interesting for Wade, for it allows him to see his reminiscences as Evelyn understands them.

So there is James, who evolves and changes in Evelyn's work as Wade relates one anecdote after another. But it is not only James who is changing. It is also Fran, for she, too, is the subject of Wade's recollections, and Evelyn's art.

Wade does not offer commentary about Evelyn's work, for that would constitute "correction." They deem it important to keep the project pure—memories verbalized, Evelyn listening and depicting.

"So it was arranged that I would have a 'helper.' At the beginning it was a twenty-two-year-old lad from Scotland. He was on his way through, the overland route to India. It was already developing then, the overland route that is. I, of course, had come out by airplane five years previous, come out to visit a mate, an old university chum. He had mentioned that there was work to be had, and as it was I had gotten in a bit of a tangle where I was employed, and they had sacked me.

"His name was Gilbert. He had been hanging out at the *Other Place* for a week or so. This arrangement with Gilbert was made just before my brother left, and from hindsight I can say that it was arranged a bit too quickly. Gilbert didn't take the assignment seriously. He wasn't dependable. A bit snooty as well. Fortunately, Gilbert didn't last long, and in that way his incompetence was fortuitous.

"As it was, four days into Gilbert's employment, I had him guide me over to the *Other Place*. It was in the evening, and Gilbert and I were sitting at a table with cans of Guinness. A man was playing the piano, and then there was a woman who began singing.

"She was younger then, you see, her voice was younger, but nevertheless it had a smoky quality, a sadness perhaps, and sadness can sometimes convey a sense of age or experience, perhaps even a sense of suffering. I sat, listening, and I thought to myself that maybe she was extremely sensitive, you know, to what she had seen on the streets.

"You simply can't come East, like these young people were doing, and not see the distress and the affliction. The overland route takes time, and it's anything but a family outing. Indeed, there is a sense of hardness or jadedness or acclimatization that sets in, particularly considering that some of these people wander around in India for months or years. Hardness is a survival technique, otherwise you'd be giving away all your money, and where would that leave you? So there's a shell that develops. But under it . . . " James trails off.

Wade sips his tea.

"She understood music and she had this voice, and she was expressing what was underneath the shell. When she finished two songs, there was silence in the room. I heard shoes shuffling, a single pair of shoes, on the floor. And then there was some clapping, some applause. I thought that perhaps she was headed back to her table. I had a picture of the *Other Place* in my mind, having spent so much time there before my accident. So I was understanding the sequence of events. I told Gilbert, 'Invite her to our table. Tell her I'd like to buy her a drink.' I heard Gilbert stand up and walk away. When he returned, I could tell by the sounds that she was with him. She sat down to my right, Gilbert across from me. I said to her, 'You have a lovely voice—a moving voice.' She said, 'Thank you.' And I knew immediately that the singing voice and the talking voice were different. She had the shell back on. I asked her what would she like to drink, and she said, 'Guinness.' Gilbert went to the bar to get the Guinness, which left me alone with her. I said, 'My name is James.' She said, 'I'm Fran.'"

"What's the timeline?" Evelyn asks. "I thought you said you ran into her in Greece."

"I did. What James was talking about was 1965, which was when Gilbert was let go and in his place Fran took over—James's helper. I ran into Fran on Crete in 1973. She had been James's helper for a number of years, and then she had tried going home, Ireland, County Cork. But she didn't stay. She came away from there rather quickly. I caught her on the rebound when she was in Greece. As it turned out, I went to Israel. And as it turned out, Fran went East again to settle in Peshawar, and to resume with James—his helper, a form of employment. And then after about a year she relinquished the 'helper' position to Brian, the man from Bath, for she wanted more independence, more time to herself. But she was still tied to James, still reaping benefits for services rendered."

"I see."

Wade sips his coffee.

"So then it was you after Brian."

"Yes."

Evelyn sips her coffee.

"You help someone like James, which is employment. But . . . You're there day after day, sometimes night after night, and you sit and you listen. You run errands, you guide them through the streets, you learn their habits, you understand their thinking—you get involved."

Between the train station and the hotel, that Wade is in quest of, Fran says, "Actually, it's not just morphine tablets that are available." Wade has mentioned that the hotel has a sign with a big red asterisk on it, and Fran knows the place, red asterisk a giveaway, thus Fran takes charge by leading the way. Fran, issuing opinion, approves of the hotel.

The street and the sidewalk along that street, the sidewalk they are walking on, are a clamor of every sort of commerce and transportation, dust in the air a glowing hue. They make a turn off that street and the commotion quiets a bit, air with less silica. Not long after this, the distance of a block perhaps, they see the sign that has a large red asterisk on it, along with the word *Hotel*. The sign is above a stairway that's wedged between a tailor's shop and a tobacconist. They start up the stairs.

At a wooden counter that serves as a reception desk, a slim, darkly complexioned man with a generous helping of hair tonic applied to his jet-black hair, hair glistening while wafting a rosewater scent, greets Fran and Wade with a questioning smile.

Wade, feeling somewhat assured because he recognizes the man from his previous stays, begins by saying, "Is room fourteen available?" The man pronounces, "Fourteen," and then, without consulting a ledger or a board with keys, says, "Yes." Wade, in contrast to standard hotel-room negotiations, which require a personal inspection of the room in order to see and to judge what is going to be bartered for, says, "Ten rupees a night?" He already knows the room from his previous visits, and he already knows the price, ten rupees a night. But now, the "questioning smile" is explained, for the man looks from Wade to Fran.

Perhaps the man recognizes Fran, or perhaps he doesn't, but in either case the issue is the same, and Fran quickly comprehends it, for she settles the issue immediately. "Twenty rupees," Fran tells the man, which instantaneously brightens his thin smile.

Turning to Wade, Fran says, "This will settle any yammering that might arise in the event of my coming and going. You're getting a room for two."

Room fourteen is two flights up and it's on the side of the building that doesn't face the street. Its one large window, which swings inward, is screened, and it is this that Wade checks by opening the window and examining the screen for holes or rips or tears. Satisfied, he opens a door and checks on the toilet, an Asian-style porcelain affair. There is no toilet paper, but there is a small spigot and an empty tin can below it, spigot a foot off the floor. And then comes a second door, concrete floor, drain, pipe going up a wall and then protruding outward, but then there's a hose attached to the pipe, hose leading down to the floor, shower nozzle attached. On the vertical pipe going up the wall there's a knob to control water flow. Wade closes that door and turns. Fran is sitting on a chair, turned-wood framing, woven-rush seat and back. Fran's one elbow rests on a table. The room has two cots, wood-framing and webbed with rope. There is a ceiling fan with a length of string hanging from it. Wade reaches up to pull the string.

Fran says, "You might want to leave that for a minute."

Wade's suitcase is on the floor near one of the cots, no mat on the cots, and no pillow. Wade's thin sleeping bag will serve as a mat, and a folded towel, also in his diminutive suitcase, will work as a pillow. All this is standard fare. But Fran's request not to turn on the overhead fan isn't.

"Technically it's called methamphetamine. But we're not into needles, are we though? They're dangerous and rather gross. Rather, we ingest it through the sinuses." And while saying this, Fran is unbuttoning the top buttons of her *kameez*, and then she is withdrawing a pouch that is on a string, string looped around her neck, pouch about the size of a mass-market paperback book. She brings the string over her head and sets the pouch on the table, a heavy-cloth pouch that is decorative but worn. There is a large button that she unfastens, flap of the pouch turned back. Wade steps away from under the ceiling fan, fan motionless. Wade goes to the table and sits down opposite Fran.

"'Go-fast,' 'up-all-night,' 'fun-time,' but it is 'crank' that is emerging as the term of choice. It's a cheap form of meth. Powdery, not crystal. We employ a straw. Are you familiar with this, Wade?"

"No."

"Do you want to try some? I'm going to do a little."

"Sure."

"You wouldn't happen to have a mirror or a little piece of flat glass available, would you now?" Fran says, and glances around the room. "They don't hang pictures in these rooms, framed pictures with a sheet of glass. It's a pity."

The room is very warm, stilled air bordering on hot, no breeze from the open window. Outside, though, it's hotter, about thirty degrees Celsius. The view from the window has rooftops, and then on the other side of the rooftops tall trees rise. They look like poplars, trees in two long rows as if lining a street on either side.

"A piece of metal perhaps, or maybe the surface of a book," Fran says. "The table's wood. Not the best thing for chopping, for we want to take the lumps out of it with the blade of a knife, or more preferably a razorblade."

In Fran's hand now there is a small glass vial with a screw-on cap, beige powder inside the vial. A short length of straw accompanies this.

Wade says, "I might have something," and goes to his suitcase and puts it on the cot and opens it, Fran having turned to watch. Wade rummages and comes up with his watercolors, which are housed in a tin case. He brings this to the table and sets the elongated tin box down, backside up. Fran says, "Perfect." Wade sits down.

She opens the vial and taps out a bit of crumbly powder on the tin and recaps the vial. From a pocket on her skirt she gets out a simple pocketknife and pulls a blade out of its wooden sheath. After wiping the blade off with her shirt, she starts chopping at the powder, which spreads the powder out while fluffing it into a finer texture that she then draws out into four small lines. The blade of the knife she runs between the pads of her thumb and index finger, and then licks those finger-pads. The moist fingers she dries on the rough-cotton material of her brown skirt.

Wade watches as Fran puts one end of the cut-down plastic straw in a nostril while closing off the other nostril with a finger. There's an inhaling sound as Fran moves the end of the straw along the line of powder with the powder disappearing up the straw. It takes no more than a moment for the line to be gone from the tin underside of the watercolor case. Fran switches the straw to the other nostril and repeats the procedure. With two lines gone, and with the straw no longer at her nose, Fran inhales strongly, which produces a snorting sound. She hands the straw to Wade and moves the watercolor box to in front of him. Wade leans forward and copies what Fran has done. Thus the remaining two lines vanish.

Bringing the watercolor case back to her side of the table, Fran runs her index finger over the area where the powder was to collect any leftover residue. Her tongue flashes onto her finger.

Wade is waiting, but nothing seems to happen other than a slightly sour taste leaking from his sinuses into his throat. The taste is not overpowering and there's not a great deal of drip.

Fran is putting things away—vial, pocketknife, and then the pouch, which goes back inside her *kameez*. She turns the watercolor box over so that its topside is up and shoves the box to middle of the table. The table is unfinished wood and the wood is stained.

"We could have the fan now," Fran says.

Wade stands up and pulls the string and the wide blades of the fan begin to turn. He gives the string another tug and the blades increase in speed, yet the speed is nothing more than moderate, if that. Looking out the window, Wade notes a late-afternoon tint on the rooftops and in the air, pastel orange. He sits down and hears the chair creak. Fran's view is toward the window. Wade looks at her forearm that is on the table. The sleeve of her *kameez* is halfway up on that forearm. Her wrist is not slim. Wade notices that he is no longer tired from the train ride and the day's heat is no longer a nuisance. He is calmly alert.

While still gazing out the window, Fran remarks, "It's a nice view."

Wade nods.

"There are also barbiturates and amphetamines, tablets. Naturally there's hash, Afghani black for the most part. Opium as well, again Afghani."

Wade nods. Vividness has entered his surroundings.

From a nearby minaret a call to prayer, *azan*, begins. Wade listens to it, and Fran seems to be listening as well. When the prayer call finishes there is a moment of silence, but this is only perceptual, for the sounds of the town have not paused. It was Wade listening to the mesmerizing call to prayer and then its cessation that produced a lag in sound. The sounds of the town return, but they return gradually.

"You were in India, I suppose."

"Yes."

"And how long were you there?"

"A little over a year."

Fran's eyes have returned to Wade's face.

"Taking in the sights, were you?"

"Kind of."

"Kind of?"

"For a lot of it, I was on a bicycle."

"A bicycle?"

"Yes. Amritsar to Cape Comorin."

"Cape Comorin?"

"The southern tip of India."

Fran is looking at him. Wade kind of smiles, which puts his face aslant. Wade notices that talking is rather pleasant and so is listening, particularly listening to Fran, whose voice is rhythmic, Irish lilt accounting for this.

"It would seem that you're traveling alone."

"Yes."

Fran raises the fingers of the hand that's on the tabletop, but the hand remains on the table. The fingers come down after a brief pause.

"There's a place not far from here, kind of a pub/tavern. The *Other Place* it's called. There is a sign there now, a somewhat recent posting, a rather quiet sign, with *Other Place* written on it. You might say, it's a discreet sign for a discreet place. You see, alcohol is served there. Would you care to trot on over? We could go together."

"Sure."

"Perhaps you could treat me to a can of Heineken."

"Okay."

"By the way, what are your plans?"

"My plans? I'm on my way back to Europe. I hope to find work there. But I might look into teaching English in Tehran on the way. I heard that that's a possibility."

"Yes. I heard that, too. But Iran is a rather strict country—the Shah, the police, SAVAK, and so forth. Drugs of any sort are a capital offense. Or so it's said."

"I don't plan on crossing that border with anything. Or any sort of paraphernalia."

"Yes, that's the effectiveness of their system."

Wade grins to acknowledge Fran's observation.

"It's not as though you have to leave Peshawar tomorrow, though, is it?"

"No. Actually, I'm planning on staying a couple of days."

Fran sits, her eyes on Wade, but then her eyes leave Wade to scan the room. She nods, a slow gesture.

"A can of Heineken," she says, view returning to Wade, "and what you put out for the extra person in the room . . . I'll leave the vial of crank with you, and some downers as well. They'll help you fall asleep, if need be."

Fran gets the pouch out again and extracts the vial and sets it on the table. Fishing into the pouch with her fingers she brings out a packet that has folded pieces of white paper, packet secured with a rubber band. She looks at this and then gets out another packet that looks the same as the first packet, but now she slips one of the folded pieces of paper out of that packet from under the rubber band. Securing the folded piece of paper is a bit of masking tape, an uppercase D written on the tape.

"Ten tablets in the paper. One tablet will relax you so that you can fall asleep. It's pharmaceutical."

CHAPTER 16

Both Evelyn and Wade are working during the day. Evelyn shows up at night. And there are the weekends. But Wade is working on weekends, so sometimes Evelyn is in the studio when he comes home, Saturday or Sunday. Wade is leaner, his arms ropey. At times fatigue is evident, and the same can be said of Evelyn—fatigue.

"Was there a reason it was called the *Other Place?*"

"Yes. As Fran explained: 'There is a more sophisticated place, a more established place, where established people gather for cocktails and beer. It's on the other side of town, but it's easily gotten to. But why should we? A stuffy crowd there. Your public servant, who might be a person of position, or your military person, or your diplomatic-related person, foreign diplomatic, which does not rule out "advisors." And then there's your professional people as well who can show up, an "educated" elite. It's not the sort of place where you can feel comfortable, because you have to be careful there. Our kind of people don't hang there, for our presence would draw attention, or suspicion—long hair, beards, local garb, colorful shoulder bags, nifty caps, sandals, a bit of smudge on the pant leg. In other words, the "overland look," which in their patois translates as "hippie"—the enemy.

"'But then there's this other place. A different sort of place, a different sort of clientele, a more diverse crowd you might say. Some of these people have money, but some carry a thin pocketbook. Of the locals who drop in, government affiliations are a little far removed, a little farther down the ladder, so there's more latitude in their appreciation of diversity. This constituency might speak Urdu or Hindko or Pashto or Punjabi or Saraiki or Khowar or Kohistani or Balochi or Dari or English. And then, there are people who are passing through, west to east, east to west. Not a lot of people mind you, for it isn't alcohol that draws the overland crowd. After all, why leave Europe or North America in quest of alcohol? But still, there are some who pop in for a beer, or maybe to meet someone, or simply for the ambiance. A mild reputation has sprouted. People on their way to and from, and having heard of... the *Other Place*.'"

Evelyn has these phrases wandering around in her brain, "push the envelope," "think out of the box," "make it new," but she has discovered that they mean nothing. They are clichés meant to dispute cliché, thus they are self-propagating. They are, if anything, an advertisement for chest thumping.

She feels that she is arguing or disputing something—a way of life, a point of view, a philosophy that calls for independence and free thinking while rewarding conformity.

Wade has taken her away from her son's death. But where has this left her? She has two sides: her job and Wade. They represent established and not established. She is grounded in one and flirts with the other.

There are a lot of pieces that she begins but throws away because she gets lost in the midst of them, subject dissolving, direction vanishing. She isn't pushing any envelopes. She is simply lost. It is this that makes her appreciative of routine, which is what her job supplies, for it is the routine of institution that gives her a sense of belonging, which grounds her.

Now and then, though, something crystalizes—some scene, some sentiment, some sliver of insight. It seems accidental, yet there is a sense that circumstance is involved. She doesn't know how to explain this, and she doesn't know how to conjure it. She suspects that there is no formula. She returns again and again to Wade's studio.

There are several bartenders, or "barmen," one of whom is Jimmy, which seems a nickname, or perhaps a school name as is sometimes employed in Hong Kong. Jimmy, by way of upbringing, has bounced between Hong Kong, London, and Peshawar, ethnic background Pakistani, perhaps Pashtun, because, in addition to Urdu and English, Jimmy can speak Pashto. Jimmy is the owner of the *Other Place*, an establishment that he began when he was a young man, and like the *Other Place* Jimmy has aged, for he is now middle-aged. Some say that it's a miracle that he's kept the place going, but then others maintain that's it's not a miracle because profits have been forthcoming. Evidence of this is that over the years the *Other Place* has expanded, walls knocked down, main room enlarged, office and storeroom and toilet facilities added on. The *Other Place* even has a refrigerator, and in Jimmy's office there is a telephone.

Jimmy has told Wade that the inspiration for the *Other Place* came after Jimmy set off from London one August afternoon with a couple of chums, one of whom was Dutch, and so necessitated a stopover in Amsterdam, after which Jimmy and his buddies continued on, local transportation utilized. As Jimmy phrased it with an amused smile, "We were on our way East, Wade."

When they reached Peshawar, Jimmy felt at home, but at the same time there was his international background, which had Jimmy coming of age in the sixties. In Peshawar Jimmy was welcomed by relatives, but at the same time he was considered a bit of a renegade, for he fancied a pint of beer.

Exploring the possibilities of alcohol in Peshawar naturally led Jimmy into the "established place," and of that Jimmy carried away a "blah" feeling, not to mention an "antiquated colonial" feeling, which hinted at arrogance.

So Jimmy made a deal with one of his relatives, an uncle, who had an abandoned animal-feed store—mice rampant, doors padlocked, windows boarded-up. A nondescript street was its location, thus a bit divorced from the hubbub of downtown, yet, in Jimmy's eyes, close enough to cheap hotels to attract the overland crowd, which at the time was starting to swell.

Rent at the beginning was zero, but there was a "promise" clause that stipulated that if Jimmy's crazy idea materialized into profit the uncle would get a percentage. This, according to Jimmy, was a "winning" setup, because if his uncle started receiving money, then the uncle would have a vested interest in keeping the place open, which meant that "gift money," otherwise known as "baksheesh," would find its way into the right hands, for Jimmy's uncle was an established businessman, which meant that he knew how things were done. Failed feed store notwithstanding, Jimmy's uncle had irons in the fire.

Jimmy, of course, wasn't the only one to see opportunity or inspiration from the emerging overland market, for along that route, Istanbul east, cheap accommodation, restaurants, bakeries, handicraft shops, soda pop factories, money changers, and dope peddlers were burgeoning, in accordance with local customs and applied law enforcement. Bus companies, too, were on the upswing.

"We started out with a plywood bar and two tables," Jimmy tells Wade. "And now look." Jimmy gestures with a sweep of the hand as if he were a proud father.

The room has eight tables and a bar with ten stools, bar-top a nicely grained hardwood with a polyurethane coating that lends itself to easy clean up and an appealing glint. There are two dartboards and there's an upright piano. A counter along one wall is fashioned for stand-up customers. At one end of the backbar there are two gas rings for heating water, instant coffee available by way of powdery Nescafe, which also serves in the making of Irish coffee. The refrigerator is down at that end, too. Through an opening where the bar ends, there's a table with a record player. LPs are in wooden boxes alongside. Jimmy claims that the record player is a "stereo." Two ceiling fans help to circulate air, while during the winter a bukhari heater warms the room. A tall bookcase with used paperbacks has a Magic Marker sign that reads: "Take what you like, leave what you've finished." Looking through the selection, Wade was amused to find a copy of *Europe on 5 Dollars a Day.*

Large jars of shelled almonds and cashews, as well as jars full of pistachio nuts and peanuts, are on the wide, bottom shelf of the backbar. As for peanut shells, they go on the floor along with cigarette butts and spent matches. Of windows, there are two openings that face the street, but they are always shuttered closed. The place gets swept out at least once a day by a boy, who doubles as an errand boy. By and large, it's a twenty-four-hour establishment.

Smoking grass or hashish is forbidden, a sign declaring this. "The place would be full of pot heads who wouldn't spend any money," says Jimmy, "and more baksheesh would be needed to cover the grass/hash privilege, you know, given the public nature of the place." Jimmy kind of smiles, and then adds, "Of course there's nothing stopping anyone from smoking in a hotel room and then strolling over for a beer."

Jimmy favors vests with impressive embroidering, primo stitch-work. He's a slim fellow with a smooth, light brown complexion.

"It took a while, and it took investment: circuit box, electrical wiring, ceiling fans, flooring, functional plumbing.

"The hardest part, though, is the booze. There is a brewery in Pakistan that produces beer, a low-key operation. Of course you know that label. We carry it here. But everything else is somewhat opportune."

"Yeah, I guess it would be."

"Actually, there's something I've been meaning to talk to you about, Wade."

"Oh? What's that?"

"There's an airline chap in Rawalpindi, eastern route, back and forth to Hong Kong. He puts aside bottles of duty-free for me, stockpiles them in his flat, Johnnie Walker and Beefeater. I was thinking that perhaps you'd like to make a run up there for me. Take a couple of modest suitcases. I have them here, supply of tea towels inside to wrap the bottles, seeing that we don't want them broken. The price is settled. I'll give you an envelope with the money. Train up, train back. No need to spend the night. I pay for the transportation. For your services you get one bottle from each suitcase, one whiskey, one gin. You can sell it back to me if you like, or if you know someone who would give you a better price, that's perfectly fair as well."

"A one-day deal, huh?"

"Yes. I'll ring up my friend, set up a day, and he'll meet you at the railway station, take you to his flat. It's not far away."

"That sounds okay, but I'll have to check with James, see if he can spare me for a full day."

"I was going to mention James. He's partial to Beef-eater, you know. Buys it from me. So you can probably sell your bottle to him for what he pays me. He does buy an occasional bottle of Scotch. I think it's just for his guests, though. I'm certain James will give you the go-ahead for the Rawalpindi run."

Wade's standing at the bar and it's nine in the morning and he's having a cup of Nescafe.

"Well, just out of curiosity, what's to stop a fellow from staying on that train through to Lahore, and then maybe crossing into India with your envelope of cash?"

Jimmy kind of smiles at this.

"Wade, you're with James and Fran, right? You've been vetted."

The sounds, the smells, the colors, the bustle—pushcarts with melons, wooden trays of flat bread balanced on the heads of boys, trishaws and motorized trishaws, burlap sacks of grain coming off of trucks, tea stalls with milky tea boiling over onto a bed of glowing charcoal, bullock carts, sugarcane squeezed into juice, a boy selling ciga-rettes, a horse-drawn two-wheeled carriage with hooves clopping, milk cans jerry-rigged onto the sides of bicycles, donkey-drawn flatbed wagons, a boy leading a brindled goat by a length of rope, red meat hanging from chrome hooks, mounds of black and brown and yellow and golden raisins, music blaring from shops selling sweets, bananas piled on pieces of canvas on the sidewalk, gaunt dogs sniffing at refuse, women with wicker baskets on their backs full of yellow grapes.

Having come from Nescafe at the *Other Place* and on his way to James's, he glides through this euphony with bounce to his step, and prior to the *Other Place* there was his waking in his room, which he now rents by the month, a discounted rate, Fran having alerted him to the by-the-month discount. And so it was, and is, that he brushes his teeth at the small sink in his room and then sits down at the wooden table by the window with a small mirror and a razorblade and a cut-down plastic straw and a vial of crank. Ten minutes later, the Nescafe settles on top of this nicely, and so does a chat with Jimmy, who's almost always in the *Other Place* in the morning, business and habit. A boy of about twelve years old is busy with a broom and a dustpan and a trash bucket. It's a quiet time of day, and sometimes Fran is at a table with one or two or three people, and it's not always men, for occasionally there'll be a female, negotiations in progress. Fran has told Wade that she no longer frequents the railway station. "It was never really my forte. I think the last time I was there was when you rolled into town."

Before reaching the doorway of the building of James's flat, Wade stops to buy a couple of pieces of warm naan, newsprint folded around them. The summer's heat has abated, and in its place there is a briskness that'll give way to warmth in about an hour. The poplars have turned yellow. The air is dry, and there is something that speaks of the Hindu Kush and the Spin Ghar, and the weather that might descend from those slopes.

And then he's at the doorway where the "concierge," or caretaker, gives him a rotten-toothed smile and says, "Good morning." The concierge's post is behind a window opening that faces the street, sliding pane of glass operable, but usually the glass is slid back and open. Wooden shutters close off that portal at night when the caretaker is asleep, shutters secured on the inside with a sliding bolt. Large jars of hard candy are set out on the wide sill of the concierge's window opening during the day, colorful nuggets that draw the appetites of children and adults both. Wade has purchased some of these sugar-coated delectables himself, for they help to keep moisture in his mouth and throat, and they taste good.

In addition to the street-facing window, there is another window, which faces the space between the sidewalk doorway and another door that is at the bottom of a stairway. The sidewalk doorway is open during the day, but the stairway door is never left open. Wade has keys to the sidewalk door and the stairway door, but he doesn't need to use them when the concierge is on duty, for the concierge will open that second door from the inside via a door at the side and rear of his station. A guest wanting to visit one of the apartments upstairs during the day must wait in the space between the sidewalk door and the stairway door, and in this waiting the concierge gets to look at and talk to the visitor, and if the concierge hasn't been alerted to the arrival of a specific guest, the concierge will pull a cord that has been rigged up to travel up the stairway wall to the apartment in question, thus setting off a little bell inside that apartment. Conversely, there is a cord going the other way, apartment to concierge's, and if pulled in response to the concierge's bell, a little bell in the concierge's cubicle will jingle, thus signaling "okay." The concierge has access to four of these bell-pulls, each numbered accordingly, for there are four apartments, two on the second floor, and two on the third floor.

If the bell in James's flat rings, and if a guest is not expected, Wade will go down to see who it is. If Wade isn't in James's apartment, and if James does not respond by ringing the bell in response to the concierge's ringing, the guest will be turned away.

Also, if James wants to summon the concierge, he pulls the string that rings the bell downstairs. This is not in response to the concierge's ringing. This is a ring initiated by James.

"Everyday life and security were inseparable," Wade tells Evelyn.

"Yes," she replies. "But aren't they inseparable here, too?"

Wade sits a moment, and then says, "Yes, I guess they are—car alarms, home security systems, armed guard response, neighborhood watch, coded-access doors, security guards, barred windows, bullet-proof glass in front of a bank teller, body-scanning machines, pin numbers, steel-meshed screen doors, buzzer-access doors, surveillance cameras, guard dogs, gated communities, intercoms, and guns."

"Even in the supermarket parking lot there's a security guard," Evelyn adds.

They are in the studio at Wade's house and it's eleven at night. Winter has set in, albeit Southern California style, forty-five degrees Fahrenheit the low temperature. The door of the studio is open, gas heater that serves the hall and living room effective, for the living room side has been vented off and certain doors have been closed to direct the furnace's heat into the studio. Both Wade and Evelyn are at the worktable, Evelyn's space, Wade's space, each with their own projects. Evelyn is working on a woman's face that shows both weather and paleness. Wade is sketching a western scrub jay, which most people call a blue jay, that frequents his chaparral backyard. Wade is working from a photograph that Evelyn took of the bird for him with her digital camera, color print a product of Evelyn's computer and printer.

"But there was this starkness or frankness about it there as compared to here, where there's a sense of subtlety, or at least an attempt at subtlety. Or," says Wade, "maybe it was that I wasn't brought up in that culture, and so things often struck me as crude. It's strange if you think about. I mean, the homicide rate in Los Angeles isn't a pleasant figure, and neither is the number of reported rapes, but somehow this eludes our sense of repulsion . . . unless we happen to be involved."

"Of course," Evelyn responds.

Wade has set his pencil down.

"So I go over to Fran's apartment with her because she needs some help carrying jars of pills. It's in the morning and there are two Mercedes waiting in front of the *Other Place*. Fran's room is an add-on at the back of a family dwelling slash business. It's a second-floor add-on. Probably someone in the family got married and they needed another room for the new family is what Fran surmised, but then for some reason the new family moved out. Maybe they moved in with the main family when the grandparents died. Who knows? At any rate, Fran is living in that room, and it's gotten to via an unpaved alley. There's an outside stairway made of steel, and at the bottom of the stairs there's a padlocked door, steel-framed with metal grating. But then there's the stairway, which is exposed, so they welded arched piping on to it to create a canopy and strung barbed wire. I looked at that in the morning light, and what came to mind was Auschwitz."

Wade sips his tea.

"Naturally there's a landing at the top of the stairs where Fran's apartment door is, a plank door with a hasp and a padlock, wooden planks painted green, but the green has faded."

Evelyn sips her tea. The cat is on the couch, sleeping.

"Around town, particularly at the outskirts, walls made of adobe bricks or cinderblocks have pieces of broken bottles, clear or green or amber glass, embedded on top, shards protruding and all glittery in the sunshine."

Evelyn's been working on some pieces that feature James's flat, exaggeration, fracturing, and cubist techniques availing. She first sketched the pieces in graphite and then used colored pencils, and now Evelyn and Wade are standing at the worktable looking these pieces, a Friday night.

"I've taken some home, and I've used acrylics in copying these images onto canvas. Acrylics give me more latitude, at least with this subject."

Wade nods.

"I don't know quite how to handle this," Evelyn says. "I mean, it's like cartoonish and fantasy and pornography and eroticism and . . . and I don't know what, colonialism or something. I can't decide how to do this, or maybe it's that I don't know what it is I'm trying to do."

"Yeah," Wade says. "You seem to be going back and forth between themes."

"I am. And what I have in my studio at home is even more divergent."

"Is that bad?"

"Well, no, not per se, but in the past I've always felt in control, you know, coming at a subject with different viewpoints and techniques. It's not uncommon. People do it all the time, and so have I."

"Okay."

"It's just that this is different because I'm not sure what I'm dealing with."

Wade nods. Evelyn shifts her weight.

"You know, it might seem weird, but I've never seen a pornographic movie."

"Oh?"

"Do you think you could rent some?"

"Rent some?"

"Do you have a DVD player?"

"Yes. I bought one six months or so before my mother died. She liked animal movies, dogs and pigs and that sort of thing."

"Well, maybe you could rent some porno and we could watch it. You know, I'd feel kind of weird walking into that special section, or room, where you got to be over eighteen. I've thought about this before, and it was having to walk into that porno section that hung me up."

Wade chuckles and says, "Yeah." He then looks at a clock that's on a shelf and says, "It's only eight-thirty. They're probably still open. Let's go."

"Okay. But I'll stay in the car."

CHAPTER 17

He is standing to the side of the doorway after having admitted Fran and a woman. The woman looks to be mid-thirties. Wade closes the door and throws two deadbolts.

Fran steps forward and says, "James, I'd like to introduce Margaret, or Maggie. Maggie, this is James."

James sits regally in his wicker chair, directing his gleaming sunglasses at the jalousies. His legs are at a forty-five degree elevated angle. A light brown *kameez* extends from James's shoulders to his knees.

Margaret is wearing a black vest that is colorfully embroidered, obviously a local product. A yellow blouse with ruffles down its center is under the vest, and then there's a loose skirt that is a deep purplish red. Her feet are squeezed into a pair of sandal-like shoes that have two-inch heels, wide straps of the sandal/shoes white, but the white has been soiled as is common with all footwear in Peshawar. The exposed white skin peeking out from between the straps is in the same condition, borderline filthy. Margaret's toenails are red, but the red is chipped. The red on her fingernails, though, is in better shape. Beads of sweat are on Margaret's forehead. Her neck, too, is sweaty, which is understandable, for the temperature outside is thirty degrees Celsius, eighty-six degrees Fahrenheit. It is the middle of September.

Fran was over to James's flat in the morning to alert James, and in a sense Wade as well, that a female guest, a friend of Beverly's, had requested an "appointment." It was Beverly who called Jimmy, Jimmy taking the call in his office and then passing the message on to Fran, who then skipped over to James's flat.

"Let's say three in the afternoon," Fran said, "just in case the train is late. Is that hour convenient for you, James?"

"Wade," said James, "is there anything on the docket from three to roughly five o'clock today?"

"No, nothing other than Hemingway."

"Well, we'll just have to move Hemingway up so that we can accommodate our guest."

"Sure thing."

"Right-o," said Fran. "I'll meet her at the station, and then when she's through here I'll put her on the evening train back. She'll be back to Rawalpindi tonight."

"Fine," James said.

"Okay, I'll just pop back on over to Jimmy's, so that he can confirm."

Margaret is looking at James with extreme interest. And James, seeming to sense this, is smiling. Margaret's features are sharp to the extent that her face appears squarish. A red flush is coming through from under her makeup, flush probably a heat flush, for her bare forearms are nearly lobster red. Evidently her train was on time, which meant that Fran had to entertain—show Margaret the town, go shopping, drop in at the *Other Place*, maybe feed Margaret some pills.

There seems to be no lack of energy in Margaret's bearing nor is there a lack of curiosity. She is now leaning forward and is peering at James's face as if examining minutiae. Pulling back and straightening, and then turning to Fran, Margaret breaks the silence that has enveloped the room in the wake of Fran's introduction. Margaret's voice has a nasal sound.

"This here is a novelty item."

Margaret gestures toward James with her free hand. In Margaret's other hand there is a large straw bag, woven straw, a beach bag sort of thing.

Wade, who is still near the door, hopes that nothing of value is in the bag, for it would be easy pickings for pickpockets, particularly those that populate the railway station, but of course Fran would have cautioned Margaret.

Wade steps further into the room, which gives him a frontal view of James and Fran and Margaret. Margaret brings her gesturing hand up and wipes sweat from her brow, and in the wake of this there are traces of smeared cosmetics and dust. Fran is looking at Margaret. Margaret redirects her eyes to look at James again.

James continues to smile, yet it's not as though he didn't hear Margaret's assessment, for his flabby lips seem to have inflated more. His bulldog-wrinkled forehead, though, remains constant.

The ceiling fan is on at medium speed. Margaret glances up. Seemingly, she's noticed the fan. Her view returns to James.

"I am so happy to make your acquaintance, Margaret. Is it a Yankee voice that I hear, perhaps East Coast?"

"People call me Maggie, and yes, I'm from New Jersey, Elizabeth, Elizabeth New Jersey, but I've also lived in Manhattan, but now I'm back in Elizabeth."

"I see. And you're a friend of Beverly's?"

"Yes."

"Beverly, if I remember correctly, is from New York."

"Yes. We met through our husbands, ex-husbands. But when Beverly and I met they weren't our ex-husbands yet. Our ex-husbands, who were our husbands at the time, worked for the same company in Manhattan. Anyway, Beverly got transferred out here after her divorce, Islamabad Airport, ground staff, or maybe it's called terminal staff, you know, airport terminal. She's been here for about a year or so, and I thought I'd come out and see her."

"Of course."

Maggie turns to Fran and says, "But Beverly didn't tell me anything about this." Maggie indicates James. Fran, in response, says, "Maggie, he may not be able to see, but he can hear."

"Well," says James, "what exactly did Beverly tell you?"

"She told me about your thing, and about your hands, and about this man who has to be in the room, Brian. I guess that's him, there." She points to Wade. "And she told me about this old-fashioned room."

"Did she tell you I was blind?"

"Yes, she told me that, and she told me about Fran. Fran's been marvelous. We went shopping today and I bought some souvenirs, and then we went to this kind of bar-like place and had a drink. Also, I gave Fran an envelope with a 'contribution,' just like Beverly instructed."

"Jolly good. Well, speaking of 'drink,'" James says, and bellows, "Beefeater, Wade!"

This resonates in the room.

"Maggie," says Fran, "I'll be back for you at five to take you to the railway station."

"Okay," Maggie says, and with this Maggie watches Fran go to the door and throw the deadbolts and leave. Wade walks over to re-deadbolt the door.

"Maggie," James intones. "Would you care for a refreshing libation? I'm having a gin and tonic, Beefeater gin."

Maggie smiles, a broad expression. "A gin and tonic? Yes. Lots of ice, okay?"

"Sure thing," Wade responds, and heads for the kitchen, which is where a block of ice sits in the sink, a towel wrapped around the block, icepick on the counter nearby.

"Wade went out about half an hour ago, Maggie, in anticipation of your visit," James says. "You see, ice is somewhat of a luxury item in the flat. We don't always have it."

"Oh. Well, ah, is that man, Wade?"

"Oh, I'm terribly sorry. I should have introduced you. How rude of me."

"Where's Brian."

"Yes, well, Brian went back to England. In his place, there is Wade."

"Well, is Wade going to be in the room when we get started?"

"Yes, Wade will remain in the room in case we are in need of anything, such as beverages or a towel or the blinds adjusted. If you have a request, simply ask Wade."

With a bowl of chipped ice and a smaller bowl with lemon slices in hand, Wade returns to the room and goes to the liquor cabinet and starts making the gin and tonics, glasses of the tumbler variety. Maggie watches this.

"The refreshing tinkle of ice," says James. "An invigo-rating sound."

Maggie looks around the room.

"Before serving the highballs," James says, "please bring a chair for Maggie and the small side table for her drink, Wade."

Leaving the drinks on the liquor cabinet's protruding shelf, Wade fetches one of the two chairs from the table near the kitchen and sets the chair down next to James's wicker chair. An end table from next to the couch is brought over and placed near the chair.

James has a way of tilting his head this way and that as if to zero in on sounds. When listening to someone talking, he sometimes cocks his head to give one of his ears the direction of the speaker. It's a listening/contemplative pose that people appreciate because it suggests that what they are saying is important, or at least important to James.

"Beverly was right. You have a lot of old stuff in this room," Maggie says.

A moment ensues, James with his head cocked as if thinking about Maggie's observation.

"Maggie," says James, "why don't you come over here and take a seat so that we can get further acquainted."

James reaches over and pats the seat of the chair, position of the chair familiar, for it is one of several designated places in the room for a chair. Maggie sets her straw bag down on the floor and comes over and sits down, perspiration on her neck and face having dried.

Wade picks up the tumblers and goes over and hands one to Maggie. Reaching down, Wade takes James's hand and brings it up to the glass. James takes the glass from Wade.

"Let us have a toast, Maggie, my dear. Let us toast to a lovely afternoon."

James raises his glass and Maggie responds with the same gesture. They drink, and then Maggie says, "Ah, that's better." James, who is smacking his lips, says, "Indeed it is."

"Maggie," Wade says, "I'm going to move your bag to over by the door." Wade picks up the straw bag from the middle of the room and takes it over to the door with the two deadbolts. He sets the bag down where all such bags are placed.

Maggie's hair is yellow-blonde and it comes to the top of her shoulders. Regarding hairstyle, there's what's left from what was once wavy, waves having been exhausted due to the onslaught of chilled, damp air in the air-conditioned uber-class coach of the train, and then the rush of dry hot air while strolling the picturesque streets of Peshawar. A few bobby pins hold her hair in back of her ears, but there are tresses that have escaped to fall over her ears. She has a habit of brushing these wayward locks to the rear of her head with a hand, the hand that's not holding her drink. But when she switches the glass to the other hand and sends the newly freed hand up to groom her hair, there's moisture on her fingers from the glass's condensation, which then registers in her thrown-back hair. Maggie's eyebrows are thick and dark, which creates a light versus dark contrast between her eyebrows and the hair on her head. The irises of her eyes are dark as well, and they dart right to left in a pair of wide sockets, eyeliner in stark evidence against the attempted white of her facial cosmetics. The scent of genuine perfume plumes in her vicinity.

While on his way to the kitchen for a can of Heineken that's nuzzling the block of ice under the towel, Wade sees James reach over to put a hand on Maggie's skirt, thigh under the material.

"Maggie," says James, "you are still clothed," intonation suggesting surprise.

"Well, yes. I just walked in."

"Don't be shy, Maggie."

"I'm not shy. Just let me finish my drink and I'll take my clothes off."

"Yes, drink up!"

Maggie and James raise their drinks to their lips. Wade, seated at the table near the kitchen doorway, does the same, but his beverage is beer.

Maggie, after lowering her glass and swallowing, says, "Aren't we at least going to do some small talk?"

James, his free hand having moved from Maggie's skirt to the ruffles of her blouse, colorful vest open and no obstacle, says, "Small talk? Well, yes. We can chat while festivities progress. No reason whatsoever not to comment on the proceedings."

James's hand is exploring the contours of what lies beneath the fabric of Maggie's blouse to the right and left of the ruffles where her chest rises, vest hardly a hindrance. This exploration, though, is not clumsy or grabby. James's large hand conveys a sense of consideration that Maggie seems to notice, as if perhaps she was expecting something else and is now pleasantly surprised. She looks down at James's hand, or maybe it is his bare forearm she looks at. Her eyes begin to settle.

Maggie raises her glass and sips her drink, ice cubes tingling. Of course James's hand has piano fingers, but they're not the lengthy piano fingers that people sometimes speak of. They're not short fingers, though, yet they aren't excessively long and skinny. They are sensitive fingers that have strength, but the strength is controlled. And beyond this, they are gathering information. They are "information-gathering" fingers, and as this term comes to mind, "information-gathering," Wade apprehends a memory from when the blind girl/woman sat next to him on the train in India. Wade of course has seen James gather information with his hands and fingers and feet any number of times, but this time it's different because there is a person who is the subject of those fingers.

"Well, where should I put my clothes?"

James's hand leaves Maggie's blouse. "Put them on one of the armchairs."

Maggie sets her glass down and steps over to an armchair, sheds her vest and then sits down to take off her sandals/shoes. She then stands up to take all of her clothes off.

While this is in progress, James says, "Wade, if you would be so kind as to refresh our drinks."

So while Maggie is getting naked, Wade is over at the liquor cabinet making drinks. Maggie glances at him, but there is no communiqué. Yet, excluding self-examination on Maggie's part, it is only Wade who can assess Maggie's physique in a visual way. She seems to ignore this, perhaps because more relevant evaluation will come when James's fingers find her flesh, and it is this that is important, for this is where the focal point rests, and to involve Wade would change things, and James would notice. Maggie has contracted James, not Wade, nor Wade and James. Wade's role is that of a domestic, faceless and anonymous, unless otherwise stipulated.

"Do you think Maggie understood all this?" Evelyn asks.

"No. And I didn't either at the time, except for parts of it, like the household-servant role. Yet I do think that all this might have been operating below conscious understanding, as can often happen. We don't necessarily need consciousness to operate within certain bounds, such as logic or consideration or manners or social contracts or . . . or evil. It's only when we put things into words that explanation develops. And, words are often after the fact."

"Yes."

"I gave James his drink and I set Maggie's drink down on the low table next to her chair, and then I went back to my place at the table.

"I should mention that my true purpose in that room was to make sure that Maggie didn't steal anything. This was protocol. James had cash hidden all over the apartment, four hiding places that I knew of, because I was the one to hide money for him, and I was the one to count the money. These caches were in addition to spending money, money for expenses. Fran was privy to this as well, privy to the logic of not allowing anyone the opportunity of rifling through the apartment. It wasn't so much that James and Fran thought Maggie and Beverly were thieves, particularly Beverly, for Beverly was like a friend. But of course Beverly was also a 'guest.' Borders and demarcations got blurred."

"Yes."

"Anyway, it was policy that if someone were in the apartment with James, then either Fran or I would be there. This was of significance when the pornographers showed up, two men, and it was of significance when other men showed up, men who consulted James about drugs or whatever else they might be concocting in a lab or a makeshift factory. Sometimes James would tell me to get a book from the shelf and read him a certain section, chemistry and/or pharmacology. This mostly involved substituting one substance for another. Quantity and proportions were critical as well. Of course James knew these people, but James was blind, physically blind, and this made him vulnerable, and he was aware of this, and so was Fran, and then so was I."

"Yes."

"So I was in the apartment when people visited. But with Maggie, and particularly with Beverly, and even with the women who were filmed for porno, my presence added this other facet, this other element, which reminds me of your story about Vicky and Randall."

"Yes."

"You see, even though I was supposed to be a nothing-presence, that wasn't possible. I was there, so how could I have not been there?"

"Of course."

Maggie is full-breasted, but this feature isn't so high on her chest. Her waist tappers slightly, but there, too, age is involved. An hourglass figure might have been her purview in the past, but the sand has lost its hour.

Maggie steps over and picks up her drink and sips. After swallowing, and while still holding the glass in her hand, a change occurs, for Maggie raises herself up onto her toes, which arches her chest outward, and she shoots Wade a purposeful glance that lingers long enough to be something more than a glance. She is checking to see if Wade is looking at her, and he is. And Maggie is showing him a pose. After confirming Wade's attention, she lowers herself onto the soles of her bare feet, thus forgoing the pose. But something has been established.

Wade, sitting at the table near the kitchen, sips his beer in an attempt to be nonchalant.

Maggie sits down next to James to accept his hand on her chest. There is the uniqueness of the room and its blind man, and there is Maggie having removed her clothes. But there is also someone sitting at a table, watching.

James's fingers have found something interesting, for they are stalled while investigating Maggie's areolas, the largeness of those discs the subject of James's exploration, pads of his fingers tapping quickly and lightly.

Wade has noticed this feature, too, wide areolas, but in Wade's case he can only glance furtively, full investigation denied him, for he can't be too overt, for that would intrude. And this is the problem. He doesn't know what to do with his eyes.

The can of beer at Wade's fingertips and the pre-1947 room and the pleasant light angling in from the jalousies help to give his eyes something to do. So to a large extent, Wade is content with these simple features that are within his vision, for they serve as mild entertainments, and this has something to do with having done a couple of lines of crank with James in the morning. After Fran left to give Jimmy the go-ahead for the Maggie visit, James told Wade to get out the crank, James's stash, while explaining the logic of having the drug peak before Maggie's arrival. Since it's methamphetamine, the leveling off and incremental descent would last and last, and it was this that James wanted to take advantage of, for it's not in the drug's upward zip that sex can be had. The body is too fast and too occupied for erection, but on the downward side of peaking, particularly if a tolerance has been built, then sex can be had, and when it is longevity comes into play because there is no rush. The body is still away from its normal self, still somewhat detached.

So, as it is, James is using this leverage with Maggie, or about to use it, and Wade is using it, too, but in Wade's case he is using it to look at his surroundings, which offer entertainment and contentment. He is fine with sipping beer and looking at that room. Yet, on the other hand, this might be interpreted by Maggie as spaced-out or zombie-like. So, another alternative that Wade thinks about is opening a book and reading, an intellectual activity. But here as well, weirdness might be what Maggie would see. Thus, as if attempting normality in a situation that begs to differ, Wade settles upon sipping beer while looking at the room and while glancing at Maggie and James now and then.

James's hand moves in a southerly direction, and regarding that hand and its fingers Maggie voices approval. "Beverly was right about your hands." Maggie continues to talk, subject matter most anything that comes to mind in addition to occasionally throwing in a comment about James's touch, a touch that employs flickering fingers and the curving of those fingers and the curving of James's wide palm, for James is compiling information, and maybe stimulation as well, which could be serving both Maggie and James.

James isn't talking. Maggie is talking, and it's obvious that she has ingested amphetamines, pill variety in all likelihood, for Fran favors selling pills as opposed to powder, yet for personal consumption Fran prefers powder because it supplies a different kind of energy. But of sales, pills are neat and simple, and their consumption is undemanding. They can be popped into the mouth most anywhere, paraphernalia unnecessary.

"Well," says Evelyn, "it would seem that Maggie was 'peaking' on the pills. So didn't that interfere with Maggie's sexual capacities, given the logic of what you said about crank?"

"You know, I asked Fran about that during the course of that winter when we huddled around the brazier in my room, just like I asked her about a lot of other things that winter, and she said that she didn't think it was such an issue with women as it was with men. She said that based on her experience that was what she had found. Certainly on that day, Maggie was into the speed and into the sex. I had a feeling that she hadn't taken amphetamines that much, for there was too much chatter. Habit and tolerance usually reduce that. But of course every person has their own way of dealing with drugs, or more precisely 'a given drug.' Actually, James warned me about that. He said that Fran had a strong constitution and so did he, 'he' meaning James. But Brian, James's previous helper, had a different constitution, and crank had caused him problems. Fran, and particularly James, regulated their consumption, whereas some people just go hog-wild."

James's fingers find Maggie's pubic hair, which is where those fingers probe. Maggie sips her drink, very cool, yet James's fingers are affecting her—tautness at certain places on her body, movement of her eyes, lapses in midsentence. Her pubic hair is dark, but of course James can't see this, just like he can't see Maggie's yellowish blonde hair nor her glowing red forearms nor her white-skinned body nor her pink-flushed face nor her dirt-striped feet.

Evelyn giggles.

"James's fingers only worked like that when he was touching women. There were times when his fingers sought information about an object, but that touching was different."

"Yes."

"He once told me, 'It's such a pleasure to put my hands on a woman's skin. My eyes can't have that now. Only my hands can have that.' James had a piece of sandalwood that he would rub with his hands before a woman came over. This was part of what occupied him on his way up with the crank. The oils in the sandalwood scented his hands, and this wasn't lost on the women. Maggie said, 'Your hands smell wonderful.' James wanted the women to like his hands."

"Maggie."

"Yes, James."

"I believe it is time to unbutton my tunic."

"Your tunic?"

"Yes, my one and only garment."

"You mean your nightshirt?"

The new year has begun, 2007, and time settles back into its preholiday routine—Evelyn at Wade's on the weekends, but sometimes at night during the week. They are both busy during the day, Monday through Friday, with Wade sometimes working on weekends as well.

Saturday night, and a light rain is falling, which has the effect of quieting the neighborhood. Wade is in his studio and he's working on a watercolor. His awareness is going back and forth between the sound of the rain on the awnings and his watercolor. He hears the screen door open and a soft knock at the front door. He leaves his studio and goes to the front door and opens it. Evelyn enters with a large square box. "Pizza girl!" she says. Wade closes the door, and he can already smell the pizza.

They eat in the studio, the two of them sitting on the couch, pizza on the coffee table in front of them. The cat, too, partakes by chewing on pieces of pepperoni.

"Della Karr came over today. You know, I might have told you about her. She owns a gallery in Ocean Park. She arrived at two o'clock and stayed until just a while ago. She looked at my work and we talked and talked, and all of a sudden it was dark, and she had to get back over the hill."

"So she liked your stuff?"

"I'm going to have a show. The opening is set for the first week of July."

"Wow! Congratulations."

"Thanks. But now there's all this work to do."

"Work?"

"Curriculum vitae, invitation list, design of the invitation and postcard, and then choosing the pieces I'm going to show and having them matted and framed. Also, I have to price them. Of course I have to meet with Della to coordinate and work on these things. She of course has a mailing list, she of course knows people, she of course knows the market. She's really excited about this."

"Great."

"I already have enough pieces, finished pieces, for the show, but there are others that I'm working on, and who knows what else might emerge between now and the middle of June."

"Of course."

"I went straight over and told my mother. She was having dinner. She nodded approval, and then I was coming over here and I saw a pizza place."

"Let us have some Faulkner, Wade."

A freshly made mug of tea is steaming on James's side table, and alongside this there is a saucer with a piece of naan on it. The French doors have been opened and the jalousies brought together in front of that opening, wooden slats with a generous angle to admit sunlight. James sits in his wicker chair, a rosy glow to his sagging cheeks. He does his ablutions in the morning, usually before Wade arrives. He conducts these rituals at the kitchen sink, toothpaste, toothbrush, washcloth, bar of soap, hand towel. Shaving, a once or twice a week affair, is done at a barbershop, Wade getting the same treatment in an adjacent chair. It's too cheap not to do it that way, barbershop for a shave.

Regarding James's toilet activities, he can handle that by himself, four-pronged cane brought into the toilet room and assisting him in stooping and rising. The same can be said for James's showering, an independent affair, tap-temperature water, hose and shower nozzle brought to use while James sits on a low wooden stool. But now, with the advent of November, Wade and James have begun to go to a facility that's beneath a bakery, shower stalls with hot water, wooden fire for the bakery ovens responsible for the hot water. There's a changing area with benches and wicker baskets for clothes. Upon entrance a man behind a counter takes money. After undressing, Wade leads a naked James to a stall, rubber flip-flops on James's feet, the same for Wade's feet. James has removed his sunglasses, and with his hands he can feel the stall's interior, hot and cold water knobs on separate pipes that converge at a showerhead. Wade goes to a separate stall, money belt in hand, which he lashes to the pipe extending out to the showerhead.

"Faulkner?"

"Yes, William Faulkner. If I recall correctly, there are a couple of his novels in the bookcase."

"Yeah, there are," Wade says. "Do you have one in mind?"

"You choose something. You're familiar with Faulkner, aren't you?"

"Yes."

Wade goes to the bookcase and selects a novel and returns and sits down. He opens to the first page and begins reading, *Light in August*.

Sharp light refracts through the glass of the window in his room. He's just woken up, a recently purchased blanket under his sleeping bag for cushioning and warmth, while on top of his sleeping bag there's another recently purchased blanket.

He has noticed something on his right foot at the top of his instep where the instep meets his ankle, the beginnings of a rash perhaps. It doesn't necessarily itch, though. He figures to leave it as is. He figures it'll go away in a day or two.

He pulls on a pair of pants and puts a pair of socks on his feet and slides his feet into a pair of black Converse high-tops that he picked up at a shop where backpacks and Levis and jackets and so forth are sold, a shop that barters and trades with people passing through. The Converses fit his feet, so he bought them straight away, didn't even bother to bargain for them. Nevertheless, the shopkeeper discounted the asking price, while exchanging a smile with Wade.

In Wade's room there is now a brazier the size of an office trash basket, exterior metal, interior a stone-like material. The short, steel legs of the brazier rest on a bed of red bricks. A boy, at the instruction of the front desk clerk, set this up in Wade's room about a week ago. Wade can purchase charcoal at the front desk, half-kilo bags. The bags are made of old newspapers, glue and folding applied, a very common product, recycling at work. As it turns out, the paper of the bags aids in igniting the charcoal.

In the interest of price comparison, for Wade had no idea what the price of charcoal was, he went to a charcoal-and-firewood vendor in the vicinity of the *Other Place* and inquired about how much a kilo of charcoal cost. Naturally there was a markup at the hotel, but it wasn't outrageous.

"Beverly was completely different. Nothing like Maggie. We so often assume that when you meet one person you think that their friends are going to be like them. But in the face of experience, and when we stop to think about this, there is hardly any reason to assume that someone's friends are going to be like them. I, for example, am not like my friends, and that has never been more poignant than now, after returning home."

"Yes."

"I wish I was like them, though."

"Really? Why?"

"I wish I had put in thirty years at a job. I wish I had that investment, that anchor, that slice of reality that serves as 'responsible and dependable.' I wish I had never left. But then that would be to wish I were someone else."

Beverly calls Jimmy and then there's Fran and confirmation, James and Jimmy part of it. Beverly arrives by train three days later, but Fran does not meet her at the railway station. Beverly, according to Fran, goes by taxi to a nice hotel, which is where she will stay for three nights, for whenever she comes to Peshawar she stays at a nice hotel, the nicest hotel in town.

Beverly meets Fran at the *Other Place* at a prearranged time, where they have a drink and conclude details before moving on to James's, which is where Beverly is introduced to Wade. Beverly, as she always does, has brought a bottle of Beefeater for James.

Beverly removes a scarf-like cloth that's over her hair. The cloth is a fashion, or a custom, that is common among Pakistani women. Beverly's hair is black and it's short and seemingly soft, very neat, a razor cut. She's dressed conservatively, long-sleeved loose shirt and long loose skirt, both dull brown. Her facial makeup is frugal, and the frames of her eyeglasses have been chosen tastefully, an academic look. She's nearly petite, and her scent is nonexistent.

Wade makes gin and tonics while Beverly removes her clothes and sits down next to James. Beverly's glasses remain on her face. It is the beginning of November and daytime temperatures are comfortable.

"How have you been, my dear?" James inquires.

"Fine, thank you. And before I forget, Maggie was very pleased with her visit. She said that she was 'deeply impressed.'"

"Indeed. I'm so happy to hear that."

Wade delivers the drinks and retreats to his table to nurse a can of Heineken. James and Beverly sip their drinks.

"And how are you doing these days, James?"

"Tiptop, thank you. As of late, Wade's been reading Faulkner to me."

"William Faulkner?"

"Yes."

"There's always some mystery in Faulkner."

"Yes, there is, isn't there? I don't know why, but it sometimes makes me think of America jazz, not Dixieland but the other jazz, the more modern one, the more mysterious one."

"Cool jazz, yes. But I've never thought of that."

"Neither had I until I began listening to Faulkner's writing read aloud. Years ago, when I read it with my eyes, I didn't think of jazz, but now, for some reason, I do."

"You've become a connoisseur."

"Perhaps I have."

They sip their gin and tonics and there's the tinkle of ice.

Beverly reaches and picks up James's hand and brings it to her breast, and in this she glances at Wade, who's looking at the rays of light slanting in from the jalousies, but his peripheral vision catches the movement of Beverly's hand, which triggers a response that has his eyes shifting to Beverly and James. And so Beverly and Wade's eyes touch, but immediately their views avert, yet Wade catches something and he looks back to see Beverly with a blush on her small face, dark eyes darting. He's not sure what this means. He lifts his can of beer and sips, view returning to the rays of light from the wooden slats of the jalousies.

Wade hears ice tingling in glasses, and he hears casual, polite conversation that is broken into convenient pieces of observation about music or literature or weather. Beverly, unlike Maggie, has a voice that is not nasal. Beverly's voice comes from the tip of her tongue, and it exits a pair of delicate lips that are neither chapped nor painted red. She may or may not have eaten some pills or snorted some crank, for she is like James, no rush or haste or overlapping pronouncements. And James, for his part, is more refined than he was with Maggie. Yet James, even though not exhibiting signs of narcotics, has prepared for the occasion with a couple of lines, just as he did with Maggie.

Wade notices a break in the conversation, a hiatus of sorts, and this draws his attention. He looks over.

Beverly's legs are splayed, her eyes cast downward, her rump forward on the chair's seat. She is casually holding her drink. Wade can't read her reaction to James's hand, which is at that critical junction where Beverly's thighs meet. James is slightly forward on his wicker chair as if he were listening to something, attentiveness in his posture. Beverly's view rises and she glances at Wade, and a blush comes to her face like before, but in addition to this there's a shiver that travels up from her belly and onto her chest. Wade looks away, for it's like Beverly's embarrassment dictates this. With his gaze returning to the sunlight, he senses that he is more involved with Beverly than he was with Maggie because his looking seems to affect Beverly strongly.

Conversation remains on leave, but then Wade hears a soft "Oh," and he wonders if this is a cue for him to look. He is somewhat divided about this. He sips his beer, and then he hears, as if he is supposed to hear, "Let's unbutton your *kameez*, James," and so he looks, and he sees Beverly setting her drink down and standing up and then leaning over James to use two hands to unbutton James's long shirt, starting with the top button, which allows James's hand to wander over Beverly's ass, as if an invitation has been issued. But it's not just one invitation but another as well, for Wade sees that Beverly, with her fashionably academic glasses on her face, is focused on unbuttoning the *kameez*, which automatically draws Wade's eyes to that same focal point because Beverly has willed its importance, and of course those fingers are on a meticulous button-by-button descent down the center of James's loose, beige garment.

James, of course, is no longer forward in his chair. His back is against the back of the chair, and his sunglasses are directed straight ahead while resting within the folds of his gnarled face. His one forearm is on the wicker chair's lone arm that is on the opposite side from where Beverly is standing, drink in the hand on that side. Wade can't help to think that James's attention is going between his hand that's at Beverly's backside and Beverly's fingers that are at the buttons of James's shirt.

It seems that Wade is welcome to more than just a glance, and so he watches as Beverly unfastens the bottom button of James's *kameez*, and when the button is undone Beverly pauses, and then her hands open the garment, which initiates another brief moment before Beverly looks over at Wade. But this time, there is no blush of embarrassment on Beverly's face, nor is there any other expression or sentiment. What Wade sees are Beverly's glasses and Beverly looking at him through the lenses of those glasses while letting the two sides of James's *kameez* fall from her fingers. It is in this way that Beverly allows James's exposure to speak for itself, and she does the same for herself as well by straightening her body and standing next to James. This lasts for a purposeful perceptual moment, and it's as if Beverly and James were posing for a photograph.

Wade hears a British accent, better parts of London in evidence. "Wade. Would you be so kind as to refresh our drinks?"

And so he collects their glasses and makes new drinks, with Beverly sitting back down on her chair. After delivering the drinks, Wade slips into the kitchen for a cold can of Heineken.

Drinks are sipped, but instead of moving to the bed and its neat patchwork bedspread as James and Maggie did, Beverly mounts James while he's on his wicker chair, a chair that's like a lounge chair and that can support the two of them because Beverly isn't heavy. With Beverly and James's movement on that chair, the chair's wicker creaks and squeaks, and this becomes more and more emphatic. The chair is now involved, and it commands Wade to look from where he sits at the table with a can of beer.

Beverly, backside toward Wade with James's hands on her hips, turns her head to the extreme, neck twisted, academic glasses in place, while her dark irises find Wade.

"Is there a common strand in this?" Evelyn asks. "Maggie and Beverly, and then the women doing porno with James, all in your presence, and then my thing with Vicky and Randall, and then this whole business with pornographic movies in general, which are now on DVD?"

"Yes and no. I ran into Beverly that night at the *Other Place*. She was sitting with Fran at a table, and James and I came in and sat down at their table, which seemed to be par for the course, Beverly coming to the *Other Place* and finding Fran there, and then maybe James joining them. Beverly was very collected, rather quiet, but I sensed she was having fun. She didn't talk much. She was listening, listening to what Fran or James had to say. She asked me a few questions, like where I was from. And then, as was often the case, Fran led James to the piano, where he started playing, and where Fran started singing, popular tunes, but some old songs as well. It was between songs that Beverly said to me, 'It's like there's this dent in the psyche, a niche, a hidden enclave that's brought forth through conflict—shyness and embarrassment and desire. And it creates this naughty arousal that sends me to a place where I'm gone. The conflict is me versus not me, and it's only possible when I can see myself through someone else's eyes, the eyes of an onlooker.'"

Evelyn nods slowly.

"She had my complete attention of course, and all I could do was to nod to indicate that I understood, which she seemed to appreciate. I think she wanted to tell someone this, someone who would understand."

The small rash-like eruption high up on the instep of his right foot does not go away. Other such skin eruptions bloom—the left foot's instep, and then up both legs to about the knees. They spread slowly, but nevertheless they spread here and there, each one about the size of a dime, but they aren't necessarily round. They are lesions, and Wade understands this, but, oddly, there is no panic, perhaps because he feels fine. And even when these skin eruptions move onto his forearms he doesn't experience a sense of panic.

People usually don't notice them, and they wane and wax in number. It is only when he scratches them that panic sets in, for clawing at these lesions with fingernails produces a soaring pleasure, but that soon evaporates into a burning sensation, his skin a bloody mess, and in the wake of this there is nothing to do but to wait for the healing scabs, which trigger itchiness that tempts his fingers. Self-restraint is necessary because he wants to scratch that itchiness.

Wade goes to a pharmacy, or as Fran and James term it, a chemist. He purchases ointment that the chemist says will cure Wade's "rashes." The ointment is meant for dry, cracked skin, which might or might not help with "rashes." Regarding lesions, though, the ointment is useless.

"How many women were there?"

"Aside from the pornography women, there was only Beverly, and of course that one time with Maggie. Fran said that there had been others before, but they had fallen away or moved away. As for Beverly, she showed up once every three or four months. The pornography deal was about the same, about every four months. James wasn't really that busy with women, and he told me that that was good because he was no longer young."

Evelyn chuckles.

"According to Fran, James had had a couple of women friends before his blindness. And then after his accident, about six months after, there was one who wanted to come over and see him, but she didn't know how to go about this because seeing James meant that she would have to undergo the concierge's questioning. When James wasn't blind the women accompanied him to his flat, so the so-called concierge was a nonfactor."

"Right."

"It was at the *Other Place* that this woman sat down and talked to Fran, and as it turned out this woman felt sorry for James, you know, his blindness and all. But she was also interested in sex with him, because that had been a thing for her before James went blind. All this was kind of a touchy topic, this woman talking to Fran about her feelings and desires regarding James. James at that time was still lying low, not venturing out much, hardly visiting the *Other Place*. So there were two sides to this, the woman's side and James's side, but in addition there was Fran's side. Fran by then was James's helper and confidant, and as Fran told me, 'The economic side of things, the money-making side of James's situation was beginning to jell, and it was apparent that money would be coming in from here and there, which was already the case before his blindness, but more so afterwards because he couldn't get out and go places and work for people. The whole thing had to be managed, and I happened to be the one managing it. And I was keen on opportunity. So I told this woman, Beth, her name was Beth, that, yes, James was having difficulties, and that any help financially or otherwise would be welcome, a gift or maybe a little donation.'"

Evelyn chuckles. Wade smiles.

"Yeah, I know, but you got to understand, Fran was really good at this sort of thing. And as she related all this to me in my room, all these stories, late at night and into the early hours of the morning, sometimes until dawn, with the two of us sitting next to the charcoal brazier doing lines or sipping beer or smoking hash-and-tobacco joints, these stories would come alive because Fran had that lilt. I could imagine her talking so confidentially to this woman, Beth, and suggesting all this in such a way that Beth would think it her idea, with Fran saying, 'Oh, that's so sweet of you.'"

"A true salesperson."

"Oh, yeah."

Evelyn smiles.

"Anyway, so after Beth 'visited' a couple of times, Beth told some other women about James, and about James's 'thing,' and about 'visiting,' and about Fran handling the arrangements."

"Even in England, when I was young, or younger, women weren't falling over me for my looks, were they now?" James says. "And as far as my income and personality and social position, all that was hardly compensation because I wasn't high on those registers. As a boy, the other kids made fun of me, my face and all. Even then it stood out, and children are rather ruthless in that regard, aren't they?"

"Yes."

"Marriage and family and so forth weren't consider-ations, and of course it's that much more so now. How could it be otherwise? It's a freak attraction here, Wade, a chink in people's minds, a cubbyhole of fantasy, that's what's brought forth. There's something in it for me of course, but there's also something in it for them."

"Did you feel sorry for him?"

"No. He wouldn't have allowed it."

"Imagine if, as has happened in the past and as is probably continuing in some quarters, these pharmaceuticals are lacking in consistency. The market, be it legal or illegal, is there waiting, which is to say that people will purchase and ingest these drugs. If the drugs are going up and down in potency, there are going to be problems. Or, if suddenly there are unusual side effects, due to faulty substitutions, then that, too, constitutes a problem."

"Was this a moral position?"

"No. It was simply a position, a position he had thought about, and had begun to question."

"Why do you say that?"

"You mean, 'begun to question?'"

"Yes."

"Because he told me this without my asking."

Two men: one slim with a white dress shirt and dark slacks, the other stocky and in brown *shalwar kameez*. The stocky one carries a small suitcase and when he opens it there is a camera and equipment, but none of the equipment is elaborate. The camera uses 8 millimeter film, home-movie variety. When the slim man operates the camera there is the sound of film moving.

A youngish woman always accompanies the two men, but unlike the men she varies in dress and build and demeanor, but she is never fat, nor is she above the age of thirty. Sometimes her hair is short, sometimes not short. Sometimes she is loud, sometimes quiet. On two occasions she is the same woman, a repeat. Other than that, though, she is always a different woman.

Sometimes Fran is instrumental in introducing the women to the slim man. At other times Fran isn't involved, for the slim man is engaged in businesses near the railway station, two of which are billed as backpacker hostels, thus attracting members of the overland crowd, who are either uninformed or too lazy to move beyond the first ring of accommodation that some people, like Wade, find distasteful because there's too much traffic, which often lends itself to sleaziness. A few blocks beyond these immediate lodgings things improve—better rooms, quieter scene, less dangerous. The price is the same.

According to Fran, the slim man sometimes finds women for his films at the hotels near the station.

So, it's always three of them who arrive, two men, one woman, and it is always Wade who sits at the table near the kitchen door with a can of beer. In these scenes James and the woman are on the bed, James with a tumbler of gin and tonic nearby, the woman with gin as well, but sometimes she has whiskey or a can of beer. The slim man and the stocky man drink Coca-Cola. The slim man can speak English. The stocky man never speaks in English. The "appointment" time is always set for one o'clock in the afternoon because the slim man wants strong sunlight that can be controlled by adjusting the slats of the jalousies.

Surprisingly, James varies his humor in accordance with the woman. Sometimes he is gaudy, while at other times he is subtle. The humor helps to make the proceedings something other than routine and/or forced.

"Was that a problem, 'forced?'" Evelyn asks.

"No, that wasn't the case. The women weren't forced because they were there for the money, and the sex wasn't forced because of James's humor, which lightened the situation and contributed to a sense of playfulness. The man with the camera and his sidekick, who always sat in an armchair, weren't into humor, so if it weren't for James things would have been really stiff."

"Did James do this for himself or for the woman or for the film?"

"I think it was all three."

"Was it interesting?"

"Yes and no. I say that because it varied. Sometimes it was mechanical, but at other times there was interest on the part of the woman and James, and by 'interest' I mean involvement, and by that I mean they sometimes forgot, or seemed to forget, that they were performing."

"Yes, I sometimes sensed that in some of the DVDs we watched."

"On more than one occasion the women would look at me while they were engaged with James, and in a way this reminded me of Beverly and Maggie. But I never saw these women look at the slim man and the stocky man like that. Of course the slim man was operating the camera. Also, I had seen some of these women at the *Other Place*. The one woman who did this twice, I talked to one night. She was with Fran, and she was mid-twenties, and she was from Denmark, and she was into morphine tablets. She was nice, but . . . she had a habit."

"That doesn't sound nice."

Wade sips his coffee.

"February of my second winter, the 'pornographers,' as James and Fran called them, showed up with a different camera. I noticed it immediately. The sound was different and the look of the thing was different. The next day when I was talking to Jimmy, he said, 'That's right. It is different. It's called a camcorder and it uses a video cassette. You pop the cassette into the camera and you pop it out. There's a machine that hooks up to the TV, like a TV in your home, and you can put the video cassette in the machine and you get the movie on your telly.'"

"The money came in from a variety of places—consultation, pornography, Beverly, Fran selling drugs. Even the tip jar on top of the upright piano at the *Other Place* was a source of income.

"I was paid via James. There'd be an envelope from Fran or the pornographers or the men who consulted James, and I'd count the money in the envelope and tell James the amount. He'd then tell me how much to take for myself. The money was usually in Pakistani rupees, but not always. Sometimes it was in U.S. dollars. Now and then James would tell me to go to the money changer and change some rupees into American dollars or German marks or British pounds or Swiss Francs. Usually, at the same time, I'd change some of my rupees into U.S. dollars as well. James had a bank account at a bank. Of course that money was in Pakistani rupees, and that was one reason James didn't utilize that account very much. The official exchange rate, vis-à-vis foreign currencies, was all wrong. The Pakistani rupee, like the Indian rupee, was overvalued. So, there was a black market rate, which was administered by money changers and taxi drivers."

"You said, '. . . one reason James didn't utilize that account very much.' Were there other reasons for not using the bank account?"

"Yes. In James's view, the government wasn't stable. This meant that the banks weren't stable. He thought it possible that they might fail, accounts frozen. And/or, he envisioned the government printing more and more money, which would further devalue the rupee officially or unofficially."

"I see."

"Also, James didn't trust the people working at the bank. Even the tellers."

CHAPTER 18

Wade leads James over to the *Other Place* on an average of four times a week, ten or eleven o'clock in the morning. Fran is usually there, and this precipitates James and Fran working on relatively recent tunes that have come into the North American and European popular music market. But it's a delayed "recent" because the vinyl or tapes need to make their way to Peshawar. Wade, with a cup of Nescafe, mans the record player, needle dropped onto a certain tune that James and Fran want to practice, LP turning. Again and again, they'll go over a piece, "Let's have it again, Wade."

James and Fran master these songs by ear, for there is no sheet music nor written lyrics, and even if there were they wouldn't be of much use to James unless Fran read the music to him. In addition to pop, they sometimes work on a jazz piece, in which case James would have instructed Wade to bring an LP from James's collection at the flat, Bill Evans and Herbie Hancock among James's favorites.

Of course it is James at the piano and Fran singing, and what Wade finds interesting is that even after they've mastered a piece they'll continue to go over it time and time again in an effort to work up different renderings.

Often food will be sent for, which is the case at James's flat as well, meals delivered via a boy who is all too happy to fetch whatever anyone wants because a small tip is involved. There is always a boy, ten or eleven years old, at the *Other Place*, who sweeps the tavern out and keeps the toilets, or lavatories as James and Fran and Jimmy term them, clean and tidy. At the concierge's window downstairs from James's flat there is a boy as well. The position of an errand boy is highly sought after, and in both places, James's building and the *Other Place*, nephews are awarded these jobs, which is not only in keeping with how things are done but also eliminates king-of-the-hill bullying that would result among street kids if those posts weren't consigned.

Kebab is popular, and so is rice with a piece of mutton, but there's also spicy chicken, and potatoes in a greasy sauce, as well as seasonal fruit.

"I take it Fran was your lover."

"No, she wasn't. But I can see how it might look that way. It was the first time, perhaps the only time, that I had a female friend like I'd have a male friend, you know, a regular friend, no sex involved."

"Why was that? I mean, why wasn't sex involved?"

"I don't know. It just wasn't. Maybe because Fran had a boyfriend who would come up from Karachi every so often. He was Scottish and he worked on a ship that plied the Arabian Sea and the Gulf, a ship that transported cattle and camels. He had a reddish beard and he'd stay with Fran for two or three days at a time before he had to return to Karachi."

"And you?"

"You mean sex?"

"Yes."

"There were women coming through, and sometimes I'd hook up with one at the *Other Place* and take her back to my hotel room. This would last for a couple of days, and then she'd be gone, on her way to India or her way back to Europe. It was fun."

"What about the local women?"

"The local women? Pakistanis?"

"Yes."

He chuckles. "Do something like that, get your head chopped off."

A good crowd, eleven forty-five p.m., and while James made his way to the upright, his hand on Fran's forearm for guidance, Jimmy came around the end of the bar with a case of Heineken cans and set the case down on a table in the middle of the room, people seated at that table pushing their chairs back to make way. Jimmy, with a generous sweep of the arm, gestured.

Wade went over and grabbed three cans and went to the piano and gave a can to James and a can to Fran. The twenty-four cans of beer disappeared in a jiffy, but by then Jimmy was rounding the bar with another case, contents of which satisfied those who hadn't gotten in on the first batch.

And so, with everyone popping the tabs on their cans, Jimmy stood, magnificently embroidered vest on his torso, cowboy hat on his head, can of Heineken in his hand. He waited for things to settle, and when they did he raised his can of beer and held it aloft in a silent tribute, everyone else doing the same. With this established, Jimmy lowered his can of beer and sipped, and so did everyone else. Even James, in his blindness, picked up on it, and sipped his beer.

The tune began slowly, and as James increased the tempo people began to recognize it. When the tune's bounce was established, Fran's mouth went to a mike, small portable amp system recently brought in. Fran did the song just like the Beatles had, James's fingers jumping at the keys of the upright. Between the ending of that rendering and the beginning of the next there was no break, James and Fran slipping into a slower version, which made the tune funky because Fran got into her smoky voice. On the third take, with still no break in the music, James brought the tempo back up while Fran unhooked the mike from its stand and held it in her hand. With James coming on strong, Fran brought the mike to her chapped lips and started singing, feet shuffling.

People started singing along, and then they were on their feet dancing, can of Heineken in hand. James, with his wraparound sunglasses gleaming and his bulldog face rocking back and forth, was singing, too. Somewhere in the midst of that tumult there arose: "Happy New Year!"

"What was the song?" Evelyn asks.

"*Get Back.*"

A moment, and then Evelyn smiles.

"A set of tabla turned up and so did an acoustic guitar. I don't know how long that song went on, but when it ended there were other songs. After a while James was replaced at the piano and other people stepped up to the mike.

"At around four-thirty in the morning, when things were winding down, Fran stood up from the table, where she and James and I were seated, and went over to the man with the acoustic guitar. She exchanged some words with him, and the man started playing the guitar. When he found the song, Fran started singing in a voice that I hadn't heard before. She was singing without the mike, and the song was *Wild Horses*."

Wade pauses, and Evelyn says, "I can hear it."

"Sometime after that we left, James and Fran and I, the three of us walking those predawn streets, James's hand on my forearm, frozen mud crunching beneath our shoes."

Winter turns that January corner where it bogs down in February, even in Southern California. Evelyn visits less frequently, but when she does they talk deep into the night and they make love in that same milieu, as if something were slipping away and they were trying to hold on to it.

Occasionally there is rain, and Wade savors it because it interrupts the monotony of hazy-sunshine, weather that repeats itself day after day as if it's lost the physiognomies of weather, just as Los Angeles has lost the features of a city in its endless suburbs.

Dark clouds roiling at the horizon, sky in transit, he longs to feel something other than the tedium of sameness.

His gums bleed at night while he's sleeping and he understands this in the morning from the dried blood on the towel that serves as a pillow cover, and he understands it in the mirror that shows him blood in sticky stages of drying on his teeth and lips. And sometimes during the day when he's out walking there'll be bleeding if his mouth is open and the air is cold and dry.

Fran has asked him if his teeth are loose, and he has said, "No, they aren't."

There are two primary colors. One is gray, courtesy of concrete and cinder blocks. The other is an earthy brown, which comes from brown bricks, fired or adobe, and of those bricks they are often plastered over with a veneer of clayish mud. On the outskirts of town pisé, a mix of mud and straw pressed or rammed into forms and left to dry, materializes as walls, walls of buildings or walls enclosing compounds. There is of course wood, but that, too, weathers into a grayish brown. Sometimes whitewash and green paint are put to use, yet in both cases dust and mud and weather reduce their brilliance, leaving them to blend with what surrounds them.

This color scheme is in no way unique to Peshawar, for countless other towns and villages in the region share this composition. Yet whenever this palette comes to mind, he sees Peshawar.

"And your second New Years? What song did Fran sing that night?"

"*With a Little Help from My Friends*, Joe Cocker style."

It rains and the streets are a patchwork of puddles and mud. At night there's a bitter wind.

A cold has dropped down into James's chest, lungs congested. He runs a fever. Fran and Wade are concerned.

Jimmy sends a boy with a handwritten note in English, along with some money, to fetch a doctor who shows up two hours later at the concierge's downstairs, bell tingling in James's flat. Wade goes down to escort the doctor upstairs, boy dismissed after Wade gives him two rupees, some of which the boy spends on hard candy at the concierge's window.

The doctor, perhaps fifty years old and in Western clothing, employs a stethoscope that comes out of a black-leather bag. The doctor's English is adequate, but he's short on diagnosis. He doses out antibiotics, and after he is paid he says that he'll return the following day to check on the patient's progress. Wade is instructed to ply James with lemon tea.

Fran comes over in the evening, and Fran and Wade and James listen to records played at low volume, but James only listens sometimes, for he is in and out of sleep. Fran leaves around midnight. At one in the morning Wade changes James's sweat-soaked *kameez* for a dry one. Damp sheets on the bed are changed as well, while James sits on a chair sipping water. Wade spends the night on the couch. In the morning, James's fever is gone. Fran arrives with warm naan and a jar of marmalade. That afternoon the doctor says that the patient is progressing. Antibiotics will continue for a week.

Taking advantage of the doctor's buoyed mood, Wade shows the doctor the lesions on his lower legs. The doctor writes a prescription for cortisone cream, which amounts to a note that a pharmacist will read, language English. The doctor, in ballpoint pen, kindly maps out directions to a specific pharmacy on the backside of the prescription. Wade thanks the doctor profusely and hands him some money.

"If any further complications arise regarding Mr. James, please send for me."

"I will."

James recovers, lungs cleared, but he remains weak for about a month, daily walks curtailed, mornings and nights at the *Other Place* on hiatus until about the end of February.

The cortisone cream is effective, broken skin healing, although not by way of scabs. The skin simply comes together, normal coloration returning for the most part. Yet the problem persists in spurts, lesions developing here and there. Thus, Wade keeps the malady somewhat at bay with the cortisone cream. When he runs out of cortisone cream, he returns to the pharmacy for more tubes.

"Do you think you could help me transport my pieces over the hill, and maybe help with hanging them in the gallery?"

"Sure. When?"

"Next Thursday. The opening's Friday evening, so that will give us Thursday, and Friday during the day if need be. Maybe you could bring a toolbox."

"Sure."

"Of course Della will be there helping out. We pretty much have it all planned, where the pieces will go and so forth, but there's always little things."

"Of course."

She reaches into her shoulder bag and extracts a white envelope and hands it to him. He opens the envelope and finds an invitation to the opening.

"And, ah, if you wouldn't mind, I'm going to be drinking wine. So if we could go together on Friday in your pickup truck, then I could leave my car at home and I won't have to worry about driving."

"Okay."

"Of course that'd mean you'd have to stick around to the end."

"What time do you figure it's going to end?"

"Eleven, twelve o'clock. You know how it is, people get to talking and so on."

"Well, if I get bored, maybe I'll take a walk or something, and if it winds up and I'm not there, you can call me on my cellphone, and I'll skip on back."

"Good idea."

He keeps a store of tetracycline in his room in case of infection. Thus far, though, the lesions have remained stable in that respect, no pus, no serious inflammation.

He often washes his feet and lower legs gently with water that he sponges from a plastic basin. During the warm/hot months, which amounts to most of the year, he regards this measure as critical, for it's during those months that he wears sandals, feet and ankles black with dirt.

"Was your second year in Peshawar the same as the first?"

"Yes and no. In a general way things rolled along in the same manner, but at the same time there was more naturalness to my being there, which meant that I was more a part of the scene.

"During my first year things were new and I was building friendships. During my second year those friendships deepened."

After the panels were arranged and the pictures hung, he took his time and walked through the exhibit, and he found it hard to believe that this body of work had been produced in about a year. Yet it didn't look rushed in the least.

Evelyn and Della were talking, which left Wade alone to meander, and even though he was privy to what had gone into these pictures it still struck him that they were mysterious. Questions and themes had been asked and proposed, but that was as far as it went. It was like a variety of perspective and technique and subject and medium had been dropped into the viewer's eye, thus leaving opinion and resolution up to the viewer. The viewer was invited in, very much in, nakedly at times, and what the viewer found were his or her own prejudices or inclinations or secrets . . . or insights. Della had told Evelyn, "This is controversial." And then she had added, "But so is everything that breaks from pattern."

Wade thought about the pricing, for he would have never dreamt to ask for so much money for a single piece. Whether this was a sales technique or not he didn't know, just as he didn't know if the show would be a success or not. The quality of work, particularly its combination of originality and applied skill, as well as its energy, warranted success. But of course he was biased, and he knew nothing about the market.

Wade and Evelyn had driven over the hill on Thursday in separate cars, so there was no opportunity to catch Evelyn alone after the show was set up. She drove back to her house in her car, and Wade drove back to his house in his pickup truck. It wasn't until the next day, late Friday afternoon, that Wade had a chance to ask Evelyn if she was nervous.

"I suppose, but more than anything I'm tired. But I think that will disappear when people start showing up and I have a little wine."

"Does Della think the show is going to be a success?"

They were on their way over the hill on the freeway, and they were in the cab of Wade's pickup truck.

"Della's a different kind of gallery owner than the others I've dealt with. The others predicted great success, but Della doesn't do that. She has opinions about the pieces, but not about the show's success. What she did say, though, is that success has a number of avenues. One, of course, is sales. But another is buzz, creating a buzz, for it's that that might pay off down the road. Della's good about that. She exercises patience. She understands that a market is developed or built, and then, if luck intervenes, it spirals upward on its own dynamics. Another aspect of success is to convince people that the artist is serious, which is what the curriculum vitae is for. Della says this can sometimes help sales, particularly with those who might be thinking of investment. People usually don't invest in someone who picked up a paintbrush yesterday. Investors are looking for bona fides. A favorable write up in a newspaper by an art critic helps in this regard as well, so that's another aspect of success, favorable reviews. And of course the Internet has begun to play into the market as well. Della has a marvelous website, and everything in this show will be on that website beginning Monday, sold and unsold pieces both. It's part of getting my work out there for people to see, not to mention people actually buying pieces over the Internet nowadays."

"James. I have something to tell you."
"Yes?"
"I'm going to leave next week."
"Leave? You mean, leave Peshawar?"

"Nearly pornographic, some of these."
"Yes, but it's like they're either shy of that, or maybe beyond it. This one here, for example, is leading you toward something you don't want to see, but then it veers to show you something else."
"Mastery of technique, particularly in these watercolors. What might otherwise be pornography is suddenly fantasy. It's like sliding from one perception to another. Her use of paints is unusual for watercolors."
"I noticed that."
"A sense of conflict, do you think?"
"Perhaps realism versus fantasy?"
"Of course she made all this up. Quite an imagination."
"I detect some loneliness here, or maybe forlornness."
"Yes, I see that too. Yes, that struck me."

Wade's been eavesdropping, meandering around the gallery after people started arriving, and he's heard all sorts of things, including one woman, early forties, say, "How did she know?" as if the colored pencil drawing she was looking at, with a younger man at her side, might have revealed a secret that the woman and the man shared. Most of the comments Wade heard were positive, but not all. One man said, "This is over the top."

The gallery is full of people, many of whom have clear plastic cups, red or white wine. A few people have bottles of Beck's beer in their hands that they must have brought in on their own, and this seems okay. Perhaps it is cool.

"Collage-like."

"Yes. But there's this suggested focal point: the man and the woman on the bicycles. The snapshot-like scenes seem to be floating around them."

Matted and framed and on the walls and panels of the gallery Evelyn's work looks all so professional and accomplished.

"The wooden blinds and the light coming in, and the man with the wrinkles and the sunglasses, what do you make of that?"

"Well, there's this woman off to the side."

"Yes, but the man isn't looking at her."

"Yes, but the man and the woman are involved with something, perhaps something that's about to happen, otherwise why would the woman be naked?"

"Yes, but then there's this guy in the corner, at a table. What's *he* doing?"

"It looks like he's watching."

The woman chuckles and says, "I get the feeling that we're watching, too."

Some people are dressed in a staged, scruffy way. Most, though, have a neat, casual appearance. Of age, it's mixed, young to old, and the same can be said for facial hair on the faces of men, clean-shaven to full beards and everything in between. A few women have tattoos on their arms. One third of the people are wearing hats. On the feet of men black-leather shoes are absent, but some women have such shoes. Chinos are on the legs of many of the men. The one constant, even though some try to cover it up with mod language, is education. Illiteracy among this crowd is a distant statistic. Educated wit is prevalent. According to Evelyn, some of her colleagues and friends received invitations. Everyone else is gallery-connected. Thus far, Wade hasn't been introduced to anyone, and he hopes that will continue because he wouldn't know what to say.

The only people Wade knows are Evelyn and Della, and Della's partner, Winston, who is allocating red and white wine from behind the wine table, a very congenial man, early-forties, which makes him a little younger than Della, for Della looks to be mid-forties. Both Della and Winston are slim, and they both gravitate toward loose cotton, solid-colored shirts of the pastel sort, pants loose as well, khaki-colored, but more expensive than khakis. Della has blue eyes and short, brown-blonde hair that's kind of tweaked. Winston has regular brown hair that's thick and cut straight across at the nape of his neck, no taper.

Winston, if not knowing someone, instantly knows them to the extent of a remark or two that brings a smile or a laugh. Winston speaks with a soft drawl. When asked about this, Winston told Wade, "Texas panhandle, flatter than that ocean out there." Accompanying this was a nod toward Santa Monica Bay, a mere two blocks away. Winston might be considered rawboned, his face in particular, and even though from out of state he is very much at home on the west side of Southern California, lexicon attesting to this. While standing near the wine table and gazing at Evelyn's paneled curriculum vitae for a third time, Wade overheard Winston talking to people about Evelyn's work, and it was clear to Wade that Winston had taken a good look at everything in the gallery, probably Friday morning or afternoon. Winston's command of art lingo is natural.

On arriving at the gallery late Friday afternoon, Wade immediately noticed that three pieces had "Sold" tags, which caused Wade to wonder about commercial savvy. Had a few chosen people been invited in for a private showing, Friday morning or afternoon, or were the "Sold" tags a fiction? Without doubt, "Sold" strongly implied that others had seen worth in the work. Fictive or otherwise, "Sold" was a come on.

As Wade slips out the front door onto the sidewalk in front of the gallery, he's surprised to see that people are still arriving.

He carries the same burgundy-colored suitcase that he arrived with. It is hot and Fran is with him. People are boarding the train. Wade has a reserved seat, and so Wade and Fran walk along the platform looking for Wade's car. And just as when he arrived, there are turbans and burqa and *shalwar kameez* and creased slacks and white shirts and babies naked from the waist down. When they find Wade's car they stop and Wade sets his suitcase down on the blackened concrete.

He lived and worked and hung out in this neighborhood: Santa Monica, Ocean Park, Venice. It was during that in-between period, that time between his first trip abroad and his second trip abroad, the second trip lasting thirty-two years.

He walks along Main Street in Ocean Park and he understands that everything has changed. The bric-a-brac shops, the beer-soaked sawdust on the floor of a gay bar, the outrageous transvestite floor show that a gay nightclub sported, the empty storefronts, the cheap rent. It's all gone, and in its place is a chic community.

He walks further on, and at Rose Avenue he turns, and soon he's walking along Ocean Front Walk, or what most people call "the boardwalk," but there are no boards. It's pavement. On one side of the pavement there is a wide sandy beach and then the ocean, waves audible, while on the other side of the pavement, and lining its course, there are restaurants and bars and shops.

He remembers the mist and the fog rolling in, late afternoon or at night, and he remembers guys drinking wine and playing bongos. It used to be quiet, commerce nil. Especially at night it was quiet.

He continues to walk, and then he thinks about walking farther on, for he had a girlfriend who lived on Venice Boulevard, a block shy of the beach, a block shy of Ocean Front Walk, which was very quiet that far south. She had two young children, and he spent a winter with her in that apartment. He stops walking, for what would be the use? There'd only be memories of what was, and what will never be again.

He's got time to kill. He turns and walks in the opposite direction, and after a while he's in Santa Monica, Third Street Promenade, which didn't exist at all when he lived a few blocks over on Ocean near the pier, sign out front of his wood-sided apartment building: *Rooms for Rent – Men Only*.

Downtown Santa Monica, sleepy nothingness is what he remembers, but now it's lively, transformation complete. There are lots of people. Bars and restaurants are busy.

He goes into an espresso café and orders a double espresso and sits down at a counter that faces a plate-glass window. He sips his coffee and looks at the people walking by on the Promenade.

Fran takes a folded, brown handkerchief from the pocket of her *shalwar* and wipes perspiration from her face. Wade shifts his weight.

"James made me promise to give you a kiss."

He kind of smiles, a half-smile, a crooked smile. He leans down and she kisses him on the lips.

"It seems like it went pretty good."

They're on their way back over the hill, traffic moving briskly on the freeway.

"It did. Della said it was a booming success. Sales were good."

"How many were sold?"

"About a third."

"Yeah, that seems pretty good."

"Winston said it was 'totally buckaroo,' and that we could expect a comparable amount to sell by the time the show closes in three weeks."

"Wow."

"And . . . Della and Winston both said that it'd be good to follow this up with another show. They were talking about squeezing it in, maybe between Christmas and January seventh when they have another show scheduled."

"Really?"

"They want to wait for the reviews, though, and then we'll talk. But they're sure the reviews are going to be positive."

He nods.
"There was a man there, Sid Lee. He gave me his card and said I should call him. He runs a gallery in Pasadena."

The train pulls out of the station and his car begins to rock and squeak. He looks out the window and he sees shanties and lean-tos and clothes vendors and stray dogs and trash and people walking, and as the town recedes so do those endeavors that cling to the rail line.

CHAPTER 19

Equipped with six large tubes of cortisone cream he goes by train from Amritsar to Jammu, where he boards a bus that takes him to Srinagar, an overnight journey. In Srinagar he takes a local bus to a village outside of town, which is where the paved road ends. He has his burgundy-colored suitcase with him and there's a daypack on his back and a colorful cloth shoulder bag hanging from his shoulder. The daypack and shoulder bag are bulging with foodstuffs that he purchased in Srinagar.

It is precisely where the paved road ends that a graded dirt track begins, and it is there that the bus stops and turns around. A few restaurants with blaring Indian music line the end-of-the-road pavement. This is a pilgrimage route and already the altitude is well above that of Srinagar and Dal Lake.

He was up here years before on his first trip abroad and he hopes that things have not changed too much. A sign where the dirt track begins is encouraging. The sign is in English and it advertises a campground: tents, trout fishing, meals, marvelous views, horseback riding, jeep rides, and so forth. He sets off on foot and after a mile and a half there is another sign that is smaller and simpler. It directs him to the left, while the dirt track continues up the valley. He notes a few tents that can be seen from the dirt track, but they are unobtrusive and well away from that dirt road, which is the pilgrimage route, and this is how he remembers the camp and its location, camp tucked onto a flat of land, alpine surroundings.

Walking toward the camp, he sees more tents, maybe ten in all, and after that the camp's hub comes into view, four wooden tables, a large wood-burning brick oven and stove, a rough-wood shed, and a large tent, which has a rainfly, just as the smaller tents, the guest tents, have rainflies.

An older man and a young man are standing near one of the tables and they are looking at him as he approaches. Clothes are hanging on a clothesline. Wispy white smoke bleeds from the chimney of the oven/stove. He walks up to the two men and he says, "Hello."

"So that's how it began?"

"Yeah."

"How long did you stay there?"

"Two months."

"Was it rough, you know, coming off the crank and all?"

"Yes, or sort of. I mean . . . it's different for different people. I met a woman in Peshawar, who was coming back through from India and who had gone cold turkey after having done crank for six months, and she told me it was hell. She said she was a nervous wreck, like she wanted to pull out her hair, and that her skin was all creepy. For her it was a horrible experience."

Evelyn nods.

"She said she'd never touch crank or any type of upper or downer again."

"Understandable."

"But for me it wasn't like that. It wasn't fun, but it wasn't like what that woman described, and I'm certain she wasn't blowing it up. When she came through the first time, on her way to India, we got together and I got to know her, which was when she was into crank. And then when she came back through en route to Europe after having cleaned up, we got together again, so I got to know her again. She was very levelheaded, very educated."

"Yes."

Wade sips his coffee. Evelyn sips her coffee.

"I had a small tent with a raised wooden floor. There were two cots, but of course I only used one of them. The cots were like old army cots, and they each had a sheepskin pad, thick and fleecy, on top of the stretched canvas, which made sleeping and lying on the cot warm and comfortable. Also, there were two heavy blankets, army issue. Near my tent there was a fire ring made of stones, so I could have a campfire. I collected sticks on the hillsides or I bought wood from the man and his son. They weren't the owners of the camp. They managed it in the summer. Naturally, like all the other tourist businesses in the area, they closed it down in the fall just before winter. That man and his son were the same two from five years before when I was there, except the son was a boy then, but this time he was eighteen years old and his English wasn't bad.

"There were hardly any people that stayed at the camp, and all that stuff on the sign—jeep rides and horseback riding and so forth—well, it could be arranged through someone who had a stable or a jeep in the village. And about the trout fishing, there were poles, rods and reels, that you could rent at the camp, and there was a stream down a steep slope in back of the camp, which was where I, and the teenage son, got water via buckets that we hauled up the slope. I never saw anybody fishing, but the older man, the father, said there were trout in the stream."

"How much did you pay? Can you remember?"

"Ten rupees a night, or about one U.S. dollar, and the deal was, if I paid with American currency I got chai and a piece of naan for free, morning tea or afternoon tea, whichever I preferred. So I paid with American money and took my tea and bread in the late afternoon."

Evelyn smiles.

"It was the physicality of camping and walking up that valley on the graded dirt track and gathering sticks in the forest and making a campfire and going to the village for food, and all the small things, like washing and getting water from the stream, that did the trick for me.

"I'd walk up the valley on that dirt road to a place that was ten miles up, which was where the dirt road ended, for the valley narrowed there, and the stream, which ran parallel to the road, disappeared there under thick ice that was a meter or more thick. The stream came out from under the ice, and beyond that there was only ice. I went down and stood on the ice, and I looked up the gorge, and as far as I could see there was ice running on top of what was a stream bed, but there was no stream, only ice, with people stumbling while trying to make their way up the gorge on that ice."

Evelyn is looking at him, and waiting for more.

"Occasionally a jeep with a driver and rich Indian tourists went up and back on that dirt track, and horses, which were like ponies, also went along that dirt road, boys leading the ponies by the reins, wealthy tourists on little saddles on the ponies. Everyone else walked up that dirt track, me included, but I stopped at the ice. Others continued on by walking on the ice and up through the gorge to who knows where. I was told that there was a cave up there, a sacred cave. These people were pilgrims—old skinny men in *lungis*, women in saris, middle-aged men in slacks. No one had proper footwear. And so they'd be out there slipping and sliding on that ice. Day after day I'd walk up there and have tea where a chai wallah had set up a stand at the end of the dirt track, and I'd look down from that chai stand and watch those people slipping and sliding and falling on the ice."

Evelyn continues to look at him.

"Ten miles from my camp to the end of the road, which meant ten miles back. It filled my day."

"Yes, I can see how it would."

"I didn't go up there every day. On average, four or five days a week. The other days I did wash or went to the village for food, or I'd go up onto the slopes of the valley in search of sticks for my campfire."

Evelyn sips her coffee. Wade sips his coffee.

"You had no drugs?"

"None. When I left Peshawar, I left without even a peck of hash."

"So what did you feel? I mean, what did it *feel* like to do that, just to stop after a couple of years?"

"It was a beautiful place where I was at—the campsite, the valley, the Himalayas. There were thunderstorms and I'd watch them as they developed over the mountains or up in the valley. It only rained twice where I was camped, both times at night, so then I was in my tent when it was raining, but the tent was good, no leaking. And I was warm in my sleeping bag with the blankets on top and the sheepskin under me, which was kind of important because the temperature dropped some nights, and in the morning I'd see snow way down on the mountains and the sides of the valley, snow almost to my camp, and then I'd watch the snowline creep up the mountains or up the sides of the valley as the day advanced and the snow melted. And I think that was part of it, part of what helped me, for if I had been cooped up in a room, for example, with nothing physical to do, I'd have gone crazy. But as it was, I was outside, and I was getting exercise, and so then I was tired at night, and it was a comfort to sit by a little campfire and drink sugared tea and eat bread with cheese or jam spread on it. I had an appetite, particularly for sweets. I had tea bags and I boiled water in a saucepan over the fire. I had rigged up a grill-like thing with some pieces of rebar I had found."

"Yes."

"There were my arms and legs that I washed gently with cold water, and there was the cortisone cream that I applied. The arms cleared up in about a month. The legs mostly cleared up by the time I left, but I had to keep with the cortisone cream on the legs for about six months. The bleeding gums lessened, but they never fully stopped until I started seeing a dentist in Penang."

He pauses.

"Little by little I started gaining weight, but the real thing for me was loneliness. I felt so lonely, so terribly alone. I missed James and Fran and Jimmy. I missed Peshawar, and it was fortunate, or maybe astute, that I had gone up into Indian Kashmir, for there were times when I just wanted to pack it up and go back. But I was too far away to do that easily, and so that made me stop and think. So in that way, one day became the next."

"Yes."

"My days were full because of where I was and what I was doing. My body was occupied, and that helped me mentally. But still..."

He pauses.

"I've always felt lonely at the end of a relationship, or after having left a place where things had happened for a length of time, and this of course was that. But this was so vivid and acute."

House painting, handyman, chaparral gardens—it's what he does, day after day. She visits infrequently, and then hardly at all.

One year becomes the next, and in his studio at night, if he isn't too tired, he'll draw or paint, cat asleep on the couch, radio tuned to a country-western station.

He sometimes has conversations with her in his head. These are mostly monologues as he recalls a place and a time and an activity.

Occasionally she calls him and they go out to dinner, usually sushi, and she tells him about her life and about her mother passing away and about how she's thinking of quitting her university job.

He comes out of the Himalayas in September, and he goes by train to Delhi, where it's hot and where it rains and where the streets run with mud. At American Express there is a letter from his mother, but nothing from Peshawar.

He follows the train line, burgundy-colored suitcase in hand—Agra, Allahabad, Varanasi, and it is in Varanasi that he walks the ghats, day and night.

He continues on, and then he's in Calcutta, which is more of what he has seen, as if what he has seen is never ending. He boards an airplane that takes him to Bangkok. He goes south by train and enters the Malay Peninsula.

At Butterworth he boards a ferry that takes him to Penang. In Georgetown he finds something that is immediately appealing. The citizenry is mixed—Malays,

Chinese, and Indians. It's an old town, and it's clean, but not too clean. There are school children in uniforms, fresh fruit galore, and cuisine that reflects the town's ethnicities. He finds work teaching English, a storefront operation termed a private school. He settles in, accommodation a room above and to the rear of a Chinese food restaurant, a restaurant with a colonial interior—ceiling fans, jalousies at window openings, grandfather clock, fishbowls of draft beer.

In his head he tells Evelyn that it was in that restaurant that he saw 9/11 on TV. The set was mounted high up on a wall in a corner, everyone gathered and watching reruns and reruns and reruns.

There were some women over the course of all those years he spent in Georgetown, and those relationships were "convenient," as both he and those women acknowledged while circling within the intimacy of alcohol.

He tells Evelyn this in his head as if she were there in his studio sitting on the couch with a cup of coffee, and it is this that constitutes conclusion. But then he goes on to relate backstory, which is how he began drinking King-fisher beer in Delhi, a harmless consolation for having walked away from crank, or so he assumed. The beer continued throughout his travels, and in Georgetown he added vodka and rum and whisky, as if to diversify. It was a long time coming before he began to feel that there was more at work than good times and relaxation, for residuals were a slow burn, just as age was a slow burn, and given the luxury of hindsight he now understands that age and hangovers were in cahoots.

This monologue plays out in his head, which is like a summation, but then things take a drastic turn, for he hears Evelyn say: "Yes. But you could have had a good life. You could have accomplished something."

And so he sits, in bewilderment.

There are other conversations, which evolve in his head quite naturally, and they sometimes involve "if," as in "if only I had...," a supposition that keeps going further and further back in his life until he is left with: "I would have had to have been a different person."

It is somewhere along in these years of working and driving on the freeways and sitting in his studio with his cat that his thoughts advance, for he now has memories of a hot summer's day, when Evelyn said, "How do we do this?"

THE END

ACKNOWLEDGMENTS

A version of Chapter Two was first published as a short story in *Outside In Literary & Travel Magazine*. A version of Chapter Ten first appeared as a short story in *Nagoya Writes*.

I am greatly indebted to everyone at Tailwinds Press for seeing this project through. Thanks ever so much.

ABOUT THE AUTHOR

MICHAEL ONOFREY was born and raised in Los Angeles. Currently he lives in Japan. Over seventy of his short stories have been published in literary journals and magazines, in print and online, in such places as *Cottonwood*, *The Evansville Review*, *Natural Bridge*, *Snowy Egret*, *Terrain.org*, *Weber—The Contemporary West*, and *The William and Mary Review*. Among anthologized work, his stories have appeared in *Creativity & Constraint* (Wising Up Press, 2014), *In New Light* (Northern Initiative for Social Action, 2013), *Road to Nowhere and Other New Stories from the Southwest* (University of New Mexico Press, 2013), and *Imagination & Place: An Anthology* (Imagination & Place Press, 2009).

www.ingramcontent.com/pod-product-compliance
Lightning Source LLC
Chambersburg PA
CBHW031150120726
47905CB00006B/1889